The Painter and the Sea

Tom Binnie

Cover: Binnie Design, Edinburgh
Cover Image: 'Surf on Rocks' (~1890) William Trost Richards.
Courtesy of The Metropolitan Museum of Art,
1000 Fifth Avenue, New York, USA

Printed in the Europe

For Natalie

EDINBURGH, SCOTLAND
1733

Prologue

There were ten, maybe twelve mourners left standing in the cemetery. None paid heed as the two diggers laboured to fill the void. James Lockhart had clung on to life against long odds, well beyond those of his friends and contemporaries. He must have led a solitary and unhappy life these last years, but no one attending actually knew; he had become reclusive. Through his lawyers, Joseph ensured that James did not want for food or shelter; that was the limit.

David Miller had no words as the unfamiliar woman at the graveside introduced herself as his sister. She was tall and youthful, elegantly dressed in black. She filled the silence in gentle, accented tones. 'I see that this has come as a surprise, if not a shock. I have no wish to trouble you, David... and I see I may have disturbed your friend.'

David saw Joseph, crouching and clutching his stomach some distance away by the wall of a crypt overgrown with ivy.

Following his look. 'Is that Joe? Here is my card. I will be in Scotland for a further month. If you wish to meet in more favourable circumstances, I would be very pleased. But I understand if you don't, and I will not inconvenience you again.' She turned away and walked to an awaiting carriage.

As she left, David found a hundred questions, and he also found disbelief. But his immediate attention was drawn to his friend and mentor, Joseph Grieve, who appeared to be recovering. He walked over to assist him.

'Joseph, are you...'

'What did she say, did she say anything, what did she say?'

'Joe, are you all right, do you know her?'

Joseph did not answer.

'Come, let us find somewhere to sit.'

David escorted him to their carriage and Joseph suggested they find an inn before reuniting with their families. They undertook the journey without speaking, David was gathering his thoughts, and Joe had gone to a place where he could not be reached.

They found a dark, smoke-filled ale house at the side of a small brewery. A few leathered tradesmen stood drinking at the end of their working day. Joe took a table at the back of the room, and they were served by an older woman who showed no sign of their patronage being welcome. Joseph asked for a bottle of whisky and two glasses: he filled them both, drank his, refilled, drank again, and refilled before David had touched his. David took a sip from his glass and spoke first.

'Joe, are you all right? Do you know that woman?'

'No, I have never seen her.'

'But the way you reacted?'

'What did she say?'

'Do not play games, Joe. Tell me who she is, and how you know her.'

'Please, David, if you tell me what she said, then I may be able to help. It was a long time ago.'

David emptied his glass. He put it back on the table and Joe refilled it. 'She claimed, she said ... she said she was my half-sister.'

'That was all?'

'Yes, that was all. And she gave me a contact address.'

'Let me see?'

David offered Joe the card the woman had given to him.

'Joe, you need to answer my questions. Otherwise, I will leave.

When you welcomed my daughter and me into your house two days ago to stay with your family, I felt I had returned home. There was a pang of regret. I could not recall how we had lost touch when I went to university, or why we were estranged. But I do now. You can be guarded, Joe. There are things of my family that I do not know, and you will not tell me. I am sorry to find this still lies between us. I am not yet disturbed by this woman. It is a curiosity that I can easily dismiss; you know that I have enough to occupy my time. Your reaction to her does disturb me. Who is she, Joe? Is there a truth in what she claims? My mother was left a widow. She was still young and attractive but also passionate and vulnerable, and sadly confined to an asylum. She passed some twelve, no fourteen years ago. I know that much. It is a miserable thought for me but, given her situation, it would not be that unusual for her to have found another. I would worry about the circumstance, but I am not going to fret over the past. If that girl, woman, is the product of an unfortunate dalliance, then it is certainly no fault of herself, and I will not blame my mother. The woman, what is her name, Tomasine, did not appear to be suffering, the opposite in fact. Joe, I need you to answer. Do you know anything of this?'

Joe struggled to answer.

'I do not know her, David, but if what she said to you is true, it is not your mother that is the mutual parent.'

It was not in his nature, but David now spoke angrily. 'What! My father, but how? Joseph, tell me now.'

'All I can say, David, is that if you share a parent with that girl, it would be your father. Did you look at her, did you not see?'

'For a few minutes only. Tell me what you know.'

'Your father loved your mother.'

'But?'

'As you know, I was apprenticed to him on our merchant voyage to Zeeland when he was lost. Tom never returned. There was a girl from the lodging house. She helped your father with the language during the trade. She travelled with us, she dined with him and they got on well. That is all I know.'

'There is more, Joe?'

Joe remained silent.

David stood. 'It is my family. I have the right to know!'

iv

'David, it is *your* family, *your* family's past, *your* family secrets. It is not mine.'

'Are you saying your family has no secrets?'

'No, I would say not.'

'Really, Joe, then who was that woman who was not introduced at your table? And Rose tells me there was a girl, not far from her own age, that your grandchildren tease as *aunt* … no secrets, really?'

David stood to leave. Joe refilled his own glass.

'Joe, it is not just that you lie to me; you lie to yourself.' David left the inn.

Returning to the Grieve house by cab, David apologised to Joe's wife, Mary, and asked if he and Rose could sup in their rooms before retiring early. They would leave to catch a boat back to Kinghorn at first light, to return to their schoolhouse in Fife.

Mary sensed, but did not ask. 'He *is* a good man, David.'

'I want to believe that, Mary. I see two men: one I love and one I do not know. I cannot reconcile this, and I must protect Rose.'

'He would do no harm.'

'But what of the harm that is done, that which cannot be undone? Mary, I thank you for your hospitality and you have been very kind to Rose.'

'Grace, my granddaughter, has grown quickly fond of her. She will desire to meet Rose again.'

'I cannot countenance that.'

'David, I see you are hurt. I am sure it is not without justification, but please do not condemn the children.'

Rose knew not to protest at the unexpected curtailment of their visit. Something had clearly happened; her father's mood swing was apparent. She re-found the concern for her father which had been absent these past months as he started anew at the burgh school. Over supper, she shared the adventures of her day with him, and was glad of a book and an early bed.

They rose at five hours the next morn when they were met by Mary and a sleepy, tearful Grace at the bottom of the stairs. Mary handed David a parcel of food and told him to take the carriage. Grace gave Rose a small packet and begged her to return.

Mary took David aside. 'Joe told me some of it. Visit the girl, David. She has done no wrong. He does not tell me everything; he never has, yet I would not change a single red hair on his head.'

'I appreciate your words, Mary. At the moment, I want none of it. I have occupation enough.'

'Please, David, give it some thought.'

'I will that. I always do. It is my burden.' He smiled sadly, his first for a while.

They hugged, and David and Rose departed to catch the ferry from Leith. Still half-asleep, Rose said little on the short carriage ride, and David gave thought to Mary's words. They quickly found a boat to take them across the Forth estuary to the Fife coast.

As the yacht left the port, David looked to the east and saw the sun rise on the horizon out of the sea to meet an infinite sky turning from pastel red to light blue. A wind blew from the north, and the light ketch tacked excessively to make headway north. Rose tried to hold on, but her journey was spent retching, her head over the rail. David stood beside her, his comforting arm around his daughter.

He enjoyed the swing of the craft, the violent lurches, the lifting and falling, the bellowing of the single sail, the salty spray over the foredeck. David had studied long and taught many tales of Greek and Roman gods; that morning it was as if they had made an appearance. How wonderful to have a panoply of talented gods to praise, thank or blame, rather than his own country's monochromatic creator. When so inspired, he would step outside himself. This early morning, he felt clear-sighted, more confident that he would be able to find a way ahead for them both.

David had not told Rose of the legacy arising from James Lockhart's passing. That was not Joe's gift, he reminded himself, it resulted from his poor late father's industry. He would not shrink from it, but he would keep the news of it to himself, for a while at least, immediately aware of the irony in *his* decision … to keep it secret.

PART ONE

VEERE, ZEELAND 1711

Chapter 1

Knowing the ebb of the morning tide, Grietje van der Meer walked down the cobbled path to the harbour. She stood at the end of the breakwater to watch the merchantman, large by the scale of Veere's small port, float silently out towards the German Sea. Grietje waved at the ship as its crew scuttled up the rigging to lower the sails. It might have been Ruud, on the aft deck waving back; even through her tears she could see it wasn't Joe.

Grietje, unwed at thirty-six, had a twenty-year history of relationships and a life of love, loss and regret. Recently, she found a new happiness in her own company. The occasional dalliance was no more than a diversion for the body, a passing fancy. She had learned through her experience and knew that she could endure, but this man, the one unseen on the departing ship, hurt. This one really hurt.

The big, rugged, red-headed Scotsman whom she met when she served in a sailors' bar, rescued her from assault when she was taken for a prostitute. The following day, Joe learned that she had taken his apprentice, Ruud, to her bed on that first drunken night and yet he treated her only with respect. He enjoyed her company for who she was, and not for what her appearance promised or how she behaved. Joe took the time to listen to her, appreciating her knowledge and ability – talents dismissed by so many before him. The pain for her was that he lived across the sea; he had a wife whom he clearly loved and four children on whom he doted.

The pain was that she did not know if he would return. They had resolved the quest to find out what had happened to his missing employer. Joe's Scottish-Dutch trading in wool, linen, leather, coal, and porcelain had now become profitable and routine. The acquisition and shipping of goods no longer required his personal supervision. He said he would return, but her own experience did not reassure her. He offered her the chance to move to Scotland, where he would employ her. But would he, in the cold grey light of Edinburgh? Would he, sitting in the firelight of his family home? Would he ... would he ever return to her? She could only wait. And what if a letter came, would she go?

Her life was far better than it had been six months earlier, when Joe and Ruud appeared unheralded in the bar that night. She stood watching the ship, now in full sail, getting ever smaller as it headed towards the horizon. She reflected on the change in her life. In her previous life, she stayed afloat financially working for the porcelain factories, which rewarded her just enough to continue to paint. But it was time that was the problem: time, energy, and tiredness. Tiredness saps energy, saps inspiration; it saps life. Then Joe arrived ... a rescuing shadow down a narrow alley on a dark night. Joe took her on as his native assistant and interpreter. He rewarded her handsomely as she orchestrated the purchase of fine Dutch earthenware for him to import into the English market. Now she could paint freely for a year at least, maybe two, and still feed herself. He introduced her to his friend Henry, who gave her a commission and promised more. Through Joe, she met van Reit, an elderly Dutchman, who was closely associated with the art world and, in bygone days, was a painter himself.

The embodiment of this change in her circumstance was the relationship she now enjoyed with the premier earthenware house, *De Porceleyne Fles*. She had laboured there, under-rewarded, for too many years. The business meetings with Joe and Henry, where she used her expertise to advise, led to the placement of substantial export contracts, and caused the Dutch company to re-evaluate her worth. They now appreciated her knowledge and influence, and regularly consulted her on aspects of quality and craftsmanship ... for this work, she was now fully compensated.

Joe had left her in body, only in body. He would stay in her mind for many a month; she knew that. As she looked to the spot where the ship had disappeared in the distant haze, she vowed not just to float, but to sail on this prevailing wind.

3

A year since, she had looked to peace, not opportunity. This was a different aspiration, a change in later life that she shared with Joseph Grieve. A single day at forty years old, Joe was clerking in a small office in Scotland. After the tragic loss of a ship, he discovered a rekindled ambition and a route to becoming a prosperous merchant. He stood up to grasp the chance; she hoped she had it within herself to do the same.

Joe left her with enough money for her to return to Delft. In their short time together there, she had not told him the depth of her past and the pain revisiting Delft had brought her, and he did not question as to why a porcelain artist would live in Veere. Yet she realised the recent adventures in Holland with Joe, Ruud and Henry had managed to dull her pain and shed a softer light on the beauty of Delft once more, rebuilding the spirit of the town within her.

Grietje had lost her parents, a sister, and her infant child. If plague, pox, and fire were God's judgement, she did not know the crime. The day she stepped off the barge from Veere, the day she travelled with Ruud to meet Joseph, she expected to see the ghosts that haunt her, and have them appear around every corner, barter at every market stall, sit in every *koffiehuis*, play chase in every garden. Yet that is not what happened. There was pain, yes, but no lurch inside, no tears, just two new friendly faces smiling at her on those brightest of days.

It was the beginning of acceptance, of assimilation. When the nights came, it was into Joe's bed she crept. It was not lust, not much anyway, and he sensed that it was protection, comfort. Nor was it an escape. Close to him, she gained a new strength. It was forward she must look and into the future she must travel blindly, no turning. The runes have given her one last chance.

If the offer of a position in Edinburgh was confirmed, her first instinct was, yes. It still was her first instinct, but she must not go for Joe. She would not threaten his marriage or even discomfort his wife, Mary. The impetus to go, leave Zeeland and set herself elsewhere, in another country, must come from within herself …

the will from, and for, Grietje van der Meer. There is professional interest for her in Delft. She will pack up her studio in Veere and move to Delft without trepidation. That might be enough for her, even in the long term. Only time will reveal the truth of that. First, a visit to the woman in the cottage by the harbour, the cart driver's widow, then she would make plans to move to Delft.

The room was small and comfortable with two fireside chairs, a table, and a spinning wheel by the single window. The woman, who Grietje now knew as Esmée, was widowed when her husband Henrik was caught in the winter flood. He had been driving Tom Miller, Joe's merchant employer, through the night in a storm when the dyke collapsed. Tom's personal effects had been recovered and delivered to Esmée's cottage. On a previous visit, Esmée produced Tom Miller's unopened satchel and handed it to Grietje. It held great value to Joe and the business. Now head of Lockhart & Grieve, Joe told Grietje that he felt a degree of responsibility for the widow, and Grietje took it upon herself to visit. Esmée accepted no offer of reward, but said she enjoyed Grietje's company. Grietje learned much about coping with grief from this calm and thoughtful woman, and a bond formed. Grietje was drawn to Esmée when she found that she would listen with understanding and empathy. Esmée remembered every detail of their conversation as Grietje found herself recounting her most private thoughts. Esmée liked to spin her own thread and wove fine patterns on cotton squares. She made a little income from this.

Grietje told of her plan to move back to Delft but promised to return to Veere and visit her frequently. Esmée said that her husband's cart had been returned; it had a broken wheel and some of the wood was rotting. Grietje insisted on fixing the wheel and Esmée said she no longer had need of it. It was kept nearby in a small warehouse. Esmée invited Grietje to use the warehouse to store any belongings she did not require in Delft. Over the next few weeks, Grietje cleared her room and made arrangements to travel. It was fortuitous that a letter from Henry arrived to say that he would like to meet her in Delft during the next month to complete the sittings for his portrait, before he put on any more weight. Grietje had replied that she would be delighted to see him, and she informed him of her plans. She also wrote to van Reit and asked if he would like her to visit him on her way to Delft. Within a week she was ready to set off on her own, taking the cart that Esmée had now gifted. Joe had left her with a pistol; she kept it concealed and within reach.

VOORNE, HOLLAND 1711

Chapter 2

It was a slow journey to Delft from Veere by cart, with two overnight stops before she reached Voorne. There had been no reply from van Reit; regardless, Grietje had already decided to call as she passed. It was a sun-blessed late morning; if he was not available, she could easily achieve Delft before sunset.

A footman answered her knock quickly and acknowledged her, ushering her in as a boy arrived from the yard to tend to the horse and cart. The footman said van Reit had received her letter and her visit was not unexpected. Grietje was shown into the drawing-room and asked to wait; a lovely young maid, one she had not seen before, brought a small dish of food and offered her a warm drink. It was half an hour before van Reit appeared, slightly dishevelled but more sprightly than when she had last visited. He was delighted to see her and insisted she stay for one night to allow them more time to talk. The old man explained he now lived in short bursts of energy interspersed with ever-longer periods of deep sleep. 'One of these days, I shall just not wake up.'

Grietje noticed that there was no emotion in his statement.

'Please forgive my lack of response. I find it very difficult to make an arrangement, but I am so very glad you called. Would it suit you if we talked for an hour or two this morning? I shall then retire awhile, and we can take supper together in the evening.'

Grietje assured him that there was no immediacy in her travel. 'I value your company and am happy to spend the time with you here.'

'I would like to know more of your work and talk about art this morning and, if you will not be offended, I would ask for news of Joe and Tom in the evening.'

Grietje nodded, she realised van Reit lived a considered life, perhaps a consequence of him living alone with limited time. Van Reit guided Grietje along the hallway to his study. It was darker –

candles were lit in their sconces – and warmer than the rest of the house. There were several fine paintings on the oak-panelled wall each side of the fireplace, and two walls with overfilled bookshelves. Two well-worn, cushioned chairs sat by the fire, each with a pedestal table; a desk with its own chair sat under the window. Van Reit sat close to the warmth of the fire and, after making sure she was comfortable, began to ask Grietje about her professional background. Perhaps it was his manner or age, or her recent visit to Esmée, but Grietje did not follow her lifetime's habit of disclosing little. She openly told van Reit of her love of art and, through her father, her involvement in painting from an early age.

'My father was a craftsman in wood; he worked in a shop, not his own, in Leiden – mostly inlays, fine furniture. I know he produced frames for the great exhibitions; we held great works in the shop. He died when I was quite young. I barely remember him as a person, but I know I played with any bit of wood that I could scavenge and picked up a little of his craft.

'After his funeral, we lived in poor circumstance for a year or more. Then my mother, my two younger sisters and I moved to Amsterdam and lived with his younger brother. I don't know if they were married; there was no ceremony nor celebration. He was a painter. I was near twelve years and I liked him as a person, sneaking into his studio whenever I was able. When he found that I was interested and able, he took me with him every day to the studio to join the apprentices, and they had me mixing the colours and preparing the boards and canvases. If I made myself useful, I was tolerated by the others and permitted to use discarded material to sketch.'

'Can I ask which studio?'

'Not an important one. Dullaert, Heijmen Dullaert.'

'Ah, not unimportant. Did he not apprentice to van Rijn?'

'So, he kept telling us. He did not appear often, and I was chased away when he came to work. It was the younger painters that made me welcome.'

'Ah.'

'It is a long story, meneer, and I do not wish to tire you with the details, some of which are painful in recollection.' Grietje hesitated. 'As you can imagine, a young girl, in the company of men whom she admired, could not separate the hand from the heart…'

'Please Grietje, I have no wish to stress you. Do not feel you need to continue.'

'I was involved with the studio work for three, four years; that was my apprenticeship. My uncle became the studio senior and supported me, teaching me many skills. He and others said privately that I had a good eye and was as talented, perhaps more so, than many of the others. However, the cause of my upset is that I then had to leave. It was my fault … and I had to leave not just the studio, but Amsterdam and my family.'

Van Reit reached across to pat her hand. 'Please do not say more.'

'It was a long time, meneer. I was with child and would not name the father. I did not know the father. My mother was not unkind but, for the family's sake, my uncle decided to send me to Delft to stay in a hostel run by nuns. There were many girls there. It was a cruel and sorry place. At first, I was sent to work in the laundry, but after a time I found a place in the potteries. It paid more, but all my earnings went to the nuns for our keep.'

Grietje stopped and took a breath. 'When I reached seventeen years, I left the hostel and managed to find a living for myself. I had persuaded a manager at the pottery, who had taken a liking to me, that I was a skilled draughtsman. He tried me on the line. At last I could draw again, and my life continued in an unsettled fashion for many years. Do not let me portray too poor an impression. I have not had a bad life compared to many, but nothing lasted. Try as I might, I did not find stable or secure situation in harmony with my own desire to paint. On the rare occasions I could find the time and money for paint, I painted.'

'You did not return to Amsterdam or find work in a studio?'

'It was not possible in the circumstances I found myself. My mother had departed, and my uncle quickly took another. It was difficult for me to find an open door.'

'Let me guide you away from this and talk about the art, and I apologise again for asking this of you. Would you tell me of your situation and work now? Do you have any paintings to show or sell?'

'I did not want to misrepresent myself to you, meneer. My past is my own; I am not embarrassed by it. And the answer is yes. I have some small paintings with me, in my case, but the larger pieces are in Veere. There are not many. Enough only for me to show competence and gain commissions.'

'I see.'

'I have managed these last few years to find a little time for painting. I have my own room in Veere, I still do some work for the porcelain factories and I have been finding work in bars and *huizen* sufficient to allow me to eat and paint. I have been successful in gaining a few small commissions but not enough to live on. That was, of course, until Joseph and Ruud appeared.'

'Ruud?'

'Joe's assistant. He is just a boy. They were together when we met.'

'Then Joseph helped you?'

'He employed me and paid me well for what he considered to be a professional service, but it was more than that. He involved me in the business dealings and trusted my opinions. Meneer, he treated me with a respect I have never had and that, I believe, has presented an opportunity to change my life.'

'In our short acquaintance, Grietje, if you'll forgive me, I can see it is a respect you well deserve.'

'So I have a number of commissions now, and Joe left enough money to keep me well and painting at least for the next two years.'

'May I see the work you have with you?'

'There are only a few pieces, mainly still life, but yes, of course.' Grietje stood up.

'Please remain. I will have the boy fetch your bag if you will direct him.' Van Reit rang a hand bell.

Standing at the desk van Reit had a footman bring over a candlestick. Tilting the paintings to get the best light, he carefully examined them as Grietje stood beside him in silence. He reached into a drawer and held a glass to see the detail.

'These are all by your hand?'

'Yes, meneer.'

'Remarkable ... the detail.'

Standing back, he held a still life composition: a candle lit apple, a torn lump of bread and a pewter tankard sitting on a pale folded cloth.

'You manage to lift these objects from the canvas, exceptional. Were you taught?'

'Yes, meneer, Dullaert was a master of *trompe l'oeil* and he encouraged the apprentices to use his techniques in their painting. I practised with them. On this scale,' she pointed at the painting, 'it is only a slight exaggeration of certain features and subtle changes of tone. Overdone, it becomes a cartoon. It is a matter of judgement.'

'Do you use measurement and geometry?'

'No, I just paint what I see.'

'And you mix your own paints?'

'Yes, of course.'

'The expense?' Van Reit queried.

'I am a thief.'

Van Reit laughed too hard; it turned into a cough and he had to hold himself steady.

'And if I may be further rude and ask one last question, is this your best?'

'Of that style, perhaps. I prefer life study, interior, em ... domestic scenes, or portraiture. I think those are where my talents lean.'

'No landscapes?'

'I'm competent, but they do not inspire, I do not consider them my signature. I spent many hours painting seas and skies for the master. Perhaps I paid a toll.'

'From life?'

'No.'

'Are these for sale?'

'I need them to exhibit my skill for commissions, so I am reluctant to part with them.'

'If I was less aged, I would offer an amount you might find hard to refuse but let me do something else for you. I know two very reputable art dealers in Delft. If you would leave the paintings with me for a short while, the dealers will attend at my invitation and I would gain their opinion. It is my indulgence, but I would hope it would give you a measure of value and perhaps lead to more work.'

Van Reit saw Grietje's hesitation. 'Do not be concerned as to the security. I will not part with them and I will return them to you at the address you leave, say, within fourteen nights regardless of anything else.'

'Thank you, meneer. I value your support. It is not that. I have not been apprenticed and am not a member of the Guild in Delft, or anywhere else, a burden of my gender. I am careful with my commissions and cannot sell openly. If I am discovered, at the least it would be a fine and a prohibition; the punishment for me would be that I would not be able to paint. Veere did not present this problem, Delft is not too stringent, in Amsterdam or Antwerp it would become impossible for me to trade.'

'I see. Pardon me, I should have realised. You have signed your work with your surname.'

'Yes, it is, was also my uncle's. If I am questioned, I say the work is his. It does not bear close scrutiny; I take pains to avoid that.'

'If my friends take an interest, and I will not reveal the true source or my own favour, a display in either of their houses would enhance your reputation and your demand. But I will take care, let me think more on this.'

'Thank you, meneer.'

'Now, I must retire. You will dine with me this evening?'

'Gladly, meneer.'

'I promise I will not interrogate; the conversation will be lighter. I will now have you shown to your room. You may want to take a walk in the grounds before supper. There is beauty. If you walk towards the sea, you will come across a row of cottages, *huisje*. This is where I used to work. They are very private and will not be secure, just a bit dusty I suspect. I cannot walk there now; I still paint a little here in this house. If you are curious, do enter; there is some of my own work there, mostly sea and sky.' Van Reit wore an apologetic expression. Grietje smiled. There was an intensity, a fervency, about this gentleman which had her fully engaged. She looked forward to the evening.

Tom Binnie

FIFESHIRE, SCOTLAND 1733

Chapter 3

Rose gripped the rail. She had yet to become accustomed to the pitch and roll of the Forth estuary.

'I'm sorry, Father, am I being punished?'

'No, do not be fretful, it is not God's doing nor is it your own fault.'

'I have nothing more to bring up.'

'The voyage will soon be over.'

David asked a crewman for a bucket, and they moved from the rail.

'It hurts, Papa.' Rose held her midriff.

'I know a trick. Sit here in the middle of the boat and look, can you see the shore?'

'Yes.'

'Just keep looking at the land in the distance, not the boat nor the sea; move if you like.' David stood up. 'Try to keep your head steady with the shore.'

Rose did as he suggested. 'How do you know this, Father?'

'Joseph told me a long time ago when I took a sea journey, my first, to St Andrews. I had just finished school.'

'I liked Mary and Grace.'

'I know, Rose, I did too.'

'Not Joe?'

'Yes, Joseph too, but there are problems at the moment. 'David had to deflect her. 'Rose?'

'Yes, Papa?'

'Why do you call me *father* sometimes and *papa* others?'

'Oft-time you are father. You teach me, correct me, scold me, and keep me right and good under God. But now, with mother gone, happen-times a girl just needs a papa.'

'You are a very wise child.'

Rose was perking up. 'Wiser than Adam Smith?'

'Hah, no, he is clever, and not necessarily wise. You are prematurely wise.'

'Maybe he could teach me clever and I can teach him wise.'

'I'm not sure if either can be taught, certainly not wisdom. Look, we are close to Kinghorn now.'

'Father, I am hungry.'

For the first time since the loss of his beloved wife, David's inner raging stilled, and he inwardly and humbly thanked his gods for their gift of this special child.

There was a trader on the ferry who recognised David and offered them seats on his grain wagon for the short journey to Kirkcaldy. The offer was gratefully accepted.

'My lad goes to your school, sir.'

'The name?'

'Symson, sir.'

'Ah, a good scholar. He works at his books,' said David

'Will he account and writ, sir?'

'He will if you help keep him to the task.'

'Thank you, I will endeavour to do so. Can I ask, sir?' Symson questioned.

'Yes,' replied David

'I heard that you take girls.'

'Do you have one?'

'I do, sir, Margaret, she's the bright one. Cheeky mind.'

'Then send her to me if she is willing.'

Symson was not sure. 'I will have to do the accounts. Business is not as good…'

'Have her come to me, Symson, and we shall see what we can do.'

'Thank you, sir. Shall I drop you at the school?'

'Yes, thank you, Mr Symson. We are in the janitor's house, in the school yard, for not too much longer I hope.'

The new school was complete and sat high on Hill Street, but the master's house, which was to be set on the same street, had only rough foundations. David was tired of nagging the Council in this regard. Problems with finance was all he was habitually told.

They arrived to find Smithy, head in a book, another by his side, sitting on the steps of the school. It was Saturday, not a school day. Rose alighted the cart quickly on seeing him and made towards the school.

Adam, barely looking up, stayed seated. 'I can just about read this; it is part way between Latin and English.'

'Hello, Adam. I've been to Edinburgh.' She called him Adam now when they spoke, but she still thought of him as Smithy. There were so many Adams, there was only one Smithy.

'There is the odd Greek word, too.'

'I met a new friend and went shopping.'

'But I don't understand what I think are the verbs and the pronouns.'

Rose continued to tell her tale. 'I saw a shop of books in the High Street, but I did not have time to go in.'

'I get lost after a few sentences. I think it's poetry. Can you help me?'

Rose knew this was a typical conversation with Adam when he was absorbed, and she also knew how to snap him out of it … with a thump … but she quite enjoyed the game. He had stopped talking, presumably waiting for an answer.

'Adam, did you hear anything I said?'

'Edinburgh, friend, shopping, High Street, bookshop. Did you get sick on the ferry?'

'Yes, it was awful, but my father told me what to do.'

'What was it?'

'Just stare at a point on the land and try to keep your head steady.

'Interesting. Can you help me with the book?'

'What is it, let me see?' Rose grabbed the book before he could refuse and sat down beside him. 'Oh, it's French. I only know a little.'

'You know more than me.'

'Can you please say that again, louder!'

Adam lifted his head and looked at her. 'You can be annoying.'

'Yes, so can you … it's not poetry. These are letters … the title is … Adam!'

'What is wrong?'

'Where did you get this?'

'It is from my father's library. I could only find these two books in French which were not biblical, that one and this.'

'Let me see … that one is a grammar book and dictionary, but this…'

Rose stood up giggling and made to walk with the book towards her house.

'Father, Father…' she shouted, but not too loudly.

'Rose, stop … stop please.'

And she did. 'What is it? 'Dearest Adam, the title is...' she announced as if at the pulpit, then looked all around to make sure they could not be overheard. '*Lettres d' amour en francais*,' and felt herself bright red.

'What does it mean, why are you behaving so oddly?'

'They are letters from a woman to a man.'

'What do they say?' Smith questioned.

'I don't know. I haven't…'

'Rose!' a deeper voice.

'Oops, oui Papa?'

'Hello Smith.'

'Sir.'

'Rose, you'll need to fetch bread and provisions for supper. Be quick. It's getting late, the market stalls may be quite bare.'

Rose handed Smith's book back and went into the house.

'What is that you are reading, Smith?'

Adam quickly switched the books and handed his master the dictionary, keeping the other behind his back.

'It's in French. One of your father's?'

'Yes, sir.'

'I know he was well travelled?'

'You knew him, sir?'

'Yes, a little. We should talk one day but now is not the right time.'

Rose reappeared with a basket. 'I'll be quick, Father. Will you come with me, Adam?'

'I will walk down with you. I think my mother will want me home.'

They walked in silence down Kirk Wynd to the High Street. They stood awhile before Rose turned left to the harbour and Smith right, towards his house.

'Adeline is coming to visit in a fortnight, I will ask her to bring a more suitable French book for you.'

'How do you ask?'

'My father writes to her father, Sir Peter, all the time. We have taken to enclosing our own notes within their post.'

'Are they not read?'

'We code our messages, so no one will know what we share,' said Rose smiling.

'What is that?'

'Always questions, Adam. We don't write what we mean. Adeline showed me how. It's clever, they often do it in France, apparently, to exchange secrets.'

'Tell me.'

'Not now. I better get to the fish stalls, else it will be lard for supper. I'll see you in school on Monday.'

'You never quite answer my questions,' Adam complained, and Rose just smiled. She liked Adam. Despite, at eleven years of age, being two years younger than her, he was by far the cleverest and wittiest in her class. She used her age advantage to tease him frequently. He did not seem to mind. As the other boys of her own age in the school grew older, she noticed that their behaviour towards her was changing. She also noticed that she had grown much taller than the boys of her own age. Oft-time, they treated her as someone separate from themselves. Adam, as yet, showed no such change. They all, however, adored her friend, the whimsical, pretty, French Adeline. It was when these thoughts, and others like them, swam in her mind that she missed her dear departed mother the most.

Rose returned to the small house with four herring in a bowl … paying the extra penny for beheading and gutting … and her small sack filled with flour. There had been no bread, but she would bake some for supper.

'Father, I will go to the farm for eggs and milk. The market was bare.' And she left again to walk up the hill. The stipend of her father's new position was improved, and it was assured. He had been released from the discomfort of chasing parents and heritors. Now, there was more than enough for good food, clothes, shoes and some furnishings.

It had been a fair day for mid-November, the leaves had all but left their branches. The paths were mushed with yellow, reds and browns. She reflected on her first journey to Edinburgh and looked forward to Adeline's visit next week. She wished she could have Adeline to stay with her, but there was no room in their small house. Her father was correct in this and she would have to wait until they moved into their larger house which seemed to be taking forever to build. The two girls were left with either staying at Dunnikier with the Oswalds' which meant they were surrounded by boys, or at the Andersons' where their movement and behaviour were more constrained. They only truly found time to themselves when she could visit Adeline in Tarvit. It was nearly a day's journey, and she had not been able to visit since moving to Kirkcaldy.

Whenever Rose was overly worried, she devised a plot. She couldn't help it; it had always been so. Ideas just popped into her head. Christmas was the opportunity … there would be a school break. She prayed that Adeline would still be in Scotland and not travelling south to visit her mother's family. They would devise something by letter. Manipulating fathers was not as easy as dealing with boys, but Adeline was expert.

Rose had managed to get pork and roots at the farm, so she could produce a good Sunday supper for her father. She would also make a pot of soup while the bread baked.

'Father, you haven't lit the fire!'

'Oh, Rose, sorry, I was caught up in my correspondence'

'Supper may be a little late.'

There were only two rooms and a scullery in the cottage, much like their old home in Cupar. The rooms were good-sized. David worked in his room, the bedroom, and Rose kept herself to the other room which contained a table and four chairs, a box-bed and a dresser. She cooked using the racks above the fire. The washing sink was in the scullery and there was a convenient well halfway down the Wynd.

It was nearly the seventh hour when Rose called her father to sit down to eat. Rose produced two bowls of thick soup and fresh bread, adding that there was smoked herring to follow. She thought her father looked drained.

'Are you ill, Father?'

'I am well, Rose, do not be of concern. I am in need of this meal and a good night, I think.'

'Did you know Smithy's father?'

'At little, he was the Custom's Officer. I will talk to Smith about it sometime if he wishes. You can tell him. You are friends?'

'I think so, you can never quite tell.'

'Well, you appear to be.'

'Have you been to their rooms and met his mother?'
'Yes, once. She is … what is the word…'
'Austere, perhaps?'
'Yes, that is it.'
'Rose, if we mention others, in my position, I have to be careful. You understand this?'
'Of course, Father, but I would ask that you trust me when you can. I would not pass on anything I have been told. I will not breach our confidence.'
'You are growing up.'
'If you could not trust me then, without Mother, who would you have?'
They sat in comfort; the log on the fire shifted with a shower of sparks and the crackling of the flames as the heat reached fresh timber.
'Smith's house has lots of books.'
'I have heard his father was travelled and well read.'
'When did he die?'
'When Smith was very young, an infant.'
'Oh, that is sad.'
'How is your catechism?'
'Now you are being a schoolmaster,' Rose grumped.
'Yes, and your answer?'
'I practise and I know it well.'
'Now you are of age, the minister will call to test you.'
'Mr Erskine?' Rose queried with a frown.
'Yes.'
'When?'
'Anytime, it might be tomorrow. Do you not like him?'
'Can I speak the truth, Father?'
'Yes'
'Without rebuke?'
'Well, I want to hear what you think.'
'I do not like the Kirk here as much as our old one in Cupar.'
'You miss your friends?'

'Yes, but I am trying to be...' Rose couldn't find the word.

'Impartial,' offered David.

'It is dour. It is as if we are always being told off, as if we are always doing wrong. Even if we are very good.'

'We are all sinners,' David said in a sombre tone, making Rose laugh. 'It is a bit dry, but as schoolmaster, I cannot agree with you.' Rose did not know if his reply was meant to be funny.

David continued, 'It is not just the minister. In these times we, all of us, need to respect and adhere to the conventions of the Kirk, whatever you think of them. Kirkcaldy is a larger and more strict community than Cupar. I did intend to talk to you about this.'

Rose now became concerned. 'Father?'

'Well, you need to be more careful about how you behave in town, more aware at least.'

'I don't understand. I do behave.'

'With the older boys and if there are men around?'

'I do.' Rose stifled a tear.

'Just remember, you are a young woman now. As a child you can walk with boys the same age and play. You can run laughing through a busy market, but you need now to become familiar with correct behaviour of young women of standing. I'm sorry, Rose, you have done nothing wrong, but I have taken this opportunity to explain it.'

'It is not fair, Papa.'

'It is not fair, and I sometimes wish it were not so or, at least, that I could explain it better.'

'But I walk with Adam Smith nearly every day.'

'That is alright because he is younger, ten or eleven I think.'

'But what about Matthew, Robert or David?'

'I'm giving guidance. You have to be careful when you are on your own. It is fine if you are invited to their houses or if they visit here. But around the town sometimes, not all of the time, you may need a chaperone. Do you not remember Mrs Anderson's housekeeper insisting on it?'

'I do. I had to walk around in an awful gown.'

'Rose, it is not so bad.'

'Do the boys need a chaperone?'

'Well no, although some could do with one.'

Rose stood. 'I will serve the smoked fish, Papa. I think I understand, it is just that I don't feel like a young woman.'

'How do you know?'

'That's not fair either.'

'Rose, I think many young women, even those much older than you, feel exactly the way you do. Only now am I realising this because of you. I am learning too.'

'What did the girls do when you were at school in Edinburgh?'

'There were no girls at my school, but those that I saw in the town were shepherded around like geese.'

Rose did not go to bed upset. She wanted her father to be open and treat her as grown up. She would have to accept the responsibilities of that position. She wanted to talk to Adeline. She would write to her tomorrow.

Sunday was, as usual, a long day. She was not supposed to perform household duties on the Sabbath, but she did. There was so much to do. If she were to continue to diligently attend the school, she could not housekeep and everything else without encroaching on the Lord's time. In her own head, she was quite sure he would understand. Apart from the two very short journeys to the Kirk and back, the parishioner's time was to be spent reading the good book and giving thanks to the Lord. No work, no play, no activity outside nor in, not even a country walk, a recreation where thoughts may have grasped the opportunity and admired God's creation.

The Kirk sat overseeing the town on the steep slope of Kirk Wynd opposite the school yards. The square belltower of rough-hewn ashlar stone held a room of office, a cell, and a secure vault. The body of the Kirk, plain walled, rectangular in structure, comprised a nave only, no transepts nor choir; its thin windows allowed in little light even during high summer. Inside presented an altar to hold the ornate silverware on holy days, a carved wooden lectern, a silver cross its only adornment, and seating for the congregation; there was no high pulpit for the minister.

Candles sat in sconces and on tall prickets, ornately fashioned by the burgh blacksmith for the end of each pew. The large carved wooden seats to the front were funded by the burghers and merchants ... no Lords and Ladies lived in this parish. Behind them, the plain pews filled less than half of the nave, leaving the poor to stand at the rear.

A grassy burial ground was bordered by trees to the north and east, perched above the Wynd. Being open to the south, it caught the full sun on cloud-free days in all seasons. It was a calm and beautiful place for contemplation, remembrance and prayer.

A small plot with a dozen or so fresh wooden crosses, unnamed, some just sticks, revealed the town's continuing tragedy of infant mortality.

That and every Sunday, a long service, a miserable sermon that lasted for well over the hour, the interminable readings and the droning of three-chord psalms to celebrate the unworthiness of man, left Rose's knees stiff and her bottom sore. It was not an example of a message of God which had inspired Rose, along with her father, to be unwavering in devotion, purity, charity, duty and sacrifice. *There is but one God...* It was a message, the haranguing, the repetition, the dirge, which left the congregation without earthly hope. And the female voice was never heard. *Cannot this kirk not have a choir?* She had been given no opportunity to sing. She now understood song as pure joy, food for the soul, not the devil's work. At least they were able to sit through it – not from entitlement – they had to pay for their place on the pew.

Rose hobbled back to the house, leaving her father in serious discourse with the minister and a few of the church elders. Rose looked for her friends, but on Sundays, even the boys were tightly reined. She had to stop herself thinking of her Cupar friends, Cora and Jess. Once released from the service, the three would chase round the churchyard, all the little ones and barking dogs joining in. They incurred many more smiles than disapproving frowns. Here was God still, and there was joy. She dares not think too much about Cupar. Her father had been promised improvement in his circumstance in this new school. She knew this, but as yet he seemed more burdened, not less.

Arriving back in the cottage, David asked again about her knowledge of the catechism. He appeared preoccupied and went straight to the schoolroom to work, although that was certainly against the Lord's wish. She wondered if he made deals in his prayers like she did. And sometimes she wondered if she had lost her mother because of her attempts to barter with God.

Rose spent the Sunday evening carefully writing the letter to Adeline. She used a crib that she and Adeline had written out. The crib gave her plain message a meaning and intent that only Adeline and herself could understand. They had done this many times before, and part of the fun was making mistakes and laughing about the misunderstandings when they saw each other. Rose was sure Adeline did this deliberately to mislead her into thinking the most awful things. It was their secret; it was their bond.

The last two letters she had received from Adeline contained more mystery than usual. Interspersed within the English, French and Latin words scattered into sentences written in Adeline's elegant hand were short words with numbers: Gen 1.1-2, Phil 3-8, Lev 4.2-5. Rose was lost. Adeline's message superficially told of her mundane days at Tarvit, but Rose knew a *repulsive pie* became an unwanted male; a *beautiful pudding that fell on the floor* was her stepsister, *sweet wine* was a desirable youth, and the message became an entertainment of the highest order. These words and numbers, however, were new and meant nothing to her.

One lazy Saturday, prior to her visit to Edinburgh, four legs dangled over the harbour wall,

'Adam?' No acknowledgement. 'If you have words and letters in a message, what does it mean?'

'What words and letters?'

There was enough sandy dirt for Rose to scratch her example in the ground.

'What message?'

'Just a message to me, from a friend.'

Smithy looked a while. 'What is in the letter?'

'Just things about my friend's life.'

'You mean Adeline?'

'I didn't say that.'

Smithy thought some more. 'Write another one.'

Rose did.

'It's the Bible, isn't it?'

'What do you mean?'

'It's the Old Testament, words from Genesis and Leviticus.'

'Oh, I see.'

'Why does she write that?'

'Adeline and I often discuss the teachings of the Lord.'

Smithy looked sceptical and Rose raised her small pointed nose in the air and wore her well-practised angelic expression. Rose was then desperate to return to the message and look up the passages to determine what Adeline had written. She suspected that it was nothing to do with God's words at all.

David came back to the house as Rose prepared the pork, beans and kale for supper. There was also some bread left over, which she reheated.

'Would you like wine, Father?' There was a half-filled flagon in the pantry.

'Not on the Sabbath, Rose.' David sat at the table.

'Have you been preparing lessons?'

'Yes … and dealing with Council matters.'

'I am happy here, father, I do not need the big house.'

'Thank you, Rose. That is one of the issues but not the only one.'

David hesitated before continuing. 'There is a new leader of the Council and Mrs Oswald is unwell. Do not worry though. It is unfortunate but I shall keep to my task. How have you occupied yourself today?'

'Father, I did only a little Bible study, but I did the translation for school tomorrow.'

'How do you know the set task?'

'Smithy, I mean Adam told me yesterday.'

'Well, that is a good use of time. Perhaps you would read to me after supper?'

'Gladly, do you not have to work?'

'I remember promising you many things when we moved here. Not many have yet come to fruition but do not give up on them just yet. The one thing I can, and will give you, is a bit more of my time.'

'Thank you, Papa. I would like to read for you. Is Mrs Oswald very ill?'

'I don't know. She is certainly incapacitated. I shall enquire.'

'We could ask one of the boys.'

'Would you ask Matthew tomorrow and I will write a note in the evening?'

'Yes, Father.'

'This is fine pork, Rose.'

'Mother showed me how to serve it.'

David went to his room while Rose cleared and cleaned up in the scullery. He returned with a volume that Rose hadn't read before and sat by the fire to leaf through its pages. Rose blew out the candles on the table and took the dirty water out of the scullery door to pour it in the yard where it found its way to the open drain threading down the Wynd. She then returned to join her father by the fire.

'I have marked some passages for you.'

'What is it, Father?' She looked at the worn spine.

'It is St Augustine. I think you will like it.'
'It is Latin.'
'Yes, Rose.'
'Ever the teacher.' She smiled.

> *What is it that I love when I love God? Not*
> *the beauty of any bodily thing, nor the order of*
> *seasons, not the brightness of light that rejoices*
> *the eye, nor the sweet melodies of all songs, nor*
> *the sweet fragrance of flowers and ointments*
> *and spices: not manna nor honey, not the limbs*
> *that carnal love embraces. None of these things*
> *do I love in loving my God. Yet in a sense I do*
> *love light and melody and fragrance and food*
> *and embrace when I love my God – the light and*
> *the voice and the fragrance and the food and*
> *embrace in the soul, when that light shines upon*
> *my soul which no place can contain, that voice*
> *sounds which no time can take from me, I*
> *breathe that fragrance which no wind scatters, I*
> *eat the food which is not lessened by eating, and*
> *I lie in the embrace which satiety never comes to*
> *sunder. This it is that I love when I love my God.*

Monday morning came and there were two sealed letters in her father's hand sitting on the breakfasting table: one to Sir Peter Rigg and one to a person, not Joseph Grieve, at an Edinburgh address. David asked Rose to take the letters to the coaching inn before school, to catch the post carriages to St Andrews and Edinburgh. She had found a way of slipping her note to Adeline into the folded paper without breaking or disturbing her father's seal. This she delicately did after her father left for school.

After clearing the pots and damping the fire, she put on her thick dark dress and cloth cap and left, holding the letters. Walking down the Wynd she bumped into Smithy walking up to school who, of course, was curious as to her opposing his direction.

'I'll come with you.'

He turned to join her, heading back down the hill. They had only travelled a few yards to find Mrs Smith, Adam's mother, coming towards them.

'Whoops,' muttered Adam.

'Adam, that is not the way to school.'

'I am going with…'

'School for you, Adam.'

Adam apologised, to Rose it seemed, and ambled back uphill in his distinctive ungainly gait.

Rose stood straight and spoke first.

'I am very sorry, Mrs Smith. My father said I was not to walk alone if possible.'

'I see. Is that the truth, Rose Miller?'

Rose curtsied.

'Then what is your journey?'

'To catch the early post horse, ma'am.' Rose showed the letters in her hand.

Mrs Smith beckoned. 'Adam, come back.'

He had not travelled far.

'I am not sure my Adam is the wisest choice of chaperon.'

Rose was not yet sure of the word or how to react, so she didn't.

Adam dawdled back.

'Rose, perhaps you need to find some female company.'

'Ma'am.'

'Adam, you are to defend Miss Miller's honour. Now, see that you are both on time for school.'

As they neared the High Street, Adam broke their silence, 'What did you say?'

'That I am not supposed to walk around on my own.'

'Oh, why not?'

'Because I'm a girl, I think. Where was your mother going?'

'To the manse. She spends much time with Mr Erskine, the minister.'

Later that day, during the midday break, Rose considered what Mrs Smith and her father had said, and approached one of the few other girls of her own age still attending the school. The girl, who usually left the yard during the mid-day break with a friend, was today standing on her own fiddling with a small cloth pack, which Rose presumed to be her lunch.

'Hello, I am Rose, are you on your own today?'

The girl was surprised by her.

'Hello, yes my cousin is unwell.'

'Would you like to come to my house to eat that?'

The girl shyly nodded. 'Do you not always play with the boys?'

'Only because I know them … all they talk about is cockfighting, shinty and Jacobites. They are fine on their own but together…' She feigned a vomiting gesture. 'What is your name?'

'I'm Isobel, Isobel Peat, you can call me Bella.'

'Come Bella, we can sit and eat, and perhaps you can tell me about the town. I am completely new to it.'

'You're quite nice.'

'I try to be. Did you think otherwise?'

'Yes, the other girls are a bit scared of you.'

'Me! I'm not scary at all.'

Bella smiled. She told Rose that her absent friend was her cousin Bessie and that she had become unwell on Saturday. She was not allowed visitors.

'Do you know what is wrong?'

'She has a bad throat. They said distemper.'

Another word today Rose did not know.

Rose asked Bella a lot of questions. She wasn't a chatterbox but didn't mind answering. She laughed at Rose's tales of her life in Cupar.

'Is it funny being the master's daughter?'

'To me, it would be funny not to be.'

'How do you know the boys?'

'I met them through friends of my father. We spent the summer at Dunnikier.'

'With the Oswalds?'

'Yes.'

'Oh.'

Rose found it pleasing to have someone her own age and gender to talk to. They were soon joined during the daily breaks by another girl, Rachel, who was in Bella's class. After eating during the break and sometimes after school, they would study together at Rose's supper table. Rose was in a higher class but was happy to have company and to help them.

As Friday approached, Rose had not seen a letter to her father from Tarvit House. She asked him at supper, 'Have you heard from Sir Peter?'

'No, and it concerns me. Why do you ask?'

'I am keen to see Adeline. Can she stay with us?'

'I have said before, Rose. This house is not suitable. You will have to wait until we move into better accommodation.' David gave her a look that was familiar to her; the matter was closed. 'Did you talk to Matthew Oswald about his grandmother?'

'Oh yes, I forgot to tell you. She is abed but sitting up and getting better. He said she was seeing family and writing letters.'

'Good, thank you Rose. I shall write to her.'

'May I ask if there is something wrong at the school, Father?'

'Nothing to worry you. There have been changes in the Council and I am having to convince them of my new curriculum, much like in Cupar. It is frustrating, and without Mrs Oswald or Sir Peter's support, it is a hard battle, particularly as I am not known here.'

'The girls?'

'The girls are safe. The Council are happy with the education of girls. We must try to engage more of them, however.'

Rose wanted to help but felt helpless.

'I also want to talk to Mrs Oswald about the lack of progress with the house. It is a delicate matter, as we had agreed terms. You must not discuss this.'

'I will not break a promise, Papa ... I do have a silly idea.'

'Tell.'

'A seasonal play, for the Council and others. They do not know you or what you do. Stand before them. Let them see!'

David thought a moment ... *and so only by my sword shall I fall...*

'Rose, you may have something.'

VOORNE, HOLLAND 1711

Chapter 4

Later, on the day of her visit to van Reit's country house, Grietje was shown to a room which had been prepared for her. It was warm, a lively fire was lit, a high bed, old linens and dark furniture. As in the other parts of the house she had seen, the walls hosted a selection of fine art. A servant entered and offered Grietje refreshment, which she accepted: an ornate thin glass of red wine with a board of bread, cheese, pickles and meat. She dozed off in a comfortable chair and woke with a moment of confusion. Beams from the afternoon sun brought life to a wall of fine dust swirling randomly between the window and the floor. Grietje changed out of her travelling clothes and into the dress she would wear in the evening. Not a fancy dress, just plain and brown, but it fitted well, and she was comfortable in it. Throwing on her cape she ventured out to find the sea and the *huisje*.

Van Reit's house sat high, surrounded by clumps of trees, the entrance near to a raised road. As she walked round to the south side, she found a formal garden. She had only seen its like in books and paintings. It was well maintained, geometrically arranged with neat rows of lavender interspersed with orange flowers she did not recognise. Small closely cropped trees, cones, were placed at the apexes of two diagonals. At the centre, a pergola with seating was wrapped in climbing roses. Plants were budding and dying, there was not a leaf out of place.

The path away from the house took her down to sea level. Once she had cleared the last of the trees, she saw a row of buildings in the distance on a raised bit of land near the shore. There was a well-worn path to follow. The term *huisjes* misrepresented the row of three buildings. She was expecting a place where a fisherman might feel at home. These were taller, stone roofed buildings made from ashlar stone. The nearest was a two-storeyed house. Of the other two, the middle had three tall windows on the north side and nothing, not even an entry on the south; the farthest had two small windows in its side wall and a large double, barn-type door which, given the wear on the path, seemed to be the common means of entry. Each end of the row was a crow-step gable with quiet chimneys; no fires were lit.

Grietje walked round to the sea side of the buildings and found an open wooden shelter with an easel and chair set such that a wide view of the open sea could be viewed and painted under its cover. In contrast to the groomed garden she had walked, the ground by the walls of the *huisje* were filled with a haphazard of wildflower, spilling out of overfilled beds before merging into clumps of sea grass which stretched as far as the seaweed on the rocks.

The tide was coming in along the wide sandy shore. A nearby bustle of silvery sand'lings followed the rushing breath of each wave, puffed-up and pecking at the servings of the wash. Grietje felt a stir from the unseasonal, warm wind. As she watched the birds, she saw that they all behaved as one, except the few which, on with the ebb, were quicker to run into the sea, the same ran further out and were more reluctant to return. Were they hungrier? Were they the young or the male birds? Were their likely futures better or worse? Which sand'ling was she?

A glance though a darkened window showed the end house to be furnished but unoccupied; it was not her interest. She pushed at the bar across the large doors at the other end of the row, and they slid reluctantly. The loud creak of the rusting hinges made the birds fly off, over her head. Swatting the cobwebs, she walked into a large open space. The studio was tidy, organised but dusty with as much canvas, chemicals, oils, paint, brushes, knives and pallet boards as she had ever seen in one place. There was also apparatus, winches, ladders, linen sheets and wooden frames. She saw that van Reit, or whoever worked here, enjoyed large canvases; one stood on an easel, its surface partly filled with blues and whites, greens and greys – it would need a stepping stool to reach to its full height. It was not her oeuvre, but she understood the challenge of the scale. There was no wall between the end cottage and the middle one, just a few wooden screens. Walking through, she found clothes on benches, lanterns, a large table and several small chairs along with pieces of carved stone, pottery, bottles, jars and metalwork. The striking feature was the light: the three great windows let in a cool even light. But it was the smells, the distinctive scent of an artist's studio that evoked her ambition. A smaller easel with a smaller canvas looked recently worked, unfinished: ominous, bulbous, darkening, grey-blue clouds over what looked like a morning horizon; a thin, calm sea with the light lines of a schooner, guides for a brush stroke. Was the ship coming or going? she wanted to know. It was an inspirational place that incongruously seemed both calm yet full of energy. She had some questions for van Reit if she was given the opportunity.

It was near four hours after noon when Grietje returned to her room. She was sitting pulling her boots off when a knock on the door brought two men, one older, one younger, carrying a half-filled tin bath. They were followed by a young maid struggling with two large jugs of water. The men placed the bath carefully by the fire and left, wordlessly. The maid curtsied and poured the water into the bath.

'Mevrouw, I am Sara. I am sent to help you bathe and dress.'

Grietje nodded as she felt her face warm.

'I will fetch more water and a tray.' Sara left the room and Grietje waited until she thought the maid was out of earshot before she released her laugh.

The maid returned with jugs refilled, placed them by the fire and left again. In her absence, Grietje tested the temperature of the water. Sara re-entered carrying a tray with bottles, dishes and a collection of puffs, soaps and stones. She placed the tray on a small table and started to chatter nervously. 'Excuse me, mevrouw, this is not my normal work. They sent me up to Constance this morning. She told me what to do. She talked and talked. I will try my best.'

Sara produced a thin shirt in fine white linen from under the tray she had brought. 'I have a bathing dress for you.'

Grietje put her hand up to make Sara stop talking. 'Sara, is it? I am not used to having a lady's maid, so we can learn together.'

Sara smiled and curtsied at this.

'Who is Constance?'

'Oh, she was the mistress's maid for many years. She stayed on after the mistress died, God rest her soul. She lives upstairs in her old room next to the mistress's room. She is old-fashioned.'

Grietje wondered what she was about to experience; presumably the bathing was meant to be pleasant. She could not help but think of Joe laughing at her.

'What do we do first? No, wait.' Grietje spotted the empty wine glass from her midday meal. 'Do you think they would bring a glass of wine?'

Sara, who was to Grietje's eyes, dressed as a novice from a nunnery, looked a little surprised. 'For the bathing, mevrouw?'

'Yes, why not?'

'I am not allowed to serve wine, but if you ring the bell.' Sara pointed to a large hand bell on the mantle. After a few minutes, it was answered by a slowly opening door.

Grietje requested wine; the footman nodded and left. 'Well, Sara, what do we do?'

'I will prepare the bath, then I will undress you.'

Grietje sat on the edge of the bed and watched Sara pour sweet smelling salts, oil and herbs into the water. Bubbles appeared as she adjusted the temperature, filling the bath with water from the jugs.

'How long have you worked here?'

'All my life, my mother is cook.'

'Is it a good place to work?

39

'Yes, the master treats us very well. He...'

'He?'

'Sorry, he says he will make sure that we will be looked after.' Sara blushed at her own words.

'Does he have children?'

'No, mevrouw, the young master died before my time here.'

'Family?'

'Not that I know ... I'm not supposed to talk.'

'I shall stop, Sara. I like your master, but I do not know him well.'

'Thank you, mevrouw.' Sara unfolded a Chinese screen and pulled it between the bath and the door. 'Your bath is ready now.'

Grietje stood as the footman arrived to leave a small jug of wine, a glass and a plate of cheese. She poured wine into two glasses and offered the fresh glass to Sara. Sara taken by surprise, took a step back.

'Oh, mevrouw, I couldn't.'

'Try it.' Grietje insisted and Sara took the glass with an embarrassed smile. 'I won't tell.' Grietje assured and laughed as Sara spluttered and coughed. Grietje put down her glass, removed her cotton cap and reached for the ties of her dress.

'I will do it.' Sara stood behind her and carefully pulled at the threaded linen strings. The dress slipped down to the floor and Sara moved to Grietje's front to undo the lace of her undergarment. As the top fell open, she stopped. Offering the Grietje bathing dress, she said firmly, 'We put this on now.'

Grietje did as she was bid. 'Do I wear this in the tub?'

'Yes, mevrouw, to preserve your modesty as I wash.'

Grietje walked to the bath. It was fragrant, the water warm and smooth from the oiled mixture. Knees up, she just fitted in. The light linen garment did not feel as uncomfortable as she thought it might. Sara brought the bathing tray and sat it beside the bath.

'My wine please,' requested Grietje, waving her raised hand. Grietje saw that Sara had sneaked another drink before she brought her own glass over. Sara began by releasing the top part at the back of the bathing dress. She picked up a soft grey-yellow object Grietje did not recognise, applied some oil and started to rub Grietje's back.

'What is that?'

'Oil, mevrouw.'

'No, the soft thing?'

'This is sponge. Am I doing it right?'

'Sara ... this is heaven.'

Sara worked her way over Grietje's body, uncovering and recovering the parts she washed. Sponge for the soft flesh and pumice for the feet and hands. Grietje sank into a half sleep, a dreamy state, so much so that she started when Sara next spoke. 'I'm finished now, mevrouw.' She stood near the fire.

'Shall I get out?'

'When you want to, then I will use anointment.'

'Sara, is it a formal supper?'

'Mevrouw?'

'Where will I be eating?'

'They are preparing the dining room.'

'Then I require a better dress. Could you fetch a blue and white dress from my trunk; it will still be on the cart. The dress is near the top.'

'The footman will get it.'

'Ah, would you ring the bell?'

'No, mevrouw, I am not permitted.'

'Would you pass me the bell?'

Sara nodded and did as she was asked. As Grietje rang the bell, she thought she was becoming too accustomed to the mores in the life of a country house. Rising from the bath, Grietje stood by the fire; she found the bathing dress less appealing when wet. Sara began the incremental procedure of applying the ointment, first to Grietje's back. Grietje, tired of the wet linen, undid the ties and pushed her dress to the floor. Sara paused and continued smoothing in the ointment.

As Sara finished, a knock at the door brought the trunk. She left Grietje naked and glowing by the fire as she fished out fresh undergarments, a light blue satin dress with a white top, and an embroidered cap. Sara's light touch was both respectful and intimate as she then dressed her lady.

'I will fashion your hair now.'

'If I ever gain my own house, I would employ you as my maid.'

'Thank you, mevrouw, I would come.'

Chapter 5

Van Reit was standing by the fire, stick in one hand and a wineglass in the other, when Grietje was shown in. The dining room was large but not intimidating. The table would comfortably seat twelve, but only two places were laid at the end nearest the fire. Although dark in décor, the room was well lit by candle and oil lamp. On the table there were two earthenware urns containing glowing coals. A footman stood in the shadows.

'Juffrouw van der Meer, I am delighted to have your company, and I apologise for this.' Van Reit gestured to the room. 'It is rare that I have an opportunity of a dining occasion. This is one of the finest rooms in the house, and I wanted to show it to you.'

Grietje curtsied. 'You have a wonderful house, sir. Beautiful. But it is not the fabric, there is something mystical about this place. I cannot define it. The grounds also, I walked them in a dream.'

'Please be seated.'

The footman showed her to her chair, then helped van Reit to his. 'May I we discuss the paintings? I am interested in your thoughts.'

'Are any of them your own?'

'No, you may speak freely.'

They both laughed.

Van Reit talked about the history and the acquisition as well as the merit of each painting. Grietje was absorbed in his knowledge and experience. Their discussion became lightly heated when they compared the older style with the new. Wine and food were served soundlessly – Grietje noticed only an occasional nod from van Reit to the footman. Large plates of meats, potatoes and root vegetables were placed on the warming urns. The footman served Grietje from one of the plates as she indicated her choice. Later, Sara arrived to clear away, giving Grietje a small smile. Light ices were brought with yet another bottle of wine, and van Reit became a little more serious.

'I promised not to question you, but may I ask about Joseph, and what you know of Tom Miller?'

'Yes, but I am sworn, and may not be able to answer.'

'I understand.'

'Can I ask your interest? You met Tom only once with Joe?'

'Yes, I question myself whether it is just an old man's whim and I acknowledge that it is partly so. Tom found the house and came in the middle of a very dark night. As he stood in the doorway, he had the look of my son, his hair, his height, even the odd mannerism. I am not deluded. I did not ever think it was him, but out of the similarity grew an empathy. We took to each other, I am sure he would agree, and sat talking through the long hours. Unlike Joseph, Tom has a vulnerability. I very much believe Joseph will succeed in this life. He is a good person; he stays on the ground. He is honourable and strong. Tom was less so. It was as if he felt he should be this successful merchant, indeed could be, but he was not actually sure if that was what he wanted. If you can follow me?'

'I think I understand what you mean, a conflict within,' Grietje replied.

'Regardless of that, I wanted to help Tom even if I could not resolve his dilemma. This is what he felt he had to do. I did not want to influence him. We talked into the night, and when he left, I felt certain that I would see him again. His look back assured me that he thought so too. And then nothing, for a long time nothing, I made enquiries … nothing, until you and Joseph arrived at my door.'

Grietje did not respond immediately as she saw that van Reit's attention had drifted. Van Reit suggested they leave the table and move to the library. A footman followed with their wine glasses and the bottle. Such is an old man's mind that van Reit said he remembered acutely his evening in this room with Tom. 'You never met him?'

'No, I only know of him through Joseph who admired him and cared very much for him.'

'He has a son in Scotland?'

'Yes, he is well. Joseph and his wife Mary see him regularly and ensure his welfare.'

'Grietje, I understand there are matters you cannot discuss. There was a girl in Delft. Janssen, my lawyer had met her.'

Grietje grimaced at the sound of the name. 'Yes, let me think a little.' She took a sip of wine. 'Six months ago, Joseph and I, not without difficulty, found where she is living, and Joe called on her. She welcomed him warmly. Doorjte lives in a small house, but he did not see any means of income. When he came back, we both went back to see her and Joe offered her support, leaving her a good sum of money.'

'You were there?'

'Yes, he left a parcel. There was nothing to note.'

'Did you talk to her?'

'Briefly, it was not a comfortable situation for me.'

'Of course. She said … she knew nothing of Tom?'

'I am sorry, sir, no, not to me.'

'It is a tale that greatly saddens me, the more so as I believe he was heading here when he was caught in the flood. I wish I could have done more.'

'There was one thing. In Veere I recovered Tom's satchel. Joe has it.'

'Did they find a body?'

'Not that I have heard.'

'I'm sorry, let us now talk of lighter things. Did you find the *huisje?*'

Grietje smiled, grateful for the release. 'Such a place; you are lucky I returned from there. I was within a moment of picking up a brush. You would have been troubled to remove me. The large painting of the sea and the sky, is it yours?'

'Yes, some time ago. I doubt I will get back to it. Where will you paint in Delft?'

'I will have to rent a place. I believe I can find something, part of a larger studio perhaps. I have funds.'

'Well, as you have seen I have an abundance of materials. I know the expense. If there are paints and canvases which would be of use to you, please return there in the morning and take what you will. In time they would just dry and rot.'

'Thank you, sir. I do have an income.' Grietje noted his hidden look of disappointment and regretted her answer. She hugely enjoyed the company but did not desire his charity. 'I do have a suggestion...'

'Yes?'

'I look around your walls and I see all manner of the finest paintings, but I see nothing of you: not a portrait, nor the house, nor the *huisje*. I wish to return to paint, with your materials, a portrait of yourself?'

Van Reit visibly brightened. 'It would delight me to see you again. Not a portrait, though, the house perhaps, or local scene, or a domestic, with one of the servants.'

'The fearsome Mevrouw Constance.'

Van Reit's laugh started his cough again.

'I am sorry, sir. If I may, you do seem improved from my last visit.'

'Oh, I am given all manner of powders and potions. If my physic would prescribe you, Grietje, I fear I would live well for yet awhile.'

'A portrait, sir. I see something of a glint that I would capture.'

'I am almost persuaded. In truth it would quickly end up in an attic, if not on a bonfire.'

'Sir!' said Grietje in alarm.

'Oh, I mean the nature of the subject, not the merit of the painter.'

Grietje laughed at her own tease. 'What of your future, sir?'

'I have less and less.'

'As do we all. There are things that would satisfy you?'

46

Van Reit was surprised and almost caught out by her interest. 'There is the foundation. I have left a sum for a new school in Delft. I would dearly like to see it started at least.'

'There is a problem?'

'My lawyer tells me they must wait for my legacy. I do not fully understand. Taxes, he said.'

'I do not understand these things. Is that Janssen?'

'Yes, an old friend, he represents my matters. I saw your expression. Did you not meet him?'

'No, Joseph had an altercation with him when he tried to enquire after Tom.'

'Surely not.'

'Joseph was turned away rudely and abruptly. It may have been a misunderstanding. I have no wish to talk ill of your friend.'

'It does sound odd; he is a valued friend.'

'A school, now that is perfect.' Grietje deflected the difference in opinion.

'Mevrouw?'

'Your portrait will hang in the school!'

Van Reit did not smile, but she could see he had shared her imagination.

'I apologise, I must abed now, Grietje. Would you please ring for the footman?'

'Of course, good night, sir. Will I see you in the morning? I hope to depart near noon.

'Yes, I have a few more words to impart; we can meet for coffee if not too early. Good night.'

'I would value that, sir, good night.'

Grietje rose at dawn, before Sara's attendance, and dressed herself in her travelling clothes. She headed out for a long walk by the sea. Full of thought, she returned by the *huisje* and walked back up to the house. She had enjoyed this visit far more than she had expected to, and she understood why Tom was taken with van

Reit. She would genuinely like to paint his portrait: an old, tanned and weathered face that still held the spark of life, a slight narrowing of the eyes, an upturn at the edge of the mouth, and a continuing interest in the new and the unusual. She did not find the resignation nor pervading cynicism which creeps into many of that age.

Grietje liked Sara and would leave her an address, although she did not know if the maid could read or write. She would also like to return to this house and the land. The place, under its own power, had entranced her.

As the footman opened the dark-oak, outer door for her, she found Sara standing in the hallway.

'Sorry mevrouw, I did not expect…'

Grietje cut her off. 'Do not be concerned. I need to pack and continue my journey.'

'I have packed your trunk; your underclothes are drying, and the horse and cart are prepared. The master asked if he may see you at eleven hours in the morning room.'

'Yes, I will go up to the room to freshen. Will you follow?'

'Yes, mevrouw. First, I will pass on your reply and bring the linens.'

Sara closed the trunk as Grietje took a last look around the room.

'Can you read and write?' Grietje asked.

'A little ... for cook, recipes.'

'Try to read books. You will find it benefits you. I will write you letters, and I expect a reply.' She passed Sara an envelope.

'Thank you, mevrouw. Thank you very much.'

'I shall go to your master now. I hope to see you again.'

Sara curtsied and Grietje found herself between floors.

The morning room was east-facing and caught the last of the morning sun. Van Reit stood easily as Grietje stumbled in a few minutes late.

'I'm sorry.'

'Not at all. Would you take something to eat?'

'No, I am fine.'

'A confection?'

'Oh, em, thank you.'

Van Reit nodded to the footman. 'I will have cook pack a lunch for your journey. I have thought over some of the things we said.'

'As have I, sir.'

He sat down and gestured for Grietje to join him.

'After you, mevrouw,' he smiled.

'With my expressions of gratitude for what has been for me an enjoyable visit, I have two things I would like to say. I am afraid you may find them impudent, but I am leaving, and you need not welcome me back.'

Van Reit's nod included an expression of curiosity.

'I did not understand the point about the school. I see it is important. They have said to you that they will not proceed with the building in order to avoid paying tax? It is not my business and I may not be familiar, but who is avoiding tax? I say this because I would like to return to paint you, at no cost, although the use of your materials would be welcome. As yet, I do not wish to paint the house, the land nor the sea, sir. I want to paint you!'

Van Reit laughed at this.

'It is not an unselfish act. If my painting is hung in a grand new building in Delft, that would enhance my reputation greatly and may allow me to trade more freely.'

'The second?'

Coffee and pastries arrived at the table. The smell had preceded them and Grietje was suddenly hungry.

'In fact, there is a third, a minor request.'

'Go on.'

'Could Sara be helped to read and write? She knows a little. If you will permit it, I would like to write to her.'

'Of course. I will see to it.'

'And the last?'

'I have thought long and examined my reasoning.' Grietje took a mouthful of pastry. The coffee was dark, rich and topped with *creme.* 'It is about Doortje. I am not breaking a confidence to tell you something Joseph and I have found out. I am unsure of the degree of your interest, but I can see no harm can be done in the telling.'

'Please.'

'She has a child. There is a young child.'

'And you think this relevant?'

Yes, the timing, and the child's name. She is called Tomasine.'

'You think?'

'I do not want to lead you, sir. I only report a known circumstance.' Grietje saw that van Reit's mind had left the room. 'I am done, sir.'

They sat in silence for a good while.

'You have some things to say, sir?'

'I need to think again. I thank you for this. I need to think on all you have said. I will write to you?'

'Of course.'

'Oh, a small point. Would you accept the company of one of the footmen for the journey? My mind would be more at ease. He will take a horse and return this day.'

'As long as it's the handsome one!'

'Hah.' Van Reit wiped his eye. 'Goodbye Grietje. May God go with you, and I very much hope to see you again soon.'

'Goodbye, sir. That is my wish too.'

FIFESHIRE, SCOTLAND 1733

Chapter 6

A *senight* had passed and David found there was still no word from Sir Peter Rigg. Mrs Oswald had sent a message saying that she hoped to be able to meet him soon, but the letter was short and left no word regarding his dispute with the Council. Rose was also disappointed that she had received nothing from Adeline.

Before school, David headed to the inn to ask if there was any post.

'There is a bag in from Edinburgh, sir, and one today due from Dundee.'

'I sent a letter to Fife last week and was expecting a reply.'

'On what day was that, sir?'

The Monday post.'

'Oh, have you not heard? There was a robbery on that day. The lad was badly done over, lost his horse.'

'What? And the post?'

'Yes, sir, not a word on that.'

'Did it have value?'

'No, not as such. I'll send something down for the lad. Has he seen the physic?'

'Aye, sir, we will look after him.'

David had heard there had been more trouble on the byways in recent weeks. It was not uncommon when winter approached. The nature of this assault sounded criminal in intent, rather than a desperate act of the poor and the needy. He could only write again, but it would be too late to expect a timely response.

'Will you still take the post?

'Aye sir. We've doubled up and they're well-armed. It will cost a bit more.'

David walked the short distance along the High Street to the notary, Mr Peat. He knew the office well and he could make use of their paper and seal to quickly write another note to Sir Peter.

'Good to meet you, Lawrence. I have only realised that I have your daughter at the school. My daughter Rose has befriended her.'

'Yes, my wife deals with these matters, but she did mention it to me.'

'I have heard about the robbery of the post.'

'Troubled times, aye, troubled times. Is there anything I can help with, is it the house?'

'Your clerk has been generous with paper and ink for me.'

'I'll dock it from his wage.'

David was well used to Peat's dry humour. 'There is something, now you mention it. Our current house is too small for us, and the inconvenience does not seem as if it will end soon. Do you know of a larger place that we may use, let us say for a year?'

'I can make enquiries on your behalf.'

'If you would, sir, please do.'

'What do you have in mind? How many rooms? Do you require land?'

'Oh, let me think. One receiving, one dining, two, no, three bedrooms and a study. At the least … and a maid's room.'

'That will not be cheap, sir. Do you have a sum in mind?'

David stood in the small, dark, fire-warmed office on a wet dull school-day morning, rushed, late for his teaching. Caught unawares in the middle of a meeting of happenstance, had he without any forethought nor consideration made a decision that would affect their lives? In the moment, it did not trouble him.

'No, Peat, there is no limit.'

'Sir?'

'Lawrence, we are in confidence?'

'Yes, sir, you are my client.'

'There is no limit. You have my assurance.'

'Yes, sir.'

'If I may, I would pen another letter?'

'Of course.'

Outside the day was brightening, but the wind had got up and the rain was heavier. David pulled up his collar and suppressed his outward smile as he walked along the High Street. He returned to the coaching inn to hand over his two letters. He was given one in return, from the Edinburgh bag. It was on fine paper, in an elegant hand which he did not recognise, but he knew who had written it

As David climbed back up the hill, he knew God or fate had intervened. He did not know which.

David heard murmurings as he stood outside the schoolroom door; at the first opening creak, there was silence. 'Thomas Oswald, your translation if you will, sir. Classes two and three, quietly attend to your reading. Class four, arithmetic tables.' Thomas stood and the others awaited their turn.

At the end of the day, David held back the first class. 'Boys.' He always addressed this nine in a group as boys even though Rose was one of them. 'I have an enterprise and I require your support. In the week before the festive break, we shall perform a play. I will invite Council members and others to attend. Each of you will be both playwright and actor of your part. I have the basis and we will jointly flesh out the substance. We do not have much time. Classes two and three will copy the parts and some will have roles.

'Will it be in Latin, sir?'

'Alas not, I fear that would challenge the audience. The occasional phrase, however, would not confuse. The play is not to be an entertainment as such – it has a purpose. This is true of many classic plays. We shall follow their path. Go today, but I ask that you stay an extra hour or so in the following days. I will not press for your translations today. There will be learning enough, of rhetoric, in this exercise.'

Smith and Rose stayed when the others left.

'Will you tell us your plan, sir?' Rose did not address her father as such in the schoolroom.

'Yes, it is not fully formed, but it was your idea. I think it would be good for the school. Let us demonstrate, by interview and by discourse, the worth and purpose of this school. Not by my pleadings, but by the words and talents of the pupils themselves. You said it, Rose, let us show what we do. Let us shine that light.'

At four hours post noon on the Friday, David gathered the group of players together.

'Last century the philosopher Comenius advocated the practice of drama and oratory in education. It is this to which we subscribe today. The set shall be entitled, *A Royal Council for Advice on the Education of Boys – a foundation for all improvements.* Class one will act as a Senate and gravely sit round a high table. Classes two and three shall approach the Senate and represent the people. They will stand up one at a time and will request advice from the Senate on matters which concern them. In this mode, the Senate will address all matters that we encounter in the education in this school, and they will rise to firmly state the case for their inclusion in our teachings.'

David paused to make sure the boys had understood his intent.

'At the first, I shall only pose the questions, and those of you who will form the Senate will make the first attempt at a reply. You could perhaps ask your fathers why they send you to this school. I know they have a good range of occupation. Succeed in this, gentlemen, and we will seek to determine our own destiny. Fail, and others will impose their will on us. Which would you prefer? So for the first class, write down these questions as I dictate them. We will consider your answers on Saturday and decide on one for each of you. Classes two and three can leave now.'

Rose waited for her father and walked across the yard with him.

'Is there a part for me, sir?'

'In the representation, Rose, they would all be men.'

'That does not seem fair.'

'That is a different issue, perhaps one worthy of discussion another day. I do not want to detract from nor confuse the cause I am trying to put before the Council members, who I hope will attend. Will you assist with the speeches?'

'I understand. Yes, I would like to help.'

As they reached the house, they found a heavy-breathing fellow at the school gate dismounting from a warm steed. 'Sir, Dr Miller, sir?'

'Yes.'

'From Sir Peter Rigg, sir. I can wait for a reply.' He handed David a fold.

'Tether your horse and come inside. I will take a few minutes. Rose, offer the man something.'

David left the room, leaving Rose standing with the tall stranger. She noticed he carried a sword, and thought she saw a pistol in his belt half-hidden by his cloak.

'Would you like a slice of pie and cheese perhaps? Oh, sorry. Hello.'

'Hello miss. Yes, thank you.'

'Are you come from Tarvit?'

'No, Balbirnie, the Andersons.'

'There is a jug of ale.'

'Thank you, miss.'

'Was Adeline Rigg there?'

'I cannot say, miss.'

'That is fine. My father will not be long.'

David came back into the room just as the courier was finishing his plate. 'I hope my daughter served you well.'

'Indeed, sir.'

'If you would deliver this to Sir Peter personally.'

'Yes, sir. Could I trouble you for water for the horse?'

Rose stood up and shouted from the scullery. 'There is half a bucket.' She took it out to the yard where the horse was keen to stick his nose in. Rose stroked the horse's neck and talked. Its ears swivelled in response. David and the man joined her.

'Thank you, miss. He is grateful for that.'

Nodding to them both, he left promptly.

Rose kept her questions for supper. 'Is there news of Sir Peter and Adeline?'

'Sir Peter, yes. He has received my second note and invited me to join him and John Anderson at Balbirnie on Saturday.'

'Nothing from Adeline?'

'Sorry Rose, no. I shall ask of her of course. If you write a note, I shall take it.'

For Rose, it had become a day of deflation. 'Can't I come?'

'No, I shall travel quickly by horse. I shall return in time for the Sunday service.'

Rose could ride but had no horse nor saddle. It was a desire she prayed for and tolerated the pangs of guilt she felt as her constant contemplation of her desire interrupted her more charitable devotions.

Rose spent a quiet Saturday tending to the house. Smithy's mother took pity on her and invited her to supper with Adam, his two uncles, Mr Robert and Mr John Douglas, their wives and the minister. It was a sombre affair but not unpleasant. The dining room was not a cheery place. Dark walls hosted grim portraits of kings, dukes and biblical figures; even the representation of the Virgin Mary looked Scottish. The minister was very interested in the school, and Rose knew to be guarded in her answers and gave her view from the classroom, not her father's. She stressed the convictions of duty, charity and piety in their readings. Mrs Smith kindly asked about her mother and their time in Cupar. This in itself made Rose a little saddened. Eventually, released from the table, Smithy's bold escort back up the hill, starting at thinly perceived threats in every dark corner, left her back at her own door in giggles.

She rose early the next day and became slightly worried when her father did not appear for church. He had crept in, still in his riding robes, part way through the service and stood at the rear until the last prayer. Speaking to him afterwards in the churchyard,

Rose thought she could detect a faint smell of whisky. David spent the rest of the day working in the schoolroom. Rose could tell he was not downhearted. Rose had prepared a chicken and found honey at the market at a price she would not declare to her father. She had made a sickly pudding cake, and they had a jolly supper together.

After school each day, the Senate met and prepared their speeches under David's close supervision. The boys had talked to their families and David guided the subjects to represent, in sum, a spread of the town's professional and commercial activities. Not all could be included. David picked only those who spoke well and had parents of standing. Matthew Oswald would talk of his father's nail factory and the need for accounting; John Drysdale would talk of mathematics; Henry Oswald, Latin and the ministry; Francis Wemyss classics for Law and Politics; Henry Love, of skills that benefit the merchant exporter, a head for numbers, language and negotiation, and lastly Smith. Smith saw himself in government. Not so much at its head but included to supply an informed and balanced analysis. The boys around the table would be supplemented in number by six others who would not have a major speaking part.

They worked hard. They were given five and no more than ten minutes each. The questions read by the class two boys sitting in the audience would be formally phrased to the Senate. Each member of the Senate would stand to give his response as naturally as he could.

Singularly, Smith was not producing any work for David to review. Instead he wandered around the classroom, scrutinising what the others were doing, discussing and helping when asked.

The boys were told to include Biblical references, where possible, to demonstrate God's influence. Rose saw it as her job to listen to the boys practise their oration.

As the end of the week neared, David warned Smith that if he did not have his speech to hand on Monday next, he would be removed. Smith's handwriting was a scrawl; his English, on paper, was such that it could look like Latin. David did not want anything to be left to the last minute when he must attend to the mechanics of the event itself, and endeavour to curry favour from the councillors. He decided he would not make a speech and would pick one boy to provide a final oratory; David would advise on its composition.

Although the act was dry for the boys, they stuck to their task. David wished he could make it livelier without compromising the message. He mentioned this to Smith.

'If we are to play the Senate, sir, can we not look like the Senate? A few sheets of bed linen will do it.'

David put the others to task, begging and borrowing materials and favours to clothe twelve Romans and more. Rose took charge of the organisation. Slowly, it was all coming together.

The play had taken over all David and Rose's suppertime conversation. Near the end of the second week, Rose was pleading Smith's case as he was over deadline and had still not produced anything on paper. David said he was left with no choice when they were interrupted by a strong and extended rapping on the outside door.

Three men stood outside. Their ill humour was apparent to Rose, who only recognised Ebenezer Erskine, the minister.

'Your father?'

'I will fetch him.' Rose did not invite them in.

'Father, it is the minister, a soldier and another man.'

David went to the door.

Rose heard mumbled words then her father shouted, 'Rose, I will see the gentlemen in the schoolroom.'

Rose, unnerved by the silence of the closed door, sat by the fire, got up, then sat down again. She tried in vain to distract herself.

The minister spoke first. 'Dr Miller, this is Captain Booth of the King's troop, from Edinburgh, and Mr Hepburn of the town guard. I don't know if you know…'

David shook his head. 'How can I help you, gentlemen? This seems a serious matter to disturb at this time.'

The Captain spoke. 'Sir, do you recognise this letter?' He handed David a paper.

'Yes, I sent this note to Sir Peter Rigg, over two weeks ago now. I have seen Sir Peter since. He did not receive it.'

'It was found in a camp. I have been sent to find the brigands who have been making pillaging attacks and looting property near the Fife road to Perth. We discovered their camp, recovered goods, and have since apprehended the band. They are presently on their way to Edinburgh and are not long for this earth.'

'I am relieved to hear this. I had heard of a robbery, but why this deputation, just to return my letter?'

'That is not the issue. Now, do you recognise this letter?' The captain handed David a second folded sheet.

'No sir, this is not mine.'

'This letter was contained within yours.'

David looked more closely. 'I have no knowledge of it. It is not my hand. I am a master; to me it looks like a child's hand.' And, as he said it, David realised he suspected the source. 'But what is the problem with it?'

'Would you read it, sir?'

It was a strange letter: odd phrasing, words out of place, some French and capitalised letters and numbers. It was addressed to, 'A'. David was now certain as to the author but would not reveal his mind until he knew more. 'It is oddly written, perhaps by a young child. Why is this a military matter? I am sorry, I do not understand.'

'I have spent much of the time of my commission in the Americas, fighting the French, sir,' explained the Captain. 'More in intrigue than in battle, I have to say. I recognise this style, it is the communication of a spy. Perhaps you have disguised your own hand?'

David felt the cold burn of fear and looked at the paper again to borrow time.

'I have the hand and the solution, sir. It is an innocent communication. If you give me a few moments, I will resolve this to your satisfaction, I assure you.'

David stood, but Booth shook his head.

David made a request, 'Mr Erskine, will you fetch Rose from the house, please.'

As he left, David pointed to the papers on his desk and stepped over to fetch the pile.

'Look, sir, this is my daughter's hand.'

The solider looked at the sheet.

'That's does not relieve you, sir. What is the content?'

'I have no idea but let us find out.'

The minister arrived back with Rose.

'I shall question.' The Captain commanded and retrieved the letter from David.

Rose was firmly stood in front of the Captain. 'Miss, do you recognise this?'

Rose started to cry.

'Rose, don't…'

'Sir!' Booth barked.

David looked to the minister, who looked away from his gaze.

'Take it … it is your writing?' the Captain instructed Rose.

Rose sobbed. 'I'm sorry,' she whispered as a stream of urine dribbled down her leg to make a small puddle on the schoolroom floor.

'Speak up!'

David spoke quickly. 'She's terrified sir.' The Captain looked at him. 'You will get no sense. Let her sit.'

Booth took his point. As Rose was given a seat, he spoke less firmly.

'Rose, this is your letter?' She nodded. 'Just tell us why you wrote it. What is it for, and what does it say?'

Rose managed to control her breathing but could not raise her voice.

'It is to my friend, Adeline.'

'Adeline Rigg, Sir Peter's daughter?' the minister interjected.

'Yes.'

'How was it posted?' the Captain continued.

Rose looked to her father. 'I put it under my father's seal.'

The minister was going to speak again but the Captain raised his hand. 'It is a strange letter. Why do you write in this way? It is full of numbers and odd words.'

'It is our own language.'

'Why?'

'So others cannot read.'

'Again, why?'

She looked at David again, who nodded for her to keep going.

'We speak of others … boys, family, people we know. Sometimes we are not kind.' Rose gasped and sobbed loudly again.

David spoke up. 'Sir, you have a child's game.'

Booth continued. 'What are these numbers?'

'This is not a bad thing. These are passages from the Bible. They show what we have been reading.'

The Captain nodded at the minister, who took the letter. 'Ah, yes, I see, but it is the Old Testament.'

'Do you know the passages?'

'Genesis, the very beginning, is the first.'

'We can verify this with Sir Peter,' David offered.

Booth stood. 'No need, I am satisfied.' Turning to the others, 'Thank you gentlemen, I have no more business. Dr Miller, I am sorry for the inconvenience, but it is my duty to act on behalf of the King.'

David stood and nodded and was very relieved to see him leave. As he turned to them, Mr Erskine and Hepburn made no move.

Mr Erskine spoke first. 'Dr Miller we are still troubled by this.'

'What? The Captain is satisfied. My daughter is no spy.'

'The letter contained many things we do not understand, words that are not of man and Biblical references which should not be used in such a pagan context. The girl herself said she was bad in intent.'

Rose began to sob again.

David put his hand forward to retrieve the letter from Mr Erskine, ostensibly to view it. He struggled to stay calm.

'Mr Erskine, here you see only a girl's simple misdeed, do not see nor look for evil where evil does not exist. You supped with her last Saturday, I believe, was she the devil then? What would you have done, lock her up in the Tollbooth? And would you lock up Sir Peter Rigg's daughter with her? I fear you would soon find yourself without support and out of office if you tried. And as for paganism, don't you dare bring a hint of witchcraft into this school.' David looked to the cross that hung above his school desk. 'It is not within these walls that the devil resides.'

Erskine looked at Hepburn for support, but he had been moved by David's case and shook his head in quiet disapproval of the minister's accusations.

'Rose must and will be punished by me, sirs,' David said more calmly. 'Mr Erskine, I would talk with you about a penance and duties she can perform for the church. But I strongly suggest that, for Rose's and our own sakes, we let the matter rest there.'

'That is fair, sir.' said Mr Hepburn, 'We are not here to punish children. I have several of my own who get whacked regularly, little the good it does.'

Mr Erskine nodded in resigned acquiescence and rose to leave. David still held the letter. Rose stood, head down, and sobbed quietly.

At the door, David saw them out of the school yard. 'I understand your fears, gentlemen, there is nothing to fear in this house.'

Rose sat and waited for her father's fury.

'Rose, come. Let us go back to the house and sit by the fire. You can read to me.'

'Father, I…'

'No, Rose. We will not talk of it. Maybe one day but not for a time yet. I shall find an amusement for you to read.'

'I will do any punishment.'

'There will be no punishment. Now let me find the volume.'

Rose sat and read to her father until she fell asleep. He lifted her into her box bed and stayed downstairs by the fire all night. Before he too fell asleep, he wrote a letter to Joseph and Mary.

David was writing a second letter to Sir Peter when Rose awoke in the morning, still in fright.

'Rose, I have to take a letter to the harbour; I will be straight back.'

'Father…'

'I will be straight back. No one will come. Bolt the door and don't open it for anyone but my return.'

David left and was fortunate to find a merchant he knew from Cupar to take his letter to Edinburgh. The merchant refused any reward. David quickly returned to the house to find Rose with a bucket in hand.

'I shall clean the school room.'

'I will come, I need to see the assistant. We will not go to school today.'

'Father?'

'When you finish, go back and pack a bag. We shall go on a journey. And pack your good clothes, even a fine dress.'

'With you?'

'Yes.'

'But where?'

'Rose, I always try to be honest with you … I have no idea.'
Rose's surprised look pleased him; she was distracted from the
events of the previous evening.

'And we shall take a ferry, so you might need that bucket.'

A cross frown and a glimmer of a smile grew.

They stood with two bags and a small trunk on the pier. David had
found a ferry to take them to Newhaven. The day was overcast,
but warm for the time of year. There was not much wind, even by
the shore. They had to wait awhile and watched the loading of the
goods.

'Are we…'

'Rose?'

'No, it is fine. There is Smithy's mother, walking this way.'
David did not know her well. She was a close friend of Mrs
Oswald and he knew her mostly by reputation.

'Mrs Smith.'

'Dr Miller, may I talk with you? In private.' She looked at
Rose, who curtsied on her approach. 'Hello Rose.'

'This is neither timely nor opportune,' David replied.

'If I may, sir, I fear I must. I will only take a moment?'

It was not really a question to be answered.

'Rose, I will talk with Mrs Smith. Will you keep the bags?'

'I will.'

Turning to face Mrs Smith, David asked, 'How can I help?'

'Please do not judge my reluctant interference. I have no wish
to intrude, but I have been made aware, from the guard, of the visit
to the school last evening. I know nothing of the interview nor the
reason, nor do I ask that. I…' It was unusual for Mrs Smith to be
hesitant. 'I was in the inn and happened to see you drop letters for
the post and I now find you and Rose at the harbour awaiting a
ferry on a school day. I find I am concerned, not for myself, but
for our school. If there is anything…'

'Mrs Smith be reassured. I am not abandoning the school nor the town. I am sorry, and I understand it may look that way, but Rose and I have to take a journey. It is an exception.' David was not totally confident of the truth of his words. 'The boys will be well looked-after today by my assistant, Mr John, and I expect to be back on Monday, as usual. There is an exhibition to produce.' David smiled as he saw her expression.

'Thank you, Dr Miller. As you can see, I am relieved. I know you have not seen Mrs Oswald. I do keep in touch with her. She would see you if it is necessary.'

'It is fine. I wish her a speedy recovery and good health.'

'Well, I wish you a safe journey.' Mrs Smith paused. 'As I take my leave, may I say something to you in confidence...'

David nodded.

'We have had problems with Mr Erskine. My mornings with him are not spent happily, more in guidance than patronage. Mrs Oswald and myself, as you know, both lost our husbands at an early age, and the town lost two good men. Men who would have guided us well into this new century. Strong men of their like are too rare in these parts. There are still some, but they are often minded for profit, not the community. They are not enlightened. We strived to guide our children and others as their fathers would have guided them. To bring them up informed and educated, and we hope to have a town that would engage them. This is why you were sought. You are very important to us Dr Miller. You have friends, sir. I hope you are reassured.'

'Mrs Smith, thank you for those kind words and your reassurance. They are apposite and timely.'

'Forgive me if I have been overly anxious. I fear that if you left, there would have been a trail of young boys shortly in your wake, my own at the head of them, much like the Pied Piper of Hamelin.'

'Not the character I would have chosen...'

Mrs Smith smiled and edged away. 'Thank you for your time, sir.'

'Your words are appreciated, Mrs Smith.'

'Goodbye, Rose,' she shouted with a wave and walked back towards the town.

Rose, looking towards them, was glad to see her father coming back to her side. 'It is time to board now.'

The crewman had taken their luggage on board. David went ahead of Rose up the thin gangplank. Turning at the end, he helped her down onto the deck. They were given a bench seat aft, in front of the tiller. The few other passengers stood, or took seat on a bale, bag or box. The ketch sat low in the water, raised its foresail and smoothly moved off on the calm water of the harbour towards the entrance to find the drag of the estuary's tidal flow.

DELFT, HOLLAND 1711

Chapter 7

Autumn fell to winter. Grietje had settled herself comfortably in Henry's apartment in Vlamingstraat. She was in receipt of a second note from Henry informing her of a further delay in the visit they had arranged for his sitting. She was concerned that the light may be too poor for the portrait if he did not appear soon. In his absence, she had completed as much of the background and his costume as she could. At least, the extra days will allow her time to remove her belongings and the clutter of her workmanship from the previously pristine rooms, so he would not see its current state. During the time she had made good use of the rooms, Grietje had filled the small study room, occupied most of the bedroom floor, and set her easel by the street window of the fine reception room, where the light was at its best in the mornings.

Van Reit, against her wish, had instructed his footman to slip a small trunk of paint powders onto her cart which was only revealed on their arrival in Delft. She was grateful, as they were of the best quality, the finest blues and yellows. Van Reit had also sent her a few art books on modern techniques, which she found fascinating: *Grind orpiment and masticot, then add white chalk to bring the purest gilt; azure, russet and turnsole will produce the most Roman purple.* He had included cobalt, cadmium, cinnabar, gamboge, and lapis lazuli, each one an expensive import from the East. She could never have found and bought their like without a firm commission, nor had she previously applied paint of such quality. Henry's scullery had become an apothecary of verdant powder, oil and gum. Trials brought a depth of shadow and a brightness of accent she had been unable to achieve in her earlier work. Used sparingly, the paints promised to bring a depth to her studies which had, hitherto, not been possible. No excuses now, she thought. If you are using the materials of the masters ... the fault can only be your own.

Henry's housekeeper, usually devoid of expression and speech, wore a deep frown at the sound of a knock at the door. Van Reit's footman delivered yet another load of canvases and frames, covered only by a short note which begged forgiveness. She wrote back expressing genuine gratitude but imploring him to leave enough materials in his cottage studio for her to visit him and paint his portrait. She further demanded that he be honest about his health, and that she would come in an instant, if his condition worsened. Grietje worried as the winter months approached. They maintained a light dialogue, one or two notes a week. Van Reit's hand remained elegant and steady. She pressed him for news on the progress of the building of the charity school, reminding him of their bargain. She waited a week for the reply.

Grietje's thoughts often turned to Joe, particularly when she walked down a street or visited a *koffiehuis* which triggered a memory of an unspoken moment. Her first week in Delft had been hell. She smelled him as soon as she opened the apartment door and it stayed with her, every day, forever out of sight, until she got used to being on her own again. It was a comforting pain; she missed him, and she would live on in hope. It was not the same as the pain she felt for those who could never return.

In the apartment, where Grietje had spent many days with Joe, they had been strangers thrown together by circumstance, sharing a day-to-day life while each fought their inner demons. Yet, they had found solace and comfort in each other's company and the simple things of life.

She had since written to him at his office in Edinburgh. She wrote formally, giving details of her visit to van Reit and her arrival in Delft. She left only a hint of her feelings, as much as she was able to in a foreign tongue. She hoped that he could discern the sense between her words.

Grietje did not forward an address, as she was still to confirm the studio and rooms that would become her new home. She also did not want to wake each morning in hope for a return message from him in case of there being none. She needed to establish herself first.

Grietje led full days, always finding some time to sketch or paint. Venturing out in her quest to find rooms, she contacted acquaintances and established studios, and dealt with the daily necessities of living alone. In the evenings, she read until she slept, the candle often extinguishing itself. She had found a few English books in Henry's library, which she knew well in Dutch and worked to improve her understanding and her expression of Joe's only language.

Grietje gained several offers of a place in established studios which would not have been available, even ten years earlier. Fine art was in decline, far from the heady days where it was the envy of all Europe and attracted talent from the most sophisticated houses. In those years the wealth of the Dutch markets produced heavy demand, the finest art and due rewards. In time, however, the Low Countries attracted too many artists, a rapid increase in the number of studios, and a glut in supply. Grietje was old enough to have experienced the change in mood, the fall in trade, fewer ships, quieter markets and in her world a drop in commissions, little demand for quality and a decline in sales.

Aware of this history, Grietje did not paint for money nor to grow a business. She was an artist because she was nothing else. Many times, in these past years, she had gone to the market to buy herself a full stomach and returned with workshop items such as a stretched canvas, a new sable brush or linseed, adding only a morsel of cheese for her sustenance.

Her feelings for Joe were uncomfortable because it allowed a division between Grietje the painter and Grietje the person: without him, there was only a painter.

She realised she wanted her own studio. She did not want to spend her time painting another's vision, or indeed take too many commissions. She may even take an apprentice. There were many studios available, most too large and others overly expensive. She had taken to visiting the Mechelen Inn where many old hands, and some new, drank and dined after a day in their studio. The talk was always of the past's better days. She knew some faces from her time working in the potteries and, after a few visits, she was accepted again into their company as an artist and not as a lone woman. Hence, she could find good company to drink or dine with. Through those contacts, she heard word of the availability of a modest first-floor studio with rooms; it had windows facing north over fields. The property lay just inside the wall off Geerweg near Paardenmarkt. It had formerly been used for stabling.

Grietje had grown confident in her ability to negotiate a bargain, due to her experience with Henry and Joe. She used the promise of an immediate entry and payment upfront at the price she thought was reasonable. Often these arrangements were sealed on a handshake; Grietje thought it wiser to insist on a written contract. She had heard too many tales of tenants and their families dumped in the streets when an unscrupulous landlord obtained a better price. Dealing with lawyers and written contracts were outside her own experience. She needed to find a trustworthy notary. Even in Delft, business and property dealing involving women, although legal, were rare.

The letter from van Reit sparked her into action. It was unusual in that it bore his seal and the footman had waited to give it to her personally. She could not extract any information from the same man who had escorted her cart to Delft; he was a servant to his master and epitomised discretion. He did not wait for a reply. Grietje, concerned as to the contents, sat at the table to open and read the few pages. Relieved that it was in his own hand, she read carefully.

Mevrouw,
I am well enough apart from cold hands and feet, but I
have a concern in trying to answer a question from
your last letter. I have sealed this letter and ask that
you keep its contents in confidence. I hope my trust in
you is not misplaced. You have given me no reason to

believe that it would be. I have had no response regarding the building of the school. You suggested I press on this as you saw it was important to me, and I am glad that you did. My communication on the matter is through my lawyer Janssen. He is an old and trusted friend. Indeed, he is involved in most of my affairs and is sanctioned, legally, to make decisions on my behalf. I have no reason to doubt that this arrangement is anything but honourable. Except, that is, for the fact that I have not recently been able to get a response from him nor his office. I have sent my footman three times to deliver a letter which has been received at the door, yet Janssen has not replied. The last time the footman was instructed to wait for the reply. He stayed at Janssen's door for a day before being chased away. The letter was unanswered. As the days wear on I become more troubled. Apart from the school and my other charities, the lack of response does not affect me, but I very much worry for his health and also that if I have more pressing matters, it would become difficult for me to act without Janssen's agency.

If I may thus ask a small favour of you. There is a further sheet enclosed under this seal. Could you possibly try to find out whether Janssen is unwell or incapacitated, and deliver this letter to Janssen personally? I don't want to put you through any anxiety. If it becomes taxing, then let well alone but let me know. Is this too much to ask?

I share this with no one else and will continue to pursue the matter by letter. As I age, I find I have fewer trusted contacts in the world of business and money.

To lighter matters, I hope you have found a satisfactory studio and will be able to visit me again

soon. I just need a day or two's notice. If there is
anything I can help you with, please let me know.
Van Reit

Grietje went to the window and saw the footman watering his
horse at the end of the street. She made haste down the stairs to
catch him and had him wait for a reply. A short note for van Reit,
to say she had found a studio and would visit him within the
fortnight. Once the apartment was tidied, she could leave with a
clear floor and a clear conscience, should Henry return.

Later that evening, after a visit to the inn, a thought about van
Reit's request occurred to Grietje. The request brought back
memories of Joe, when she had helped him in his quest to find
news of the disappearance of his friend, Tom Miller. Joe had
approached Janssen and others and been sorely rebuffed. He could
make no ground and was on the point of giving up. Grietje, on the
other hand, had been able to observe and question without
suspicion. She gained useful details and made good ground. She
dwelt on the reason for this. She was Dutch. In Delft, there was
nothing out of the ordinary in her appearance nor how she behaved
and spoke. She was a woman. In that guise, she could approach
servants, tradesfolk, innkeepers and maids, as if she was kin. After
a short conversation and a sharing of empathy, secrets were
shared, confidences divulged. Men were different. Their talk was
usually guarded, business-like, trying to best the reap while
belittling the sow. What they sought was knowledge, power in
their eyes, and would only be traded for profit. There was far more
indiscreet talk among the fishwives at the harbour than round the
tables of the *koffiehuis*; talk that was beyond the reach of men.
Grietje also had no qualms about playing the innocent, the coy or
the plain stupid.

Grietje thought again of Joe and how much she had enjoyed
their visit to the village where news of Tom Miller was likely to be
found. She would return to Joe and sit with him at the table, that
table. She looked over at it, cluttered with her papers and paints.

74

She would sup with him. Was that part of it, this bond she felt? She was losing herself to sleep.

She woke early, before light. After a piss and a wash, she raked through her trunk, as yet unpacked, for trim and smart clothes. No maid nor painter today. She wrote a list for herself and a letter of introduction. Janssen's premises, a house and an office, she believed, sat in a grand street, just off the marketplace. Fortune had provided a pastry stall at the end of the street.

It was not yet eight and there was much activity as traders carried their dawn deliveries to the houses. The street was swept of the night's deposits and a milk cart stopped at each house. There was life behind Janssen's door, and the ordinariness of the circumstance removed Grietje's initial trepidation. A pull at the bell was answered by a woman; it cut her preparation short.

'Good morning, I enquire in regard of some legal business. I require a document signed and registered by a notary and request an appointment.'

'Is it for your master? It would require his signature.'

'No, I am the leaseholder. There is no master. I would be the co-signee.'

She was then fully surprised to be invited to wait in the hallway. She offered the letter, but the woman did not take it with her. Grietje carefully took in all about her. There was not much; two doors off the hall and a wide stair to the first floor, and a third door behind it, presumably leading to the rear of the house. The house was well kept. Paintings adorned the walls, and a white tiled floor and highly polished dark wood doors and fittings added to the impression of status and authority.

'Good morning, Mevrouw,' said a young man, long hair, smartly dressed, not unappealing.

'Van der Meer, Grietje.'

A brief shake of the hand. 'Meijer, Rolf Meijer. How can I help you?'

'Sir, I am taking a lease on a property. I require a notarised document for my protection.'

'I can do that for you. The cost is fifteen florin plus three for the registration.'

Grietje strove not to flinch at the extortion in order to maintain her impression of wealth and professionalism. She nodded.

'Please come into the office.'

Meijer shepherded her to go ahead of him. You have the details?' Grietje showed him the paper.

'Excellent,' said the notary, indicating a seat by a desk as he walked to the other side. Meijer went through the details with her.

'Fine, I shall prepare the papers and have them ready for your signature on Monday.'

'Friday.'

'Monday is the earliest...'

'Friday.'

'I will see what I can do. Will that be all?'

At that moment the office door opened, and an elderly gentleman leaned in and barked at one of the clerks, who visibly jumped. The gentleman left, banging the door behind him. Grietje heard a second door bang after half a minute, and the victim of the rebuke scrambled some papers together and followed out of the door.

'Your employer?'

'Yes, meneer Janssen. He is not the easiest ... we do not see much of him. Is there anything more?'

'No, thank you, Meijer, I shall meet with you on Friday afternoon.'

As they both stood, Grietje bade Meijer stay seated. 'Please stay, I can see myself out. You are clearly busy.'

Meijer hesitated, but sat down again as she turned quickly to leave. There was no one in the hallway and Grietje paused only to look up the stairs before leaving. She remembered Joe's tale of barging into his employer's solicitor's office in Edinburgh but thought the better of it.

The rest of Grietje's week was spent in hard labour, packing and cleaning. The arrangement with the owners of her new studio was that she would move in on the Saturday; her occupancy would start on the first of the month.

She duly arrived at Janssen's on the Friday afternoon and was shown directly into the office. Meijer stood to greet her with a half a smile. 'Mevrouw van der Meer.' He offered her a seat.

'Mijnheer Meijer,' greeted Grietje.

'I hope you are well?'

Grietje nodded.

'I have the documents ready for you. I expect you would like to go through them first.'

Grietje nodded again and Meijer took her through the salient points in the short document.

'This is a regular agreement. The other party did not promote any exceptions. I asked for a three-month notice of termination for you, whereas I think you will need to set a fire to the place before they can legally remove you. Further, you are not required to pay a year in advance, three months at a time is sufficient. We can administer that for you. Does that seem satisfactory?'

To Grietje, it did seem so. The young man appeared to have negotiated on her behalf well and genuinely.

She still hesitated for effect. 'It does. It is also beautifully written. Is it your own pen?'

'No, the scribes do the scripting.' Meijer nodded towards two men standing at high desks.

'I have had the other party sign the documents in anticipation of your approval, so it only requires your signature now. However, you may wish to take a copy for consideration and return to sign on Monday next.'

'May I read through it carefully, while I am here?'

'Indeed, let me show you to a private office where you can take the time.'

Meijer stood up and took Grietje across the hallway to the door opposite and into a grand office. He put her papers on the desk and lit an ornate oil lamp, although there was already good light from the two windows.

'You can sit here undisturbed. If you ring the bell when you are finished, I will hear it from my desk.'

'This is a fine room ... the paintings,' Grietje remarked.

'Yes, it was my employer's, but he now mostly works from his apartment on the first floor.'

Grietje was taking in this information and intended to approach Janssen on van Reit's behalf, but she still did not have a considered plan. Perhaps it had been a mistake to involve her own contract work with this office; she was no longer anonymous. She was actually annoyed that the young notary, Meijer, happened to be kind and had looked after her well. She put her mind to completing her own documents. She went through them quickly, reading nothing that troubled her. Standing up, Grietje took a look at the paintings hung on the walls of the office. There was some fine work. As she moved along, she leaned in to look closely at the brushwork. Looking down absentmindedly, she pulled at the handle of a drawer in a long oak cabinet that sat against the wall beneath the paintings. Locked, she tried another drawer – locked.

Grietje stopped to listen for any movement in the hall and quickly pulled at the handles of all the drawers, nine in total. One opened, and a quick glance showed a bundle of sealed scrolls indexed, alphabetically it seemed, with names, beginning with the letter 'M' and ending with 'P'. She went back to the desk. Sitting down she rang the bell before she noticed the desk drawer. She pulled it open, a bunch of keys. Too late, she heard footsteps crossing the hall and quickly closed the drawer.

'All well?' asked Meijer.

'Yes. Do you have a pen and ink?'

'We need a witness to your signature. I shall call one of the juniors. I will sign as the notary at the bottom.'

Once completed, the junior left.

'Do I take a copy?' asked Grietje.

'You can, after em...'

78

'Oh, of course.' Grietje pulled out a purse.

'We can keep a copy on your behalf and manage the transfer of funds, paying the rent when it is due and so on.'

'Is that usual?'

'More so than not.'

'And the fee for that service?'

'That would be five percent of the annual rent, per year.'

'Three?'

Meijer laughed. 'It is usually ten.'

'You offer me a lower fee?'

'You are a new client. I am trying to grow the practice. May I ask, do the commissions from your painting provide the funding?'

Grietje thought that was not really the business of Meijer but it might be in her own interest to give a good impression of her professional position. She gave an embellished account, and a route to helping van Reit grew in her thoughts.

'No, it is not. We are in confidence?' she replied.

'As your representative, yes.'

'I act as an advisor and agent for a Scottish trading company. They bring coal, salt, tobacco and finished linen, then purchase pottery, fine art and embroidery, exporting from Holland to England.'

'Oh.'

'You are surprised?'

'Yes, I admit to that. A woman with such authority is unusual. The company has representation in Delft?'

'No, the contracts are agreed and signed by the business owner. He is experienced. Not myself, I don't sign, I only advise.'

'Perhaps, in the future they may need...'

'Indeed.'

'Then I will strive to serve you well. Can I ask the name?'

Grietje cut him off. 'I think that is enough at present.'

Meijer acknowledged with a nod. 'The offer to administer the funding?'

'I shall decide and let you know in a few days. Tell me, you hold the funds and the contracts, and I pay a fee?'

'Yes.'

'And should I stop paying?'

'You can't, because we have the authority over the money and we would take what is due, while it sits with us.'

'But I could request the return of funds and terminate the contract?'

'Yes, at any time, although there is generally a period of notice on any change ... by either party. Can I ask where your funds are held at present. Hopefully not under your bed?'

Grietje smiled. 'No, they are with the Scottish Bank in Veere.'

'Oh, interesting. Then the arrangement would be similar. They deduct a fee for their service. My argument would be that here might be more convenient for you.'

'I understand. You are a good salesman.'

'I have to feed my family. Is there anything else I can do for you today?'

Grietje had relaxed; she felt far more comfortable in the role than she had anticipated.

'Mijnheer Meijer, if you can spare a little more time, I think there is.'

'It is late on a Friday, I do. Would you like some coffee?'

'Yes, thank you.' Meijer rose to ring the bell. A clerk arrived and was dispatched to find the maid.

Grietje stood to stretch her legs. 'This is an impressive collection of Dutch art.' Grietje gestured to the walls and walked over to the paintings to view a seascape more closely. 'Van der Poel?'

'I'm afraid I do not know. Meneer Janssen specialised in artwork and personal legacies for many years. I have joined recently, to broaden the clients into, for example, property and commerce.'

The maid arrived with a jug of coffee and a warm plate of small pastries. As she poured the two cups, Grietje had time to think.

'This may be a delicate matter. It is outside my own business but involves this practice. I have a good friend and sponsor who is a client of Janssen. It is he that recommended I come here for advice.'

'His name?' Meijer asked.

'In a moment. I left him a little concerned as he had sent a letter perhaps two which were unanswered.'

'Ah.'

'He has asked me to deliver a further letter to Janssen. I have it with me.'

'May I see?'

Grietje took out the letter from her satchel. 'It is sealed and is for Janssen personally. His name is van Reit.' Grietje looked for a reaction but saw none.

'I do not recognise the name, but, as I say, I am a recent addition. I can ensure the letter is given to Janssen.'

'Would it be possible for me the meet him, to deliver it personally? Van Reit was concerned for Janssen's health and would appreciate if I can report seeing him well.'

Meijer sat thoughtfully for a moment.

'Is there a problem with that?'

'It is a reasonable request. I shall call Teuling. He is Janssen's senior clerk and deals exclusively with his business. He will suggest what is best.'

'Is he the one that was summoned with a shout on Monday?'

'Oh, you saw that. Yes, Monday, Tuesday, any and every day,' resigned Meijer. 'Janssen, although very senior, is not as he once was. He is often tired, absent and forgetful. I don't know the full situation, only that Teuling suffers under him. I must emphasise that any business of yours with me, will not go by way of Janssen.'

'Thank you for that reassurance.'

'Shall I call Teuling?'

'Yes, do.'

Teuling duly appeared, and when Grietje mentioned van Reit's name he looked forlorn.

81

'Can I see him in his office? Van Reit will be saddened to find his friend ails but I feel he must be told of this.'

Meijer nodded looking at Teuling, who just looked blank. The three left the office and together went up the stairs to the first floor. Teuling bade them wait on the landing and knocked quietly before putting his head round the door.

'Meneer Janssen.'

There was no audible response.

As he entered with Grietje immediately behind him, she pushed the door further open to see an old man asleep, his head on a messy desk strewn with papers. His dribbling mouth was open and leaking onto the parchment. An ink bottle was spilled, and a candle burned down. The smell of the room was not pleasant.

'Is he?' She stood back as Teuling approached Janssen and shook him gently.

'Mijnheer?'

'Eh, what.' Janssen sat up with a shake of his head and a momentary look of confusion. He found his voice. 'What is it, Teuling?'

'A letter from van Reit, sir.' Teuling looked to Grietje to hand over the scroll.

Janssen threw it aside and spoke with increasing volume. 'Another one! I'm dealing with it, I'm dealing with it.'

Grietje spoke. Meijer was standing beside her. 'Sir, if you would just...'

'Who are you? Out, out, all of you, out!' he shouted.

Grietje bent to pick up the scroll and put it back on the desk in front of Janssen. She nodded to the others and led them back down the stairs.

'I am sorry, mevrouw, we caught him at a bad moment.'

'I understand, mijnheer Teuling, thank you for allowing me to see him. Can I ask, have you been involved with van Reit's business?'

'I cannot say, said Teuling. 'Mijnheer Janssen deals with his affairs directly. Van Reit is his personal client.'

Teuling returned to his office, leaving Meijer and Grietje in the hallway.

'A sorry end to a good afternoon,' said Meijer.

'Yes, and I am the instrument.'

'You will report to your friend?'

'I would have your advice first if that is possible? My friend is an old man and I know he will seek my counsel. He has known Janssen many years and will be saddened to hear of this, but he will not want to make things difficult.'

'Thank you. I would like to protect the office as much as I am able. Teuling is an apprentice.'

'Of course, but...' Grietje raised her eyebrows.

As he opened the door, Meijer saw it was dark outside.

'I can walk you...'

'There is no need.'

'I'll collect my coat. I promise not to talk business.'

Grietje acceded and they took the short route to Henry's apartment. Meijer told her of his young wife and their child; another was expected. He lived with his family in rooms in the north of the town; he had followed his father and grandfather into the legal profession. They stopped at the steps of Henry's house.

'You live well!' Meijer remarked, unable to temper his surprise.

Grietje did not acknowledge that the apartment was borrowed.

'Thank you for the escort. We can meet ... next Wednesday morn?'

'Yes, that would suit.'

They parted after shaking hands warmly. As she stood awaiting the maid to open the door, her mind idled through the afternoon's meeting. She startled from her comfort. She had seen something, but what? It was hazy. The image was there, but not the interpretation. Something had sparked a memory perhaps. She knew it would worry her through sleep, until she remembered.

EDINBURGH, SCOTLAND
1733

Chapter 8

The glossed black carriage sitting at the end of the pier looked incongruous against the bustle of the busy fishing port of Newhaven. A uniformed footman was attending to the horses. As the ferry approached the small harbour, David saw a second footman standing looking out across the Forth estuary. Rose had not been ill on the voyage, but she had been quiet despite David's attempts at distraction. She still bore the discomfort of the previous evening.

As the ferry docked, one of the footmen approached and David thought he recognised him.

'Dr Miller?'

'Yes.'

'Mr Grieve has sent the carriage at your disposal. There is a message.' And he handed David a folded paper.

> *David,*
> *I am truly sorry to hear of your experience and am worried for it. I thought you and Rose were well settled. I send my carriage and implore you to come to us. Of course, Rose is welcome to stay as long as your need is such. Can we set our differences aside, and if there is anything else I can do? I hope you and I can talk again. Regardless, you are both very welcome in my house.*
> *Joseph*

David nodded to the footman, who took his bags and helped Rose over the gunwale.

'Are we going to stay with Grace?' she said, visibly brightening.

'If you would like that?'

'Oh, yes, yes please, Papa.'
'Then we shall.'

As the carriage climbed the steep hill to Edinburgh, Rose gazed out of the window at the fishermen's cottages and the undulating countryside. The road to Canon Mills was busy with travellers, barrows and wagons making their way to and from the small harbour.

Sitting in silence, with Rose distracted and more content, David had time to think about their situation. There was too much in his mind, but he managed to grasp the important aspects of his own and Rose's futures that demanded his full consideration.

There was conflict. Conflict between his personal beliefs and his duty as a father and a teacher. Conflict in his ambiguous feelings for Joseph and his family. Conflict in his spending of unearned wealth. None of these conflicts had a ready resolution. He did not want any path to be taken without forethought. He did not want to find himself nor Rose in an unsatisfactory position due to whim or circumstance. Yet, is that not where they now stood? With Rose, the school, Joe and even himself, he found he was no longer had a firm platform.

When David spent his five schooled years in Edinburgh, each day started with him donning his uniformed garb and heading down the spiral stairs to the garth, to stand firm and strong on a flagstone numbered 33. Regardless of all the tensions in school and the problems with his family, or the lack of it, a belief grew within himself, during his most vulnerable period, that he would wake each morning and stand secure on that stone. He would attend church; the masters would teach; his fellow pupils would game and tease, but also support and encourage. He would set his moral compass on Biblical teachings. David stood on firm ground.

His transition to university, it was only half a league from the school, and thence to teaching, and even his marriage to Janett had been natural, without any question or doubt. Of the last, he filled the role Janett had expected of him. She had acted with such surety in the arrangement that he happily relinquished any independent consideration of the matter. And on to the school in Cupar, his valued position as the schoolmaster in the small town, and the immediate arrival of Rose. Not without problems, but all without doubt, without fear.

Then last year's loss of Janett; the ground shook, not an earthquake, but undoubtedly a strong tremor. The ground shook. Change was necessitated, mandated, and taken. Yet the tremors did not stop.

In these low moments, he wanted to return to his own school. He wanted to stand on that stone. He wanted the shaking to stop, at least for a while, to allow him to think. *God gift me the time and wisdom to think.*

The carriage arrived at the Grieves' refurbished house, now devoid of the scaffold which encumbered it on their last visit. Joe had said the frontage and the rear terrace were being remodelled. It was now a more impressive building, with a hint of Rome or Greece in style. David had only seen its like in engravings, certainly nothing in this country. Mary, Grace and two Irish Setters were waiting in the pillared entrance as Rose opened the carriage door, jumped down and danced up the stone steps. Before David could reach the portico, Rose and Grace had disappeared into the house, the two dogs galloping after them.

'I am so glad to see you both again,' said Mary, clasping his hand in hers.

'Thank you, Mary.'

'I am sorry for your circumstance. Joseph said there was some difficulty in Kirkcaldy. He regrets not being here to receive you. He went to his office this morning but will return as soon as he can. I have sent word of your arrival.'

'You are very kind. I will tell you of our experience. I suddenly felt fearful for Rose. It, it was...'

'Later, David, later. Come in, come in. You will stay of course.'

'Thank you.' And David felt that singular sense of home, of which he had become aware on his last visit.

'Do you wish to settle in your room for an hour or so. Call for me when you wish. I will send a warm drink up to you. Have you eaten?'

'I can wait, I don't know about Rose. A little time would be most welcome. I would like to write and think awhile.'

'Of course. Make use of the desk in the library. Joe is very proud of it, although I am not sure that he has picked up a book.'

David smiled and followed a maid carrying his bag up the staircase.

The next thing he was aware of was a knock at the door. A maid entered with a jug of warm water.

'Sir, the mistress says that lunch will be served on the hour.'

David checked his fob; he had slept for two hours.

'Thank you, I shall come down. Do you know where my daughter is?'

'She is in Miss Grace's room, sir. Shall I fetch her?'

'No, it is fine. Thank you.'

Lunch was a mayhem of food, chatter, grandchildren, and dogs. Joe arrived to meet a barrage of demands and questions. There were no demands on David. Joe simply walked across and, looking him the eye, shook his hand firmly. 'You are always welcome here, David, both of you.'

David was moved and, not trusting his voice, nodded in gratitude. David knew Joe and Mary's family during his school days, visiting for supper two or three times in the month. Their four children were ages with him, but he had yet to sort out the next generation in terms of their names and who belonged to whom. It did not matter. There was a chaos of vibrant life; the children in twos and threes each had their own important demand and battled to be heard or attended to. Not that they cared much if they were ignored, which was usually the response. They just changed course and carried on with their enterprise, plot or industry. Rose charged in, absorbed in some intrigue with Grace or another. She coddled a black kitten high, keeping it away from the curiosity of the dogs. Rose copied the others; they grabbed easy food and raced out before Mary's chiding to sit could be heard and adhered to. She had neither noticed nor acknowledged her father. Today, this pleased him. It reminded him of their days last summer with the Oswalds in Dunnikier.

Joe stood up from the table pre-emptively.

'A long walk is now commanded! All children and animals. Those over twenty-four at their pleasure,' he said in a voice that would reach throughout the house.

David laughed but excused himself. It took more than the half hour for all to be gathered in the kitchen corridor. The boot room held a full complement of boots, cloaks and sticks. David went down to find that Rose was one of the keenest. Kitten deposited safely upstairs, she had now adopted a hound by means of feeding it the remains of her pie. David withdrew to the library, taking his journal to compose and note his thoughts.

It was a fine room with two long windows and an open outlook to the north east. The shelved books were dusted but largely undisturbed. The volumes covered a broad range of disciplines and included some rare editions.

On that afternoon, he found himself sitting in this room in reaction to an event. There had been a real threat to Rose's safety and indeed to himself, so much so that he had needed to act quickly. He was not going to stay in the burgh and wait on the possibility of a recurrence. These few hours had greatly assured him that Rose was safe and protected in this house. Importantly, Rose had realised that too.

But it was more than that. On a previous visit, David lost his trust in Joseph; he felt Joe had deliberately withheld important information about his father. As to Rose's wellbeing and care, however, seeing Joe, Mary and their family, he knew that there were no others he would trust more. He had friends in Cupar, but he did not think that Rose herself would make that choice. She lived in a larger world now. It was, for him, a sorry admission, but he knew there was security in wealth and power.

In the short term, Rose was safe. David had his duty to the school and the children. There was a moment in his fury, before Mrs Smith had hurried to talk to him on the pier, that he thought he might abandon Kirkcaldy and the school altogether. But he knew in time, that would not sit well with him. He would go back, but he wanted Rose to stay safely here, for a while at least.

In the background of all this, in his mind, was the discovery of the money that Joseph's company held for him on his behalf. The news of it had been a shock. He had resolved not to do anything with it. He was not comfortable, he felt undeserved of it: the money was not earned. Yet, he was committing all he could to the school and the Council. He had moved town at their behest and left behind a good community. Now the burgh Council kept him in an inadequate house, played politics, were slow to respond to his letters and were beginning to question his teaching. He was short of allies.

Faced with this, he sought sanctuary in his new wealth, finding a new house even though there had as yet been no signed transaction. He had promised Rose a better life, and at his wife's graveside he had also promised Janett. Rose should not lose out because of his failings.

He retained a fear though, that by spending the money, he would drive Rose into an unequal world, away from an understanding of the deprivation and the poverty that was endemic in the Scottish towns. It is too easy for those better off to ignore the poor. This, after all, is the reason he was drawn to teaching, and why he had sacrificed a substantial amount of his school's fee income to take in as many unfortunates as he could. He suspected this was the cause of some of the Council members' frustration and their discomfort with him.

And therein lay the deeper conflict within himself. There was no easy resolution. It was a hard admission though, that his real joy in teaching was not the teaching of those less able to read and write, rewarding as that may be. His driven ambition, rather, was to inspire the greatness within exceptional pupils such as Smith, Drysdale, Ramsay and the Oswalds. Under his influence, he felt he could turn boys with their innate abilities into men of vision, men of purpose, men for the nation.

These were clever boys, receptive to his teaching, and responsive to his questioning and measured provocation. Under his mastery, the burgh school could achieve both, if it had support. He needed the support of the Council and the community. He had seen this in his own schooling, and at university. If he had to make use of his money to achieve that aim, then that is a good, and he should not be embarrassed by it. It was becoming increasingly clear to him that wealth meant influence, however reluctant he was to be tarred with that brush.

He dearly missed his talks in Tarvit with Sir Peter and John Anderson. Educated men, they had been his sages in the past when he was lost in thoughts which confounded him, and clarity of purpose was beyond his horizon.

David flipped to a new page in his journal. His issue with Joe was one of the distant past and his father's life, or rather the end of it. It seemed of little importance in this day's context. It would not disappear however, and it was still a barrier between him and Joe. At some time, it must be breeched.

He had written to Tomasine Miller. She had his father's initials. Even thinking of his name on her card disturbed him greatly. Not at this moment, though; he would leave his questions and the contention of her claim awhile yet. Since he met the woman, his thoughts had occasionally drifted in that direction. Did he really have a sister? Again, regardless of his own feelings, Rose had a right. He had decided not to apportion blame to Joe. He must bear no grudge. Whatever the history, whatever the truth, Joe was not the instrument; he was merely the witness. And, he was assured, Joe was a good man, of good heart, and his intentions, although he did not fully understand them, were honourable as far as he could judge.

To Rose then: he would speak to her and have her stay awhile. As for his own action, the school and a play awaited his direction. Meantime, all else would sit in abeyance.

As a clock somewhere chimed the half hour of four, there was a gentle knock at the door. Mary looked in.

'Would you like some Chinese tea?'

'Thank you, Mary. Won't you join me and sit awhile?'

Mary went to the fireplace to pull at a handle on the wall.

'What is that?' queried David.

'It is a bell-pull; we have had them installed. It rings a bell in the hall for the servant. Something Joe had the ironmonger make. He had seen one in the Americas.'

Mary sat on a well-stuffed chair by the hearth.

'Joe will be back soon. Will you tell us, David, so that we may help? It is lovely to have Rose here again. Grace has burst into life.'

'Yes, shall we wait for Joe? I am settled to it now. It is a sorry tale. We had a fright, that is all, I hope. Your house and family are as a magic balm to Rose's sore.'

There was clatter and yelping in the hall. They were back.

Joe came into the library carrying their teas on a tray.

'I have found my position,' he grinned.

'Does he ever stop joking?' David smiled and looked to Mary.

'Not when the children are around. Sit down, Joe, or we'll have you pouring the tea.'

Joseph did as he was bid.

'How was Rose on the walk?' David asked.

'She was fine with the brood. She bubbles with an energy I have long lost.'

'I am glad to hear she was engaged.'

'One of the boys said something about soldiers?'

'Ah,' said David, surprised. 'I'm glad she talked of it. I will tell you both why I asked to come to you.'

David told of the evening in the starkest terms. Joe stood and walked over to David to put a hand on his shoulder.

'That is awful. I cannot imagine how you must have felt.'

'Joe, Mary, I confess there was a moment, just a moment, when I thought they, the captain, might take her away.' David strived to control his emotion, his eyes filling. 'I could do nothing, I was helpless.'

David paused to regain his composure. 'Fortunately, the captain was a sensible chap and saw the letter for what it was, a childish game. Then as I said, just as we thought we were through it, that ignorant minister, and I do not use the word lightly, with the town's guard in tow, started harping on about Satan: *the devil's work,*' he said.

'Rose must have been terrified,' said Mary.

'Yes, we have yet to talk of it. She stood brave and told the truth.'

Mary reassured, 'The young are resilient, as I'm sure you know. Rose is certainly no exception.'

'Thank you. I hope so. Sitting here feels a world away. I want to ask you both. Would she be able to stay with you awhile? I will return to Kirkcaldy. I want to assess if there is any continuation of the minister's accusations, and I await a letter from Sir Peter before I'll consider taking her back there. I will not have her punished by the kirk.'

'Are you sure *you* will be safe?' asked Joe.

'Not entirely, I shall keep my awareness.'

'Do you still have the letter?'

'Yes, with me. Do you wish to see it?'

'Only for curiosity, there is no need.'

'Joe!' Mary scolded.

Joe continued, 'Were there other letters?'

'She said it was the only one.'

'But had she received any?' Joe asked.

93

'That is a good point. She has, and I don't know where they are. I shall ask her. The other girl, Adeline, is French, the daughter of Sir Peter. He told me she is not presently in Scotland. I have written since, telling him of the incident. He is a Member of Parliament. I do not think they would impose on him or his family so readily.'

'Of course she can stay,' replied Mary, 'for as long as needs be.'

'Thank you, I appreciate your kindness. I will not mention it to her until the morrow, to make sure she is settled.'

The children ate early in the kitchen before retiring. Mary's cook was a mother hen. David was pleased to see Rose's desire was to sleep in Grace's room and not to seek him out. He checked on her before the adults dined at eight.

Three of Joe and Mary's children plus their spouses sat round the table. David was content to listen to the family chatter. There was little formality; the reason for his visit was not brought up.

David caught up with Joe as the men withdrew to the library to smoke. The women had withdrawn earlier to enjoy their own company. David pulled Joe aside.

'Joe, I have put... em, the other matters aside.'

'There is no need...'

'I want to express my gratitude for receiving us, but also to assure you. If I do contact the woman, Tomasine, regardless of what it reveals, I would not let it be a barrier between us. You and Mary have become too important to myself and Rose. Our views may differ, but ... well, we will talk again, I'm certain.'

Joe expressed a sympathetic smile and wrapped his long arm round David's shoulder.

'Come, I have a strange distillation from the other side of the ocean that you might quite like.'

All were out of bed promptly the next morning. At breakfast, David talked to Rose about staying.

'No, Papa, I will come with you!'

'You will be fine here.'

'Yes, but who will look after you?'

'I will manage for *senight*. Then I will come back,' assured David.

'You promise?'

'I promise.'

'But what about my schooling?'

'I have already prepared work for you, and I will be strict about its scrutiny.'

Rose sat quiet.

'Rose, I need to confirm that you will feel safe.'

'I will not worry for myself.'

'Good. Now I have a question. What happened to the letters that Adeline has sent to you?'

'I brought them, I have them with me.'

'I think we should put them in Joe's vault. They will be safe there.'

'I want to keep them.'

'Yes, we will keep them safe for you. They will be well away from prying eyes. Come now or we will be late to church.'

'Which...'

'Not in Kirkcaldy, we are going to the church in Edinburgh where I met your mother. We both sang in a choir.'

'Papa.' Rose stepped forward and leaned into her father.

It was only a few months previously that David had first walked the streets of Edinburgh in the company of his daughter. He had not been back since his university days. At that time, he had reflected this in his conversation with Rose, but it was his daughter's first trip beyond Fife, and she had never been in a large town before, never mind a place as imposing as Edinburgh. She had exhibited no interest in his tales of adolescence or scholarship. This time it was different. He caught her attention when he told her that he and Janett were the same age that she has now reached when they first met. She was receptive but struggled to imagine her parents as children. He wistfully remembered his school-day walks with Janett, to the kirk for choir practice. He now walked the same narrow streets with his daughter.

Oddly he thought, he was not overly saddened. Janett was very much there with them. He told Rose of the day he met Joe and Mary, but he did not reflect on the sense of loss and loneliness he remembered feeling at the time.

Joe and Mary had travelled ahead of them, and now walked towards David and Rose as they arrived in the churchyard; the three adults shared a single memory.

'Well, the singing will be better this time.' Joe always had an interjection to steer away from sentiment.

The service was fresh and light. There was a young choir who sang beautifully.

Warming rays from the sun met them when they filed out of the church at the end of the service. The younger Grieves ran around the yard to find friends. The minister introduced himself to David, paying Rose particular attention. David wondered if he had been primed. David told him he would be spending his Sundays in Edinburgh and would endeavour to attend regularly, as would Rose. When David's words had run through Rose, she became desperate to sing in the choir where her mother sang, interrupting to make sure her request was heard. The minister assured her that she would be made welcome.

David resisted travelling back on the Sunday to avoid any more ructions. He was not sure there would be many boats to the Fife coast. Instead he rose early on the Monday morning and did not arrive back to the school until after the morning's tenth hour. With the promise of his return the following Friday, he had left Rose content in the company of Grace, another girl, Benthe, and the rest of the Grieve family, dogs, cat, and horses, in their grand house near the Canon Mills.

DELFT, HOLLAND 1711

Chapter 9

Dawn broke on the Saturday morning, and a cart, partially loaded with goods from storage, and two hands arrived at the front of Henry's apartment. The men quickly carried the cases Grietje had packed down the staircase to fill the wagon. She travelled with the load, calming her inner thrill to maintain sensibility and authority over the men. Grietje had not seen the studio since the afternoon she spent viewing – then it had been dark and overfilled with another's goods. It was a short journey; the men opened the tall doors, which were large enough to allow a small gig, and Grietje stopped to take in the vast open space. Dark initially, she went to the shuttered windows, removed the rusty bars, and pulled at the edge of a tall wood panel. Light from the brightening morning sky illuminated the floor with a yellow glow. Grietje smiled. It was hers, all hers, for a while at least.

'Where shall we put these, mevrouw?' Each man held a box.

Grietje looked around. 'Stack them in that corner.'

It did not take long for them to unload the cart. Grietje returned with them to the apartment to fetch a further load. It was rushed; she was aching to spend time alone in her studio. At the street door she instructed the men to go and find a coffee as she needed time to finish packing her things. When she climbed the stairs, she found Henry's door open; inside she found a maid with a brush, bucket and cloth.

'Oh, thank you. I would have seen to that.'

'I don't mind, mevrouw. I don't have much to do. I am sorry to see you leave.'

Grietje found it odd that they were having their first conversation at this moment and was surprised the maid thought well of her. Previously she had seen only expressions of disapproval, or so she thought.

'I believe Henry, I mean meneer Egerton, may return soon.'

'Yes, he will. He has sent a message.' The maid almost smiled. 'I am glad he has not seen my mess.'

The men were soon back, and after what seemed her twentieth trip up and down the stairs, she was ready to leave. The maid stood at the door.

'I have left a note of my address for meneer Egerton, and if you have any need to get in contact. I will see you again. Thank you for your help.' Grietje gave her a few coins.

'Thank you, mevrouw.' She curtsied.

On the second journey, the men sat her in the middle of the bench seat, more for their pleasure than hers she thought, though they were not at all rude. The cart was quickly unloaded, and the men dispatched with some extra stuivers. She closed the street doors and stood quiet in the centre of the space.

Grietje's new rooms lay above the studio. The entrance was a narrow door from the street which led directly to a single staircase. There were three rooms. Two had shuttered dormer windows to the front and rear. The walls and ceilings were daubed in plaster and white, the beams blackened by smoke and age. She would live in the main room, which had a large fireplace with a wooden mantle, a washing sink and a cabin bed. The owner had left a good-sized table, a few chairs and an oak dresser. In the smallest room, which sat between the other two, there was a hatch in the floor which opened on to a ladder down to the studio; she hadn't noticed this before. The rooms were too large for her purpose, but she enjoyed the feeling of space.

Grietje realised she had not labelled the crates, nor had she asked the hands to bring her domestic goods upstairs. The rest of the day and the evening was spent finding, sorting and carrying. She found she could quickly slide down the ladder then exit to carry the next load up the stairs. It kept her warm enough to leave the fire unlit. The exercise, she saw, puzzled some passers-by in the street who stood for a while to watch her antics.

Finding her bedding late in the evening made her realise how tired she had become. She removed only her shoes and her top dress and fell into the cabin bed to sleep soundly until dawn.

As she woke, Grietje lay with her eyes closed, taking a sleepy minute to remember where she was; her other senses told her she was not in Henry's rooms. As she remembered, she curled up in the warmth of her bed, her nose sensing the cold of the room outside the cabin; she dozed off again into a dream-filled half sleep. Henry, van Reit, Meijer, Janssen all played parts in her drifting, mindless theatre. Sometimes she was the pawn, sometimes the queen. She was in her castle – then a cabinet, a drawer, the drawer, an open drawer. She woke properly with a start and felt unease. 'Miller!' one of the scrolls, the scrolls in the drawer. The drawer she had pulled open in Janssen's office. One of the scrolls was labelled Miller, or had she dreamt it.

There was much to do this day. Grietje knew it would take time. Heat, food and a letter to van Reit were her priorities, and she set to task. It was a bright morning and she took a detour to find a well, and what stalls could be found within a short walk of the studio. She smelled her way to a bakery and found a *koffiehuis* by the *Paardenmarkt*. She kept her letter to van Reit brief. Her intention was to visit after her meeting with Meijer and stay only one night.

Grietje had become quickly fond of van Reit. They were forty years apart in age, but shared a life's passion for art. Although their views distinctly differed, each coloured by experience, influence and culture through their own generation, they respected and had an interest in the other's interpretation. This gave rise to boundless conversation. It was not only the art that formed a bond. The link had begun through van Reit's interest in Joe, or more correctly Joe's friend and employer, Tom. She worried about van Reit's questioning on this matter because of her sworn confidence;

one that she would not break. Such were her thoughts as she turned the corner into the street where she now lived.

When Grietje returned to the studio and saw a carriage outside, her first thought, unsurprisingly, was of van Reit, but it was the beaming smile of her tardy English sitter that stepped down on her approach.

'De heer Henry Egerton! Where have you been?'

'You do me too much honour, mevrouw.'

Grietje offered her hand but was enveloped in a bear hug. She couldn't help but laugh in his squeeze. He pulled away and held her hands in his.

'I came straight here, when I heard, to see the studio of the famous artist.'

'You are too much a tease, sir,' Grietje scolded.

'I wager you are too expensive for me now.'

'Oh, that may be true. The delay will surely cost you dear.'

Henry stood back and looked at her properly.

'Grietje, it is very good to see you ... and how well you look.'

'And you, sir.'

'Enough of the 'sir' now, you are no maid.' He smiled.

Grietje gave a slight nod.

'Can I see inside?'

'I have just unloaded, there is nothing…'

Henry waved his hand and marched towards the door. Grietje was taken by his interest in the building and her boxes. He poked around curiously to see what the cartons held.

'So when can you sit?'

'Is there light, you were not sure?'

'Here, yes, not the apartment. I have the background and I have dressed you well.' She moved forward and touched his face. 'It is these lines of great experience I need to capture.'

'They are lines of decadence and decay!'

'Exactly,' she replied, but that was not what she saw.

'I am in Delft for a while. I have travelled a long way. As you know, I come here to rest. Wednesday?'

'No. It can only be Tuesday this week, early!' Grietje replied.

'Then Tuesday it is. Now, will you dine with me tonight? I compliment you on your health, Grietje, but you are thin. You need filling up ... at my expense. Tonight? I cannot see much food here.' He looked around. 'The Toren? We can talk more then.'

'That would suit me well, sir,' she said deliberately. 'But not the Toren. I am known at the Mechelen now and we would not stand out.'

'The Mechelen it is.'

The postern got down to open the carriage door, but Henry dismissed him and said he would walk back to his rooms. As he turned to wave, he shouted, 'And I want to know everything!'

A few familiars nodded to Grietje as she walked past the servery to find a table in the back room near the fire. Henry had not dressed in finery and they went unnoticed in the bustle of the popular eatery.

'Henry, the use of your rooms was of great benefit to me, and I shall pay tonight in small recompense for your generosity.'

Henry bowed his head. 'Thank you, that is kind of you. I shall, I hope, be permitted to return the gesture.'

'Of course.'

A waiter Grietje knew attended them, and she spoke too quickly in Dutch for Henry to catch the conversation. She was on home ground.

Grietje told Henry of her business activities. 'When Joe returned from Scotland, we stayed in your rooms while he conducted his trade in porcelain.'

'Ah, I met with Joe before that. He said he was returning. Did it go well, the commerce, I mean?'

'Yes, after your help with the first trade, we, I mean he, was confident in the task. The potteries were pleased with the sale. The Englishman, Clerk is it? took all we could carry.'

'He is Scottish, I think.'

'You were a great help, Henry.'

'We were a good team.'

'Still, I hope!'

'Indeed, mevrouw, we are a good team. Can I ask of the other matter?'

'Of Tom Miller's disappearance you mean?'

'Yes.'

'Perhaps, after a little more wine, but first you must tell me of your travels.'

A sizzling grid of venison was brought to their table. Henry looked surprised and delighted.

'This is unexpected. Food fit for princes!'

'They knew you were coming.'

Henry laughed. 'I'm only the poor fourth son of a lowly Earl, remember.'

'It is a speciality they serve only on a Sunday, I thought you would approve.'

'Indeed, I do.' Henry was already serving onto Grietje's plate. 'I have been spending my time in England working for my anointed elder brother, John. We, the family business, need to move the coal from mines on our land to the towns, where it will be sold and burnt. Moving it by wagon is slow, cumbersome and expensive. It eats up our profits when others are sailing their shipments directly to the ports. Hence my interest in the Dutch canals.' Henry opened his arms. 'Alas, the English countryside is far from flat. But my nephew, Scroop, will not let go of the idea. The Dutch waterways are excellent, but they do not have all the solutions. So, I travelled to France where there are examples of aqueducts and tunnels. Forgive me, once I start it is hard to stop. As you gather, I find it an interesting challenge.'

'I am far from bored. But you are a man of art?'

'Well, they are not so different. It is man and nature after all.'

'You make me think. So, you will need to go through and over hills.'

'Yes, and that is very expensive. We do not have the expertise. The frustrating thing is that the Romans did, with many fine structures still in existence. So, it is possible. It will take time.'

A bowl of root vegetables was served, and their flagon of wine refilled.

'This is a fine inn,' said Henry.

'Yes, it was popular with artists and patrons. It was once owned by the de Meer family, not my own.' Grietje pointed to the works on the wall. In high times, accounts were paid by oil on board.'

'Not so now?'

'I haven't tried, perhaps I should. It may come to that yet.'

'Will you tell me of Joe's other matter. Did you find news of Tom, Tom Miller was it?'

'I must not say too much, Henry. You would need to ask Joe. We found the girl and a baby. Joe was happier.'

'And you are not?'

'It is not my business, but I am more curious, yes. I met the girl, Doorjte, and felt...'

'I understand, no matter.'

'I would tell you more of van Reit though. Do you remember, Tom and Joe sought shelter in his house on their first journey to Delft and it was on Tom's return journey to that house, that Tom was caught in the flood. Joe had travelled the day before, I think.'

'Yes, Joe told me some of this. I know it troubled him.'

'I met van Reit when I accompanied Joe, and he and I have exchanged many notes since. He was a successful merchant but now reads and paints a little. He is talented but unknown. No family remaining. We get on well. I tell you as I would ask for guidance, if I may? It is important to me.'

'By all means.'

'He is an old man. I am not sure of his health; he certainly has poor spells. He confided a desire to donate money for good works. He lights up when he talks of this. The problem is that his lawyer is obstructing and will not respond to his letters, despite repeated attempts.'

'This lawyer is in Delft?'

'Yes, a traditional office with a good reputation. I am trying to help.'

'The lawyer's name?'

'Janssen.'

'I have heard of him. Private clients and high value art dealing.'

'Yes. I visited the office the other day and saw Janssen briefly. He did not seem at all well. It is the kindest way I can put it.'

'Ah, then it sounds like van Reit requires a new lawyer.'

'Yes, but how easily can that be done by letter? He is out of touch now and feels vulnerable in this regard. He does not want to be encumbered by meetings with people he does not know. How can he trust them? And he cannot travel.'

'How can I help?'

'Do you know a legal office in Delft that would take this on discreetly and securely? On this issue he is not patient, he does not think he has time. I am to visit him in a few days. I will tell him of Janssen. It will upset him, and I would like to suggest some more positive way forward.'

'I do not do much business here, but I do know a reputable firm. Meijer & Meijer,' Henry replied.

'Meijer & Meijer?'

'Yes.'

'How odd.'

'Pardon?'

'Nothing, it's nothing. And can they be trusted?'

'Yes, they have a good reputation and are not centred around one lawyer. They act for several important businesses. I believe van Reit would be safe in writing to them.'

'Thank you.'

'You are a good and kind person, Grietje.'

An apple pudding arrived with a jug of cream.

'We are eating well tonight!' said a delighted Henry.

'Do not think me too kind, I have some interest.'

'Oh?'

'I have insisted on painting van Reit's portrait – after yours is complete. I see him as my next commission, but he would not sit. He did not see the need.'

'And?'

'Well, we had had a few glasses after a supper, and I asked more of his charitable work. He has given substantially to the town, the church and the poor – his good works. He has become frustrated at the lack of progress on a school, a school for the poor. This was his largest project. I think he sees this as an enduring legacy.'

'I see. Please continue, I am intrigued.'

'I have an image of the school hall. In my mind, I saw it, and on the wall was a large portrait of the founder. I told him and we agreed a bargain. He would allow a fine portrait of him to hang in the school hall if it could be built, and that I would paint the portrait.

'Then he told me more of the problems and the lack of progress. There you have it, in truth.'

'A new built school is not cheap, van Reit has this money?'

'I do not know; his house is not so large, but it is rich in adornment. The grounds are extensive and well-tended.'

'Such a worthwhile cause and clearly a worthy gentleman. Grietje, I am on board. Anything I can do to help, I will.'

'Thank you, Henry. But first I need *you* to sit!'

'Tuesday, you suggest?'

'Yes, I am not sure I will be set in my studio. I have hardly had a moment. It would need to be early'

'Shall we meet for coffee anyway and you can see how the day sits? I have time here, I can bore you with culverts and bridges, pumps and wind power.'

'Yes, thank you. I am tiring now. May I tell you more of Joe another day if you have the time and the patience?'

'Gladly, you will brighten up my visit. Shall I walk you to your new home?'

'Thank you, kind sir.'

Grietje had kindled a fire earlier in the day and the room retained some warmth. She put on a log hoping it would catch. Although bed beckoned, she wanted to sit by her own fire for a while and look at a book; she lit a candle. Her few books along with many other things were still in the workshop downstairs. Heading to the ladder, she realised she would need to improve the access. Candle, hatch, ladder, a long skirt and too many glasses of wine do not mix well. There was no doubt that she would reach the studio floor.

The first two boxes were paint powders and cooking pots; the third held, under a pile of linens, a pile of books. As she pulled at the cloth a pair of eyes sparkled in the light of her candle. She jumped back. A small head appeared above the box. Grietje relaxed when she saw it was not a large rat. The cat jumped out, stretched languorously, and sat near her feet. She reached down to grab it to throw it out, but as her hand went down the cat stood up on its hind legs and pushed its head against her hand.

'Who are you? This is *my* house.' Grietje wasn't sure of this. The cat seemed more at home than she felt.

'Sleep here then, and I shall deal with you in the morning.'

As she took a book under her arm and went back to the ladder, the cat followed. Pausing halfway to look down, the cat was two rungs behind her. It waited for her to settle in her fireside chair, then claimed her lap. She fell asleep.

EDINBURGH 1733

Chapter 10

Despite being left unsupervised, there was no sound from the schoolroom as David waited outside the closed door. The boys looked up as he entered, and Smithy began to thump on his table; the others joined him enthusiastically.

He struggled not to respond with a smile.

'All right, all right. Settle boys, settle. Mr Oswald, stand! Read me your prepared translation.' Matthew Oswald did his master's bidding.

When they met when the school broke up at midday, Samuel John, David's assistant master, batted David's apologies away. Samuel said he had been aware of some pupils muttering about David's sudden departure; the older boys were genuinely concerned.

'I shall be here a while yet, Sam. I do, however, need to carry out business outside the school. I can employ a second assistant if you find yourself overburdened.'

'I'll see how it is. As long as they have set work, your boys are diligent. My lot are also well behaved, the good ones aspire to be in your room and most of the others are persuaded of the merits of writing and accounting for their future occupation. No need for God's wrath.'

'Good, em... for the future, I would like to steer a course clear of using God's wrath within the school. We will promote his good word of course, but I don't want the church to be used in school as a threat or means of control. I now see it as an affront to faith.'

'I understand your view. Our minister takes a different stance.'

'Exactly.'

'Your play is being much discussed. If I can help...'

'Good and thank you.'

'Are the parents to attend?'

'Yes, very much so, and more. It is not really an entertainment, more a presentation, an exhibition in defence of our teaching. If you can attend the rehearsal Tuesday next, I would appreciate your view. And an extra pair of hands on the day will be welcome.'

'Gladly.'

'Thank you, Samuel. I am sorry I do not know this, but where do you live?'

'We are in a room on the High Street.'

'We! ... you are married?'

'Yes, only a year past.'

'Your good wife's name?'

'She is Flora, sir. She has been helping with the costumes.' David paused.

'Well. I think a boarding room is insufficient for a young married teacher. If you leave it with me awhile, I shall arrange something. The school will take the expense.'

'Thank you, sir. I don't expect...'

'Now, I will leave exercises for my room when I am absent and scrutinise their completion. It will be a few hours only, on Mondays and Fridays, until the end of the trimester.'

At the end of the day, David gathered the boys back to go over the play. He had not found any time the previous day to review the boys' work, which he had taken with him. He had leafed through them and there was still nothing from Smith.

'Mr Smith, I have no submission from you?'

'I brought it to school on Friday, sir.'

'That is very dangerous ground, I insist on the truth.'

'I did bring some notes, sir. I have them here. I am not done, they are incomplete.'

His head down, Smith handed the pages over.

'Very well. For those who are prepared, stand and deliver what you have. Smith will prompt with the questions. Remember, we have these six days only, the final rehearsal is next Tuesday.'

Instinctively, David thought about adding the Saturday and then remembered Rose was not with him.

Nearly all the boys spoke well. They were gaining in confidence. The questions, from a merchant, a lawyer, a minister, a captain of the sea, but also a shopkeeper and wagon master, were all framed in the same way: *This is my need – example – how does this school serve me?* The boys had clearly asked their fathers for help, but in the structure and persuasion of the argument, David detected Smith's hand. The examples the boys had chosen covered his own message to the Council. He could not be hard on Smith; he saw that he had been working with the others on the oratory. He held him back, however.

'Smith, your introduction is fine. It takes a bit of scrutiny, yours is not the clearest hand. You have set the scene, the rationale, and the method. I like the Latin phrases but remember this is a school for all. The end piece is only notes.'

'I will write it, sir, I would wait until I see all the speeches, in order to encompass the whole and draw it together.'

'How long?'

'Friday, sir?'

'It has to be Friday morning. I leave at noon. If I do not have it, I will write it on Saturday and Ramsay will read.'

'Sir.'

'Do you know anything of the dress?'

'Yes, sir. The others were sewing on Friday and Saturday. They are ready apart from the ill-fitting.' Smith lowered his voice. 'Rose was not there, sir. Will she return?'

'In truth, I do not know, not for the play.'

'Oh. Can I ask, is she unwell?'

'There are no concerns as to her health. I cannot talk more of it. She is perfectly content.'

'Thank you, sir.'

Smith walked home down the Wynd with dropped shoulders. He turned and ran back to catch David at his door.

'Sir, may I write to her, Rose I mean?'

David considered. 'Yes, as long as it is an open letter in plain English. If you pass it to me by Friday, she will receive it promptly.'

Smith was puzzled. 'Thank you, sir,' but he left brighter.

David entered a cold, dark house with an empty larder. As he lit the fire and did some clearing up while the room warmed, he realised he did not know where dishes were kept or even where he could find food at this late hour. He wanted to work. He was thinking the inn was the only option when he heard a knock at the door. David chilled at the thought of finding the minister, but he opened the door to find a woman with a pot and a bag.

'Yes.'

'Sir, I am Mrs Smith's housemaid. She has sent up a pork stew and bread. Shall I prepare them for you?'

'No, I can manage that. This is very welcome. Would you please express my gratitude?'

'Sir, I am also instructed to attend in the morning to fetch the pot and clean up.' The maid curtsied and turned.

'Oh. Thank you.'

On the Friday, David left mid-morning to visit the notary, Lawrence Peat, on his route to the harbour. David instructed him to find a house for Rose and himself outside the parish boundary.

Alone on the ferry, unable to work or even read on that morning's sea, he found it the perfect environment for him, ironically, to find firmer ground for his thoughts. He had not notified Joseph of his expected arrival as he still felt an embarrassment of being met by a coach and footmen. Instead, he found a trader who was heading up the road towards Calton Hill and paid him two pennies for the ride. As he walked up the short drive to the Grieve house, a draughtsman was sketching its frontage.

The door was sitting open, so he walked into the hallway and shouted. A flustered maid arrived. 'I'll get the mistress, sir.' Mary was already coming through the hall towards him.

'David, how lovely. You are earlier than expected.'

Mary bellowed up the stairwell, 'Rose!'

They both laughed at her indecorous behaviour as she forgot to send the maid.

'Joe would have me be a proper mistress. I will never get used to it.'

She embraced David lightly as a bundle of girls bumped down the stairs.

'Father!' Rose jumped into his arms. 'Can I go horse riding tomorrow with Grace and Bene ... Please, please?'

'I will see your work first.'

Rose dropped down from his arms and raced back up the stairs.

'Come and sit, David, I will arrange some coffee.'

Mary insisted he use the house as his own. 'You will have your own days. Do not be obliged and uncomfortable.'

'Thank you, Mary, I do have work and some business to attend, and Rose of course. We would come with you to church.'

'Joe will be late tonight. We have guests tomorrow evening, you are welcome at our table. There will be no children.'

David spent the next hour with Rose. Her work was not up to her usual standard. It was not for lack of effort, more probably the loss of the school environment. She knew it.

'I know it is difficult, Rose. Do I understand that neither Grace nor Benthe study?'

'They do, but not Latin and Greek. They have a tutor for reading and writing, and they play pianoforte and embroider.'

'I think you need a tutor here. One day in seven, perhaps.'

'Am I staying forever?'

'Not forever, no. I am not fully decided. But until the end of the year, I think. Then we will see. I will not decide without talking to you.'

'Father, you will visit each Saturday and come to church on Sunday?'

'Yes, that is my intention.'

'That is fine for me, Papa.'

'Now let us go through these texts I have given you, then you can go riding on Saturday morning.'

'But I would spend it with you?'

'I have my own work and business to do. In the afternoon we can take a walk and you can tell me of your week.'

He would leave the delivery of Smith's letter until later.

The early morning was gloomy. Even the midday light had a cloak to it as grey clouds filled the dark sky. David set off on foot for the college, forgoing Joe's offer of a carriage or a horse. He was glad of his long coat as he strode up the steep climb to Calton Hill. The narrow road from Canon Mills joined where the cart road and the walk road from Leith converged. Terraces of part-built workman's houses lined the road. Passing the burial ground and the churches of Lady Orchy and College, he walked by Trinity Hospital, up Leith Wynd, across the High Street and down St Mary's Wynd. These were the streets he frequented as a student. He travelled along the Cowgate until he found a close which led down to the new infirmary; thence along a newly sett road to arrive at his old University College.

'Doctor Miller, it is good to meet with you. How long has it been?'

'Twenty odd years, I think, sir.'

David had sent a note to his old school friend Robert Hunter. He had known him first as a High School boy during his later school days. They had then studied together at the College, often finding themselves adversaries in academic debates. Robert had now risen to become Chair of Greek at the University.

'And you are master in Kirkcaldy now. You were born for that.'

114

David nodded.

'I would tempt you here, but if I remember correctly, you enjoy a larger and perhaps a more impressionable audience.'

'That is still true. I am at home in front of a class of fresh minds, unhindered by too much learning.'

'Fresh for you to influence...'

David laughed. 'You haven't changed, Robert. I tell you I have a startling bunch at present. Some, I hope, will attend with you in a year or so.'

'If you are impressed, then I will surely be. I confess, they will be well received. We are in grave need of able students. Not one new entry this term past. Is this why you have come?'

'Not at all, I come on a very minor matter. We had digressed.'

'As ever. Shall we walk to the coffee house in the High Street? It is more hospitable and there is always a fire lit. If you have the time?

'I have the morning,' replied David.

'Have you been there before?'

David elbowed him gently in his midriff, remembering the hours they had spent drinking together in their youth.

'You have to be careful, David, I think I can have you held in the stocks for such.'

There were a few looks and nods as they walked into the smoky, crowded coffee house, mostly students, David thought. Robert, wearing his college gown and long wig under his tricorn, walked to a busy, small table by a window. The students looked up, then stood to offer the master and David their table.

'Professorial privilege,' quipped Robert as they sat.

David saw that the hostelry had barely changed in twenty years: the cauldron over the fire, coffee pots on the mantle and in the hearth. He thought the yellowed paintings hanging on the chimney breast and the walls were the same. Two pot-serving maids and a third, dispensing clay pipes with tobacco, attended the tables. There were many more newssheets and pamphlets strewn on the tables than he remembered.

'Tell me, how is Janett?'

'I am afraid to report, I have lost Janett. More than a year now.'

'I am so sorry. I didn't ... do you have family?'

'Yes,' David said with a soft smile, 'a rebellious daughter. Actually, she is the cause of my visit to you.'

'I cannot quite take your sad news in. I remember you came as a pair.'

'It is true, I am but half. There is a pain inside that will not be quelled.'

Robert waited for David to continue.

'When Janett died, shockingly sudden, it was difficult for us to stay and live in Cupar. By luck, or so I thought at the time, I was offered a better position in Kirkcaldy and we made the decision to move.'

'That could not have been easy.'

'No, but we, that is Rose, my daughter, and myself thought it wise to move forward.'

'Of course, how many years has she?'

'Thirteen years. The good of it has been that, as I have said, I have a fine classroom of children and a new school building. The councillors presently are not as – how shall I say – as liberal or enlightened as I had been led to believe. No matter it is early days yet, and I am not done with it. As well, I am only beginning to appreciate the ease of getting to Edinburgh from Kirkcaldy and visiting old friends.' David gestured towards Robert.

'You can find the time?'

'I am making the time. I have decided to let the irked be irked. I shall not be troubled by them.'

A maid served a coffee pot and two clay cups.

'Well, I am sorry we can only drink to you in coffee.' Robert raised his cup.

'And you Robert, you are doing well?'

'Yes, you know I enjoy the bookwork and writing. But there are many old hands leading the College and without a vibrant number of students, it is not easy to make changes or progress.'

'It seems we share similar frustrations. Maybe our chance will come.'

'We can live in hope. It is good to see you David, you have shaken me out of my torpor. Now, how can I help you?'

'It is a small thing. I shall not tell the full tale, but at present it serves us to have Rose in Edinburgh. She is staying with friends in a house near the Canon Mills. I set her work and visit Saturday and Sunday, but she is in need of a tutor for one or two days in between. I would pay well. I just ask if you have someone who would suit. Oh, I should add, in Latin, Greek and French if possible.'

'She is accomplished?'

'Yes, she has surprised me and challenges the boys' class. There is only one who is the better of her.'

'Does she not discomfort the boys?'

'No, and that is not the reason. They are well accustomed to her now. It is the girls that are the more puzzled.'

'You have girls and boys. I am the more curious, but it would be rude of me to question more. Personally, I do not have anyone, but...' Robert paused while he thought. 'John Stewart in Religion has a bright young man who has tutored. Yes, if I recall correctly, he has taken on pupils to gain funds in order to travel abroad and may have tutored the sons of gentry while he was in France and Italy.'

'He sounds ideal. Is he studying in Edinburgh now?'

'I think so. Not for a degree, but he writes papers, uses the library, and gives an occasional talk. He is not, how shall I say, well supported.'

'And his character?'

'He is a little eccentric in nature, a very original thinker. I think you would find him academically challenging. His personality is amiable and entertaining, when not deep in thought.'

'My only concern then, is that you say he studies in Religion, I do not require a preacher.'

'Ah, no, the opposite in fact. He does come from a strictly Presbyterian family, but he now struggles with the discord between the beliefs he grew up with and his current thinking. There is nothing of that nature to concern you.'

'His name?'

'As yours. David, David Hume.'

'If I could leave a note for him with you?'

'By all means. It may take a day or two to find him.'

Tom Binnie

DELFT 1711

Chapter 11

Grietje awoke late, in bed, although she could not recall how she got there. There was a small tortoiseshell head pushing at her chin and soft white paws padding at her undergarments.

'You are too familiar with me, *Katje*. We have not been introduced.'

She shooed it away while she made use of the bucket; she washed, then dressed smartly for her meeting with Meijer. Rekindling the fire, Grietje heated water in the kettle and sat by the table to eat a bowl of warm oats. The cat appeared on the opposite chair and waited patiently for the scrapings.

Grietje pulled at the contents of her trunk. If she was to play the professional and not the artist, she must acquire a smarter countenance. In her second trunk, along with a few other garments she had bought from the markets, just because they were beautiful, she kept a muddle of clothes which she had used over the years to dress children for portraiture. In that trunk, she found a small man's doublet, finely embroidered with blue, black, and purple silks. There were breeches to match. These had been used, she remembered, in the painting of a young man. They were a little tight on her but there was a smartness about them. After letting down her waved auburn hair, Grietje added a shirt with frilled sleeves and a wide-brimmed feminine hat in place of her usual cloche, all to give an impression of business. This she hoped, at the very least, might unnerve the young lawyer. Grietje considered adding a sword, but she only possessed a wooden proxy.

'Well, what do you think, *Katje*?'

On the floor beside the hearth of the dying fire, the cat raised its head and offered an aloof look before curling back to its slumber. A knock at the door brought a messenger with a reply from van Reit. Grietje threw on her long cape and picked up her satchel. Stopping on the canal path at a coffee stall before heading to meet

Meijer at Janssen's offices, she drew not a sideways glance from passers-by, apart from one small boy with a hoop who returned her smile.

At the legal offices, the woman who answered the front door looked at Grietje twice before taking her cape and asking her to wait in Janssen's office. The woman explained, with Meijer's apologies, that he was detained with another client but would not be long. Grietje declined the offer of a coffee and was left alone.

Less apprehensive than on her last visit, Grietje peeked out of the office door to find the hall quiet and empty. She retreated back into the room and went quickly to the cabinet drawer she remembered. It opened easily and the papers were still there. On instinct, without reason, she gathered the papers that were marked with the name, *Miller*, and secreted them into her satchel. She closed the drawer quietly and went to sit by the desk to await Meijer. She contemplated the action she had just taken. In truth, she could not account for it, even to herself. Grietje thought it might only have been curiosity; she also worried that it might have been devilment.

Standing in the centre of the room, Grietje looked again at the paintings that covered the office walls. Meijer entered. 'Mevrouw, I am sorry. A client, a recent widow, I had to attend...'

Grietje waved away Meijer's apology and smiled as she turned to see Meijer's open-eyed stare. She could not interpret his expression. Was it admiration, ridicule, or a hint of lust? She did not know which and feared the last.

'Is all well, mevrouw?'

'It is and I am. I would ask a few questions of you. I will visit van Reit on Wednesday, returning Friday. I want to be sure of my advice.'

Meijer nodded and they both sat at the desk.

'Before I begin,' said Grietje, 'I confess that I have taken independent advice from a reliable associate.'

'And?' queried Meijer.

'We, that is, I, cannot see how van Reit can continue to be represented by the lawyer, Janssen. The least of it is that van Reit requires prompt legal work regarding the transfer of substantial sums. I stress prompt: the requirement is now. Did you happen to have sight of the letter?' asked Grietje.

'I cannot answer you with honesty.'

Grietje continued, in the firm serious tone she had developed for use with inebriated customers in her past life serving at an inn. 'It is not just paperwork. There is need for counsel and discussion with the authorities, all on van Reit's behalf.'

'And you do not envisage Janssen as being able.'

'That is the sum of it. If I measure correctly, Teuling is an apprentice and you have not yet the experience ... there is no one else?'

Meijer shook his head in agreement.

'But I do need you, mijnheer Meijer.' Grietje smiled, leaving Meijer looking relieved. 'Would you advise me? How can the authority van Reit has given Janssen be transferred to another office?'

Meijer thought on the question. 'A dated and witnessed letter, authorised by a notary, making clear the request.'

'To Janssen?'

'Yes, and I can see your thought. Janssen may not respond. The letter would be lodged with the civic office and if not heeded, a legal process would follow. That would involve the judiciary.'

'He does not have this time. Can Teuling not assist?'

'Formally, he does not have the authority.'

'And informally?'

'To whom would you be transferring the authority?'

'I do not know, but that does bring me to my second query.'

'Go on.'

'There is a firm, Meijer & Meijer?'

'Yes.' Meijer looked embarrassed.

'Your father?'

'My family, yes. The office is named after my grandfather and my great uncle.'

'Ah, they have been recommended to me,' said Grietje, 'but why... well, the obvious question?'

'I dare say I will end up there eventually. I desired experience elsewhere. I have older brothers who are senior there, and...' He stopped with a shrug of the shoulders.

'There is a rift?'

'No, not at all. As your friend has said, they are a good office with many important clients. So, do you think van Reit would choose them?'

'I do not know. I do not want to stretch beyond my personal experience, but I know he will ask. I have enough to report. If you can consider how we might proceed, we can discuss it again. Is that reasonable? I will pay for your time. And, er ... could you gain sight of van Reit's letters to Janssen? Not to break confidence, but it may confirm our, I mean his, intent.'

'You are my client now, mevrouw, I will look into it. I do have a question.'

'Yes.'

'What does van Reit desire to do? I presume he has left a legacy.'

'He desires a school to be built. Now. He does not want to wait until he is beneath God's earth.'

'In Delft?'

'Yes, an orphan school, for the poor.'

Grietje rose early the next day to sort the studio into a functional workshop. She had formed a setting, a space with a chair and side table, where the sitter could position himself comfortably. The morning light shone indirectly across the floor. A knock on the door came as she was laying out her easel, chalks, and brushes. A well-dressed gentleman stood expectantly on the threshold.

'Henry, in perfect time. Are you well?'

123

'I am,' he exclaimed. Henry embraced Grietje, adding a kiss on her cheek. 'Mevrouw, whatever you require of me ... do I smell coffee?'

'Yes, I shall fetch it down. Now, I am nearly done, I needed to see you again.'

'Oh, Grietje...' Henry laughed.

'For the painting!' Grietje remonstrated, 'Sit!'

The scolded gent obeyed her bidding.

'Now change that look or I will paint it.'

Grietje brought her sitter a coffee. 'I will just sketch this morning. And I want to find your tone in this new light.'

'I am at your service. When do I view it?'

'Not quite yet.'

Henry knew to sit quietly while Grietje worked at a sketch. She had prepared and mixed a board using the powders van Reit had gifted. She hoped to bring a strong sense of life into Henry's expression. Her portrait placed Henry in a room similar to that of his apartment, furnished with objects she felt represented his status and occupation. This was a risk, but she could easily trim the canvas into a simpler portrait if Henry did not approve. They took a break and went up to the apartment to be nearer the fire. The coffee pot was still on the hearth-plate, the cat settled near the grate. They stood by the fire to warm themselves.

'Did you meet with your counsel?' Henry asked.

'Yes, yesterday. It went well, I think. And I thank you for your good advice on the matter. I find I now have three matters with lawyers; it is not what I would choose to do.'

'But it went well?'

'Yes, my own business of a simple contract is free of problem and I will use young Meijer as my own notary and accountant.'

'Meijer?'

'I didn't mention to you that the notary who I have engaged for myself, is a Meijer. He is of the same family as Meijer & Meijer.'

'Working for Janssen?'

'Not directly, but in his office. Regarding van Reit's worry of Janssen, I have brought it to young Meijer's attention, and he is going to raise the issue with Janssen's apprentice.'

'As I have said, Grietje, if I can help in anyway, a meeting perhaps?'

'Thank you, Henry. I will visit van Reit tomorrow and stay a day. I will act only on his direction. Your suggestion that van Reit uses Meijer & Meijer, was understood by my notary and it has his support. I will suggest as such to van Reit.' Grietje paused. 'But...'

'But?'

'It is not what I want to do, Henry. It is not what all this is for. I want to paint.'

'You are being of great help to someone who you hold as a good friend, without interest as far as I can see.'

'Not wholly...'

'Oh.'

'I have a guilty intent.'

'Tell uncle Henry.'

Grietje laughed. 'Not yet. When I return if you will wait.'

'Of course, I'm intrigued. You said three issues. May I ask the third?'

Grietje's expression betrayed her indecision. 'You know much of the story; it is in regard of Tom Miller.'

'I thought that Joseph was resolved in that issue.'

Grietje hesitated. 'Yes.'

'Oh, well I will not press you.'

'Have you heard from Joseph?' Grietje asked.

'Yes, we exchange letters often ... business. And you?'

'No, I have not written. I do not wish to disturb him.'

'And he has not written to you?'

'He has not my address.'

'Well, I am not supposed to say, but he always asks if I have seen you and expresses his concern for your welfare.'

'Do you tell him?'

'Yes, of course. Grietje, may I tell him of your whereabouts? If nothing else, I believe he has business for you.'

Grietje took a moment and very softly replied to Henry's request. 'Yes, you may.'

They stood quietly for a few minutes, draining their cups before Grietje regained her purpose.

'Right! downstairs, Henry Egerton. Now would you prefer van Rijn's gravitas or Hal's chortle?'

Henry smiled. 'I am a serious man, mevrouw.'

Van Reit's carriage and footman were waiting outside the studio when Grietje woke early the next morning. Head a little delicate resulting from her supper with Henry, Grietje sent the footman away to find his own breakfast while she prepared for the journey. She was relieved that the footman, with whom she had become familiar, was now less formal with her. He reported van Reit to be in better health and looking forward to her visit.

Arriving at van Reit's house half a day later, the carriage wheels crunched up the short driveway. Van Reit stood stick-in-hand at the door, appearing in better health than Grietje had ever seen him. Sara was also there, standing to the side and slightly behind him.

'Sir, have you found the elixir of life?' she enquired.

'I have. She is walking towards me.'

'You do me too much honour, meneer. I am but a maid.'

Van Reit nodded to Sara who curtsied to Grietje as she fetched her bag. He grasped Grietje's hand in both of his and kissed her on each cheek before shepherding her into the hall. 'It is good to see you again.'

'And you, meneer.'

'I will leave you awhile with Sara. I am managing a short walk in the garden each day. Would you accompany me, in an hour, perhaps?'

'It would be my pleasure.'

126

Van Reit needed help down the steps, but he walked well with the aid of his stick on the flat. Grietje noticed he was working at straightening his back and trying to lengthen his stride. She offered her arm and took his stick.

As they slowly walked the garden path, she sensed the weakness in his movement and the need for her supporting arm. They stopped occasionally to rest and admire the crisp, white, winter beauty of the unfallen leaves and iced seed heads suspended until spring. A low frozen mist sat near the ground as dew, vaporised in the early morning sun, was caught mid-flight in December's breath; there was no wind to wisp it toward warmer climes.

'If I could capture this in paint, I would have no other ambition,' said Grietje.

'A challenge indeed. I think we can only show one side of nature by hand, and there is a multitude. I have news. I have engaged a tutor for Sara. You were correct, she is a bright and able girl. I am sorry I did not think of it; I hardly knew her.'

'Thank you, you cannot be expected...'

Van Reit waved his hand. 'We can talk of other matters before supper, but I am impatiently curious. Did you see Janssen?'

'Yes, I have news too, not all good.'

'Ah, well, let us not spoil our walk. I can make it to the *huisje*. They will send a chair for me to return.'

'That is very good, meneer. Let us stride on!'

Grietje found a quiet companionship in the elderly gentleman, particularly when they talked of art and painting. Van Reit enjoyed telling her of times past, Grietje prompting on occasion for more detail. Van Reit's sedan awaited as they reached the *huisje*. The walk had taken them over an hour. Although tired, van Reit insisted on going inside his studio. He showed Grietje the focussing glasses and demonstrated how she could make a projection of a well-lit, inverted scene onto calico. She had not

seen this technique in practice before. Van Reit left her exploring
the old building, returning to the house to rest.

Grietje dressed or rather was dressed for supper, a giggly Sara in
attendance. 'The master asked to meet you in the library before
sitting to dine.'

'Thank you, Sara. How is your writing? And I hear you are
studying English.'

'Not too well, mevrouw. I enjoy it though.'

'Well, stick at it.'

'I will, I promise.'

Van Reit was sitting by the fire when Grietje was shown in.

'I thought we could talk here a little before we sup,' he
suggested.

'You want to hear of Janssen?'

'Yes, if you do not mind. Pray tell me your thoughts, if you
will, along with your experience.'

Grietje told van Reit of her meeting with Janssen in detail. She
told him of her impression of the young Meijer, of Henry
Egerton's reflection and his offer of assistance. She informed van
Reit of Henry's aristocratic background, business experience and
his relationship with Joe, helping him in the early trades, refusing
any reward. She said she trusted Henry's view.

Van Reit's first concern was Janssen's health.

'You think he was ill?' he asked.

'According to Meijer, he has good days and bad days, but yes, I
have seen the same in others. He is ill.'

'And not competent, you say?'

'Not in the sense that he could act promptly to a reasonable
request. When I saw him, albeit briefly, he would not behave in a
responsible manner to myself nor his apprentice.'

'My poor man, I am sorry to hear this.' Van Reit's look expressed his sadness. 'I am at a loss now. Did the apprentice or, who is it, Meijer suggest anything?'

'They now understand the situation and wish to help. I left them trying to engage with Janssen regarding a change in authority. They wish to protect the legal office as well as their own livelihoods.'

'That at least is reassuring. I cannot use you as a go-between, my dear. You are so kind, and you have my trust, but there will be complication and your time should not be wasted in this way.'

'But you must preserve *your* time, sir, and I am concerned for your worry.'

'Indeed, I have no need for the strain, nor do I have the mind for it. Let me think a moment. Would you ring the bell for me?'

Grietje stood to fetch the bell from the mantle. The footman appeared in less than a minute, Grietje was convinced this house was run by magical devices.

'Would you bring us a bottle of the Spanish sweet wine?' requested van Reit.

Once they had a glass in hand and after Grietje had taken a sip, van Reit spoke again.

'Forgive my tiredness. Let us not be downhearted. Your lawyer, he would visit here?'

'I am sure he would.'

'Perhaps the apprentice, I'm not sure, and what about the English adventurer, meneer Egerton?'

'I have no wish to burden you, but I believe, meneer, that Henry would delight you and you him.'

'He would come?'

'I am sure of this also.'

'Then let us arrange that. Not the apprentice then, and can I humbly request that you also attend?'

'You do not need to ask.'

Van Reit finished his glass and asked Grietje to reach again for the bottle.

'Well, let us gather and enjoy a good dinner in this house. It is near Christmas after all, like old times. Does Meijer have a wife?'

'I believe so, I have not met her.'

'Well she must come, else your youth and beauty will be spread too thin.'

Grietje laughed. 'She will be a bit younger than I.'

'There, I will look forward to that, and before then I will carefully consider and write of my intent, so we will not be overburdened with contracts and legacies. Perhaps my contribution can be no more than a signature or two.'

Van Reit was tired and a little subdued during the supper, but he did not let the conversation drop. Instead, he told Grietje of his wife and their happy partnership over many years. At the end of the meal, he apologised, saying he must early abed.

At the table, he again took her hand in his. 'If you would see me through this, I would be most grateful. So many of my ... well, they are all gone you see, and I find myself apart, estranged from what was once my whole life.'

Grietje squeezed his hand in return. 'Meneer, for reasons other, I understand you more than you may think. An accidental meeting brought about a change to my life. I do not think that I am doing much for you, but if I can play this role, I am content to be here and offer all I can.'

'Thank you, Grietje. Now I have some other news. It is both good and bad.'

'Meneer?'

'The art dealers, my friends, have visited and I showed them the artwork that you left with me. I gave them no information as to their provenance. To the good news first, they were delighted with the quality and suggested that, at a price that I felt was fair, they would exhibit them. Even in these strained times they would expect a sale or two, but...'

'I think I can guess...'

'I felt obliged to mention that the artist was not a member of a Guild and they apologised, sadly in fact, and said in these times, they could not consider taking them.'

'I am not surprised, and as you say, it is rewarding to have their professional appraisal.'

'The Guild could put them out of business. In more prosperous times they would not have been so strict, but these days...' Van Reit sighed.

'I understand, meneer, and I thank you. I am encouraged, not the opposite.'

'Well I must to bed now. I may not see you in the morning, but I will prepare some papers for you and Meijer. If you will keep me informed by letter?'

'Of course.'

Grietje was back in her own studio by the Thursday and had arranged to meet with Meijer again after noon on the Friday. An early hour knock on the studio door, brought Henry with pastries and two hounds. The cat flew up the ladder at the sight of the dogs.

'Do I interrupt?'

'You are always welcome, Henry, the more so when you bring food, but I am afraid the cat does not share my sentiment. Shall we go to the fire upstairs? I will pour coffee.'

Grietje looked to the ladder, then decided to take Henry out to the street and back in via the other door.

'I walk the dogs daily to the town wall, and you are now conveniently on my route. How was your visit with van Reit?'

'He was well. He is tried by this legal business. He has given me a note and papers for Meijer, the young Meijer. I told him of your interest, and he expressed gratitude for your offer of assistance. Shall I tell?'

'Do ... go on.'

'In short, he wishes to update, rewrite his legacy and he wishes to ensure that his own staff are cared for, for their lifetime.'

'He is a generous man.'

'Indeed, he further wishes the endowment for the building of the school to proceed promptly. He wants to see it rise from the ground. These matters are all sitting with Janssen. I am taking this to Meijer tomorrow.'

'Janssen is effectively in control of the funds?'

'I do not fully understand these things, but it would appear that way. There are standing contracts, but nothing is being done in their execution.'

'Shall I come with you to the lawyer?'

'Your presence would be a welcome reassurance. Now I must chase you away, I have work to do.'

Meijer hesitated when he saw that Grietje, wearing a heavy green dress, arrived accompanied and in a carriage. He warmed, however, when Grietje introduced Henry as a businessman associated with the Scottish company that required representation. Henry had, in his own business, met Meijer's uncle a number of times.

'Mijnheer, I find we cannot keep calling you Meijer as we have too many in this business. Is there another name?'

'Rolf ... meneer, mevrouw, please call me Rolf.'

Grietje gave Rolf van Reit's papers and he took a few minutes to read through them.

'You are familiar with the content?' he asked Grietje.

'Yes, we are in confidence with van Reit.'

'My information is not good. I have spoken briefly with Janssen. He will not countenance my interference, as he terms it. Even after I stated my intention to act in his interest. I fear he does not trust me.'

'That is unfortunate. Now you seen van Reit's requirement, what do you advise?'

'I have also spoken to Teuling. I put the case that Janssen's behaviour is affecting his own future. I did not have anything firm to propose, but he made it clear that he will only act under that authority of Janssen.'

'Despite Janssen's incapacity?' ask Grietje.

'Yes, it is the sworn duty of an apprentice. I cannot fault it.'

'He is a loyal apprentice,' observed Henry.

Meijer continued. 'The legacy is not a problem. Van Reit has given the details in these papers. I can draw this up, and if it is notarised it will supersede any prior testament.'

'It doesn't require Janssen?'

'No, I can notarise, but it needs two witnessed signatories at best along with van Reit of course. A minister or a surgeon and perhaps yourself, meneer Egerton. We all need to be present at the signing.'

'I think van Reit had realised this, he extends an invitation to you both to his house, if you can spare the time, for a dinner.'

The two men looked and nodded to Grietje.

'For the other matters, I do not see an easy way forward without recourse to the judiciary.'

'Never a quick route to anything,' Henry muttered. 'Can I ask?' Grietje nodded.

'Do you hold a ready account for van Reit's estate? If Teuling, could, without compromising his position, report this to you?'

'I can ask, but I don't see...'

'Perhaps we can find some middle ground that Janssen would accept. Surely, he would not relish a judicial review. If he would release the authority that van Reit demands, but retain some control of other, perhaps less consequential matters?'

'I will talk to Teuling further.'

Henry continued. 'If your family firm was instructed by van Reit to take an interest, say in regard of the building of the school, would your own position here be compromised?'

'I would step back from that. I would not take that instruction. The legacy is a simple matter of administration and registration, not cross representation. I do, however, wish to stress my independence regarding any other matters of mevrouw van der Meer and your own business.'

Henry looked to Grietje. 'We understand this and do not wish to compromise you, Rolf. Your advice is appreciated. We must then try to maintain a dialogue with Janssen through Teuling.'

Grietje excused herself to visit the backroom, leaving Henry and Rolf discussing Teuling's position. She had not seen the housekeeper and the hall was quiet. She tiptoed upstairs and turned the handle of Janssen's office door. As it opened a crack, she heard only heavy breathing. Apology at the ready, she looked in. She found Janssen once again slumped over his desk. He was deeply in sleep. She crept over and looked at the jumble of papers covering his desk. Grietje only saw that his recent attempts at writing were scribbles and indecipherable. As she left as silently as she had entered, she glanced around at the paintings on the wall.

'I worry that there is little progress,' Grietje confessed to Henry once she had returned downstairs and they had left the office.

'These things always take time. Rolf does not understand why Janssen is obstructive, he cannot see the benefit from it. He is embarrassed and as frustrated as we are. Now, let me take you to supper.'

'Thank you. It is the time that worries van Reit.'

'I did like Meijer. I made an informal offer of other business for Meijer, including Teuling if they can ease our path. I just get the feeling there is something we are not seeing. You left the room?'

'I looked upstairs. There was nothing of import.'

They talked of other matters over supper and once Grietje had finished her second glass of wine Henry, who had had one or two more, chanced a few personal questions.

'My dear friend, are you still bothered with the Tom Miller business?'

'Yes, the more so. It is not a worry. In consideration of it I shall return to Monster for a day or so, to paint in this winter light.'

'My curiosity is sparked.'

'You must again be patient. Nothing, is more the likelihood.'

'What then of your guilty deceit? You have to tell me something!'

'No, I don't. But I will, for you Henry, tonight.'

'Baited, I await.'

'I am driven, as you know, to aid the building of the school...'

'It is to your credit.'

'...because I desire to paint van Reit's portrait, to hang in the hall therein.'

'Again, due credit.'

'A masterwork ... to be hung in a public building, exhibited.'

Henry puzzled for a moment. 'The Guild...'

'Exactly.'

'If you exhibit a masterwork in the public building, you can apply for acceptance to the Guild of St Luke.'

'And it is rarely refused.'

'Then you will be able to trade openly... *mon dieu*, you are a devious girl.'

'Oh, don't Henry, it is my guilt. I did not quickly see it. I did not plan it. I do very much care for van Reit and for the orphan school. Am I wrong to also want for myself?'

Henry smiled at her as he ordered another bottle.

'Sir, I have to stay clear headed!'

'Grietje, your artwork is not for you. Your paintings are a beauty you give to us all and ultimately leave for all beyond our selves. As long as it is in exhibition, a painting can never be a selfish act.'

'You are a good friend, sir.'

'Let us drink to that.'

'Let me ask you then, what would you do with Janssen?'

'I fear it may end in court. Teuling is entrenched and Rolf cannot interfere. I understand van Reit's concern, but he may need to raise a formal action if he wants progress.'

Henry dropped Grietje off at her studio, where a hungry cat and her own warm bed awaited. She would write to van Reit and to the inn at Monster in the morning.

EDINBURGH, 1733

Chapter 12

David headed to Edinburgh's High Street, where he hoped to catch Joseph in his office. He wanted to talk to him without the family around. He needed some guidance on financial matters. Joe was at his desk.

'David, this is a surprise.'

'Am I disturbing, I would value your counsel?'

'Not at all, I am done for this day. Please sit.'

'I know we are overdue a talk, but I have some pressing issues.'

Joe nodded for David to carry on.

'I would speak to you more on my situation another day, but I have come to realise that the money you have told me of...'

Joe interrupted, 'It is your inheritance, David.'

'Yes, thank you. In the circumstance in which I find myself, well, it would be of value to me. I can put some money to good use to help the school, to follow my own ambition and, perhaps most importantly, release Rose from my own burdens. I am coming to terms with this.'

'Yet you seem concerned?'

'I am divided. It is not the creed I have followed.'

'So, you want to make use of the money?' Joe smiled. 'That is fine. You will need access to your own funds, of course, even if you wish to give it away. That is your right.'

'I don't even know the means.'

'Do you have a lawyer?'

'Yes, Lawrence Peat. His office is in Kirkcaldy ... the High Street.'

'Well, we, the company and myself, that is, use the New Bank. Are you aware of it?'

David shook his head.

'It is a longish tale and I'm hungry. Shall we go out for luncheon?'

'By all means, but I told Rose I would be back.'

'I can send a messenger and then we can return to Canon Mills by carriage.'

David accepted the proposal and they walked together up the street to the Sailor's Tavern, where Joe was clearly well known. The dining room was on the first floor.

'I will eat a little; I am full of College coffee.'

A maid was quickly in attendance. David ordered a small platter and Joe did not seem to order any food or drink.

'Shall I tell you some of my background?' offered Joe. 'As you have come to understand, you are now a man of wealth. It is necessary, therefore, for you to know where your money is held and how to use it, even if you choose not to.'

David accepted Joe's point.

'I was in ignorance when I started trading. It was a small world in Scotland, where we dealt in coins of different heritage, promissory notes or just the straight-forward exchange of goods. The agreements were often based on personal trust. My life changed when your father took me to Veere and the Low Countries. He knew much more than I. Yet he learned much there too. The seven states have a sophisticated banking system. I mean the issue of notes, foreign currency exchange, credit notes and so on. Trading becomes quicker and easier. In simple terms, the merchant did not need personal trust. If the bank trusted you, then you could trade freely. The system meant you could also arrange for money to be provided in any town with a banking office. Sorry, if this seems far from your question but I thought, as your father...'

'I am interested ... in your past too, Joe,' David added. 'I have been in ignorance.' He viewed Joe as a different person at his desk, in his business environment. In the past, David had heard him say that his wealth was due to luck and happenstance, he now saw that this was far from the truth.

'In short, in Scotland,' Joe continued, 'we are catching up. I have played a small part. I believe our new system is quicker and more convenient than England's.'

David's platter was served, and a meaty dish was placed on the table for Joe along with a jug of ale and two unusually large glasses.

'You will not have tried this. I acquired the recipe and imported the hops from northern Europe. It is called Pilsner. As you see it is served in a glass.'

'You have a hand in everything.'

'Edinburgh is a small place.'

David sampled the amber liquid and screwed up his face. 'It is quite sweet.'

'The New Bank is formally, *The Royal Bank of Scotland.* Myself along with a few other merchants were concerned about the Jacobite influences within the *Old Bank,* the Scottish Bank, although I still keep money in both. A bank can have no hint of uncertainty, particularly if it is to be respected abroad. This second bank was established with the King's sanction, oh, about five years ago. The Scottish Bank was not, shall we say, very cooperative. There was an extensive battle with our rival over the distribution of the new notes. Huge sums were risked as we nearly pushed it into bankruptcy.'

'How do you bankrupt a bank?'

'We borrowed and bought all their notes, took them out of circulation, replacing them with our own. I digress; both banks have survived, and I think, on reflection, that is a good thing. Both notes are now accepted, here and in England, but, alas, not by each other that may be a year or two yet. A merchant does well to keep a foot in both camps.'

They paused to eat, then Joe continued.

'I have already set up an account for you in the New Bank. Your money is held there. The company pays a credit to the account each month. You are free to take sums out at any time.'

'I just walk to the office and ask?'

'In principle, yes. I will have to introduce you personally, and I would bring your lawyer. He will alleviate the burden of larger transactions and prepare contracts, but you need to be able to trust him fully. Is he well established?'

'I don't know. He is young.'

'For small deals you would use the Bank's new notes. Have you seen one? They bear an engraving of the King's head.'

Joe took out a fold and produced a note for ten pounds. 'But for larger trades, many hundreds, the Bank would write a paper for the purpose. Both bank offices are near here, off the High Street, on opposite sides.'

'I see.'

'Will you tell me of your plans?'

'They are not yet firm, so I will tell you of my thoughts. Perhaps I can do that in the carriage?'

'Of course.'

Joe waved his hand to get the maid's attention.

After five minutes or so, the wench told Joe that his carriage was waiting, and they got up to leave.

'We do not pay?'

'There is an account.'

'You lead a different life, Joe.'

'From what?'

'From your ill-lit, two-room flat off the Cowgate.'

They sat in an open carriage and headed north in light rain towards Canon Mills.

'I have engaged a tutor for Rose. Do you mind if he attends her for one day initially?' asked David.

'Do you know him?'

'We have not met, but he is at the university and comes with a strong recommendation from a trusted old friend.'

'Then by all means.' Joe paused. 'David, there are so many longer discussions I would have with you. My grandchildren, for example. The girls are not schooled. They just learn to dress and entertain.'

'There is no wrong in that.'

Joe moved on. 'What of your plans?'

'The building of a master's house has stalled. I think I said. There is no janitor. My assistant master has a wife and lives in one room ... I could go on. Now, I could harangue the Council and the ministry for months, or, with the money you say is at my disposal, I can make provision myself.'

'Would you charge a fee?'

'No, it would be a charity.'

'A worthy deed, David, but do not let the people who obstruct you off too lightly.'

'I am not sure I am minded that way, but let me say further, that the important thing to me is that Rose needs a good house. With the loss of Janett, I am in danger of letting her slip into her mother's role of housekeeper and looking after me. And she would do so without complaint. I have seen this so many times, the maiden daughter. It is a limited life. With this wealth you say I have, she need not be confined to this, nor should she be. She wants to grow and study, to stable a horse, to entertain friends such as Adeline and Grace. They cannot come to our two-room hutch.'

'I see.'

'If I am truthful, they would not be embarrassed. It is me. I would be so, on her behalf. And they will soon reach an age when they will question.'

'Tell me then, without Rose, you would be happy in your ... hutch?'

'Yes, I don't see why I wouldn't, my head in a book, an eager class next door.'

The carriage drew up at the house door.

'But scholars I know thrive in fine libraries and invite erudite friends to their table, to be well fed and engage in heated debate?'

'That is a heavy blow, Joseph!'

Joe's broad grin appeared as a gaggle of children piled down the steps of the house.

'Where have you been?'

'You're late!'

'Daddy!'

As they were both pulled up the steps, Joe added, 'David, I have two guests this evening.'

'Yes, Mary said.'

'One of them is Edward Clerk. He knew your father. I thought I should alert you.'

'Oh, I see. Thank you.'

Rose brushed David's suit as he, looking in the glass, tried in vain to make his wig acceptable.

'You are now handsome, father.'

They heard the carriage arrive and felt a draught from the opening front door.

'Enough, I shall go down to meet them in the hall.'

Joe and Mary received the guests warmly, but the table was set only for the men tonight. Young Joe and Hugh walked into the hall from the drawing room as David reached the bottom of the stairs.

'Joe and Hugh, you know.' The two men nodded. 'And this is David Miller.'

Edward introduced himself, shaking David's hand.

'Not the notable schoolmaster, Dr Miller of Kirkcaldy?' said the second gentlemen who held a bundle of large scrolls.

'You are ahead of me sir, you look a little familiar, but I can't...'

'I am William Adam of Kirkcaldy, more recently relocated to Edinburgh.'

'Oh, sir, of course. I have met with your family at Dunnikier. You are the architect.'

Joe answered, 'William has remodelled our frontage, and he now has designs on the rear.'

Mary looked up the stairs and saw Rose, part hidden on the landing, had been listening. Mary looked to David who nodded as he surmised her intent.

'You can come down, Rose, and greet the gentlemen properly.'

The pink-faced girl came slowly down the stairs.

Joe performed the introductions. 'Miss Rose Miller, this is Mr Clerk.' Rose curtsied to Edward, who was staring. She then turned to the next. 'And this is Mr Adam.' Rose managed a smile and shook William's hand.

'But we are met. I believe, Rose, you attended Gladney house this summer past with young Smith, to see my boys.'

Rose nodded.

'Hello Rose. It is good to see you well.'

'Thank you, sir. Are the boys...?'

'They are well. Thank you.'

David interrupted. 'All right, Rose, this is not a family occasion. Off you go, and to your room, not the top of the stairs.'

'Yes, Papa. Sorry, Papa.'

Mary excused herself and Joe organised the party.

'Gentlemen, we shall have dinner. But first we must view the drawings. David, William has brought plans for the house, Edward too has an interest. The younger men will re-join us at the table. You are free to...'

'I am interested, if I may?'

David accompanied William. 'I have admired the new frontage. You are building fine proportions into tired Scottish buildings?'

'I try, and I am astounded that the design is proving popular. I am so overtaken by demand I will soon need the assistance of my boys.'

The four gathered around the table in the library as William went through the details of his modelling. William's style achieved a sense of grandeur, proportion, and elegance, without demanding an increase in scale. The windows were tall and many, the rooms behind would be well lit; large fireplaces were included to match the detailed embellishment of the interior, not extravagant nor overly ornate.

Joe went over the drawings with William while Edward explained his own interest to David. 'It is my eldest brother, Sir John, who is the architect in our family. He and William have recently worked together on Mavisbank. I don't know if you know of it?' David did not. 'It is yet incomplete, but it is worth a visit. John now has grand plans for Penicuik.'

David declared his interest. 'I am in need of a new house, on a much smaller scale. I understand little and this evening is a valuable lesson, indeed.'

'Did Grieve tell you that I knew your father?'

'He did.'

'Not well, but his reputation was such that I invested in his first overseas venture, a tragic loss. Grieve has always credited him and that venture for his own success, from which I too have benefited. Seeing your daughter, I believe I may have met your mother also, many years ago.'

'Thank you. My return to Edinburgh has brought the past near to me. I last saw my father when I was aged ten years. Such were those times that he was more in business than at home. At his loss, my mother suffered greatly. As you say, it was a long time ago. Do you have family?'

'Yes, a wife and a brood of four. We stay at Penicuik with my father, mother, many of my brothers, sisters and their kin.'

'And you are a merchant?' asked David.

'Yes, I am very far down the family pecking order; I am thus charged with earning my keep. Grieve and I have a long and I may say successful history.'

'We are done, gentlemen,' announced their host. 'Let us to the table and see what cook has provided for us tonight.'

The evening was both involving and entertaining. David was pleased that he had accepted Joe's invitation. For him, the three men, he realised, were illustrious company. The table conversation was serious, initially. He felt the younger members of the family, and perhaps even himself, had been invited as part of their growth, learning the ways and means of a commercial society and the habits of a merchant businessman. The young men stayed quiet unless addressed directly. They left the company when the four men withdrew to the study to sample Joseph's fine assortment of whiskies.

There had been no serious disagreement among the three. They knew each other well, and appreciated a diversity in opinion, laughing at times at one or another's entrenchment. Yet, as David looked on and listened, he realised there was a sure unanimity. None of these men held strong positions on the conventional principled stanchions of society. The Gods of others were of no import. Presbyterianism, Catholicism, or the Episcopalian were of no matter. A Tory, Whig or Jacobin did not concern them. Kings, queens, north or south, were only of passing interest. The Old Bank or the New Bank, they would use either or both. It was progress, growth, trade and the flow of money that was their doctrine.

The Union, however, had been important to them. Peace meant good international trading relationships. It was vital for progress. They quietly worried about the highlanders; despite the debacle of 1715, they were still a threat to civil rule, investment and progress.

What these three shared was a drive to industry, to manufacture, to mining, to building roads, burghs, and communities. They shared an ambition to export and import from Europe, the Americas, and the East. Yet this impetus was not solely for their own importance. Indeed, they shied from ministry, public authority, Council and parliament, merchant bodies, and talking shops. They saw the accumulation of wealth as of much greater benefit to their world, to Edinburgh and Scotland, than any political or religious movement. They just wanted the freedom to get on with it. Further, and this surprised David, they saw education as one of the keystones. The trader, merchant, owner, or businessman needed educated people working for him, men of talent and ability, men who were open to innovation and new ideas. These were good men, *eudaimonia*; they strived for *the good life*. David sat at Joe's table and saw his own philosophy reflected back to him.

As the whisky began to take its effect, Edward included David's role. 'You see David, we have three cornerstones laid, but we three do not have the means of education. There is no snap of the fingers, political shift, nor investment that can instantly produce an educated population. William is building a new school in Aberdeen, but if the boys are taught poorly, the bricks serve no purpose.'

David responded. 'We have the Education Acts?'

'Indeed, but are they working? I have heard schools are not well funded despite the law, and the masters are poorly rewarded. I would happily hear your view.'

'It is very much dependent on the burgh and thence the Council. You are right to have misgivings.' David paused. 'There are some very good schools. We better the English and many others on this. It takes time – eight years – longer if your requirement is ministers, lawyers and professors.'

'Then what would you advocate?' Edward asked.

'More grammar schools and trade schools. Therein is the lack. And you are correct in regarding the staffing.' David was glad of their interest but did not want to stand too long on his lectern. 'Is it a merchant school you have newly built, William?'

'Yes, Joseph has said you attended *Heriot's Hofpital*. It is as much the same.'

'Well, the school served me well, as did the teaching of classics in the High School.'

There was a lull as Joseph summoned a footman to top up their glasses.

'Prey tell us more of your play, David.' William asked.

'You know of it?'

'I still have an ear in Kirkcaldy.'

David gave details of the background and his intent. He admitted to some nervousness for the event. He was aware he had held their attention for too long. When he had finished the summary, he invited them to tell of their own school and university days. Their embellished and amusing tales told mostly of antics outside the classroom.

It was well after the twelfth hour when the men convened in the hall to extend their farewells with much handshaking, back slapping, and jocularity.

'William, why not bring your family here, one Saturday or a Sunday perhaps, after church? The boys would surprise Rose. Sorry, David, is that acceptable?'

David hesitated. 'Yes, it would be ... after term? Then, yes. She would be thrilled, I expect.'

David rested well but was rudely woken by Rose pushing at him. 'Father, Father you need to rise.'

'It is still dark. It is too early, Rose. What hour is it?'

'It is seven hours. I need to go early.'

'But why?'

'It is a surprise. You need to rise. There is a carriage at the eighth hour.'

David groaned and rolled over. He had had five hours sleep.

Rose was to sing in the choir. David was pleased, but at that moment he could not express it. He half-slept at the end of a pew at the back of the church as the choir practised, much to his daughter's embarrassment.

When the congregation started to arrive, David found he recognised familiar faces, more than he had expected. The church was full and warm, and for once he enjoyed the quiet solemnity of the sermon.

There was a note waiting for him when they arrived back at Canon Mills; it was unusual, being a Sunday. It was from David Hume: a letter detailing his somewhat extensive experience and a second sheet giving his circumstance and willingness to take the position. David showed Joe the letter and they agreed that Mr Hume would attend as a tutor for Rose on the Wednesday.

In the morning, after leaving Smith's message and one from himself beside his daughter's sleeping head, David caught an early ferry. He hoped for a calm crossing to gain rest before he faced the next five days as master of his school.

DELFT 1711

Chapter 13

Since the vicious assault she suffered in Veere, Grietje had become wary when travelling on her own. She decided, for the second time, to dress as a man or at least cloak herself in ambiguity. She wore her dark curls down to her shoulders and donned a black velvet tricorn. A loaded pistol was tucked into the garter of her breeches and a slim dagger sheathed on her belt. Grietje boxed her sketching tools, paper, board, and a small easel, and loaded them onto the cart. She included a bag for herself with pen, parchment and ink, her linens, and a single dress.

'And what about you, *Katje*, will you starve without me? I think not, but you'd better come, else I will worry.'

She whisked up the kitten and enclosed her in a box with straw.

Using the old cart, the one Tom used and Esmée had given her, Grietje set off towards the coastal village. Once clear of the town port, the horse sensed the route and she let her mind drift back to her first journey to Monster with Joe and Henry. Would that those heady days of summer could return.

The road was pitted, and the land became low and flat. As she neared the coast, the cultivated pastures by the roadside diminished and were replaced by long grasses and marshland. At this time of year, the raised road seemed to be the only sure ground. The third hour brought distant sight of the neat coastal village on higher land. Ten, maybe twelve cottages together and several others outlying, along the shoreline. A new church was half built; its aspiring tower dwarfed the other buildings. A single line of white stucco formed a street, reaching down towards the pier and the sea. The harbour wall must have struggled to keep the drift sands at bay.

She stopped the cart to the side of the inn. There was no hiding place for strangers in this village: a boy appeared and said he had been sent to tend the horse. The nag would be stabled in an outbuilding nearer the harbour. Grietje nodded in agreement and checked that the cart would be safe where it stood. As the boy unharnessed the horse, she lifted the sleepy cat out from the box and enclosed it in her bag before walking into the public room of the inn. In an instant, a memory of Joe formed substance. In that moment, she could see, hear, smell, and feel him, her stomach empty.

A cheery elderly housekeeper looked hesitantly at her garb, then gave a welcoming greeting. She showed Grietje to a room at the rear of the inn. It was larger and more comfortable than she had expected, with a good bed and a roaring fire. Once alone, she opened her bag and the cat peeked out, then tentatively crept, paw-by-paw, crawling low around the room, starting at any sharp noise, on occasion looking back to Grietje and sounding a mewling cry. Grietje sat, then lay on the bed. The cat jumped up beside her, and immediately changed its mind. Preferring the fireside, it cleaned itself with a lick, then curled up in a contented purr.

On the hour, a maid arrived with a rich fish soup and some bread, which brought the bat back to life. With *Katje* on her lap, Grietje sat on the single wooden chair by the fire to satisfy the demands of two empty bellies.

The light was fading when Grietje walked towards the harbour and turned along the shore, all the time looking out to the endless sea. The narrow path, bordered by tall grasses, thrided down through sea-smoothed rocks, hosting pockets of water and tangles of gulfweed, to the flat, white sands beyond.

Her artist's eye appreciated the challenge of the sky and the sea, the light and the land, the difficulty in making waves sink and soar. She had seen many works of the old masters and gasped at their controlled expressions of freedom and subtlety in their tones: creams, blues, pinks, and purples. The highlights were shadows, opposites, and contrasts: ochre, blue, and grey, not the yellow, gold, and white of the Renaissance Tableau. But it was only recently, in her new-found maturity, that Grietje was beginning to sense an inkling of the inspiration to which van Reit sang his evening song.

She sat on a fisherman's upturned basket and took up chalk, paper, and a board. She let her companion out of her confinement. *Katje* stayed close and played at hunting; whether real or imaginary prey, Grietje did not know. As Grietje waited, she practised her art, concentrating on a narrow field: ropes and creels, nets and sailcloth, rocks and sand. She often paused to look up and out to the pastel shades in the sun-setting sky, changing every minute: every glance left a new impression.

She was not able to paint on canvas here, nor could she sketch the breadth of the scene with sufficient acuity to paint-in from an outline, once she had returned to her studio. This was not a portrait. The masters and their apprentices would occupy a building or a shed by the shore to paint these scenes from nature, much as van Reit had used his *huizen*. She needed a warm kettle and her jars, powders, pots, mortar, oils and pastes.

Her cat did not stray, nor would it be caught: the failing light brought out the tiger. As Grietje walked back, *Katje* followed whilst pretending not to; each time she looked back, its body was stilled. At last, she managed to grab its scruff and despite a spread-eagled protest, the feline was squealed back into her bag.

Grietje spent the early evening exchanging a few words with local fishermen who did not baulk at, nor question, her androgyny. She took a supper of bread and cheese before going to bed early with the intention of rising early to catch the breaking day.

When the first pink glow appeared on the horizon, Grietje and the cat sat by a rocky outcrop near the breakwater. The fishermen and their nets were already gone; their small boats were enveloped in sea mist. She put crayon to paper, but this vista needed a larger canvas and oil paints of rich and subtle hues. As the sun rose, she turned instead to sketch the string of houses down the village street, and capture the sloshing of buckets, the tying of wash lines, a maid at her duties, a wagon waiting for the trawl catch, and the early morning stretch of the everyday.

Then a man's figure echoed, stooped, with a limp and a slow walk. The children went to him; even at a distance she could hear their chatter. He laughed with them. The man she knew as Tom was walking towards her.

Sketching was such a good disguise. You could stare in apparent composition and not cause offence nor brook any enquiry. She felt a degree of guilt: she knew so much of him, although they had never met. He would not know her at all, she assured herself. He had an obedient collie at his side. Grietje looked for the cat and, finding her sleeping, lifted her back into her bag. Tom nodded absently as he walked by, giving her no other attention, though the dog left his side to sniff at the bag, quickly obeying when called back.

Twenty or so minutes later, Tom walked his return. Another ten and the aromatic lure of fresh bread and coffee called to Grietje's needs, and she started to pack her things. Looking up too late, she saw a second figure with a quizzical expression approaching her directly. No time to compose on paper or in mind. The woman's eyes narrowed.

'Is it Grietje?'

'Hello, Doorjte.'

'You have returned?'

'Yes, I live in Delft now. It is not too far.'

'You will visit?'

'If you would ... em ... I did not intend to intrude.'

'It is not an intrusion. I would like to thank you for the drawing you left, although I have a question or two.'

'Of course. I am going to the inn for some bread.'

'Come to us. I have this minute opened the oven.'

'Oh ... well ... thank you. It will take a moment to pack.' Grietje was trying to buy time to think.

'You know the house?'

'Yes.'

'Well, come when you are done. Em, your bag is mewing?'

Grietje laughed an opened a peephole to show a demanding furry head.

'Hah, Tomasine will love her. Please bring it.'

'I will, thank you.'

Grietje watched Doorjte walk back towards her stilted house turning to smile and wave as she approached the wooden staircase. She had to remember that Doorjte and Tom did not know of her connection to Joe. Yet if they had deduced, and if they asked, she must confess it. She would not entertain too much deceit. But, initially at least, it was not that way. The dog, the cat and Tomasine kept them all amused. The collie assumed she had been given a new puppy; Tomasine had a new friend, and *Katje* was excited to enjoy both roles. The house was comfortable but tired and not well furnished. Grietje suddenly had a worry that they had not received the money Joe had left. She also remembered that the children had called Tom, David. A father after his son, she did not fully understand why. She took care not to show any surprise or shock at his appearance. He was scarred down one side of his face, as if by a burn, and the arm and hand on the same side as his limp were noticeably disabled. His eyes were bright though, and he shook her hand before leaving her with Doorjte to sit and talk at the table.

Grietje saw her drawing was crudely framed and mounted on the wall opposite the single window.

'I was going to write to thank you, but the moment passed. It was kind of you. Tom loves art, yet he has no talent himself.'

Grietje dismissed Doortje's gratitude and drank the last of her cup.

'Perhaps we could walk the sands together if you have finished. I can leave Tomasine with David, and I will bring the dog.'

They put on their cloaks. The cat was content to stay. They walked first in silence, until they had cleared the village.

'Grietje, there was a bag of money from Joseph Grieve, do you know of it?'

155

Grietje took a long time to answer. Doorjte was sympathetically patient and did not quickly press her.

'Yes, Joe was there. I was with him. He told me you had met and talked.'

'You have seen Tom now?'

'Yes, Joe left you a note?'

'He saw Tom?'

'No, but I did, and I told him I had seen him, or more correctly, I described the man I had seen walking with you and a child.'

Doorjte was shaking.

Grietje reassured her, 'Doorjte, I am not here to disturb. And I know with certainty that Joe is not ill intended.'

'Did Joseph not send you?'

'No, he may well be angered if I tell him.'

'Then why?'

'Not much more than an instinct. I know Joe. I now know him very well. We have spent many days solely in each other's company.'

'He is here?'

'No, I have not seen nor heard from him in months yet, to me, he is always near. Aside from Mary and the children, the only time he openly expresses his feelings and his love is when he talks of Tom, and David.'

'Then he knew of Tom and did not seek to talk with him?'

'No, he thought long on it, but he saw it surely as Tom's decision to make, and not his. I can say more.'

'Go on.'

'I think at first, he did not understand. Then he slowly began to. He does not apportion blame. Over time, a comprehension, perhaps an empathy, grew within him.'

'Did you help in this?'

'I don't know. I may have, I suppose; we talked late into the evenings on many occasions.'

'Are you ... is Joseph in love with you? Oh, I'm sorry.'

'It is fine. I don't know. Neither of us dare confess it. I am older, Doortje. It is better that way.'

Grietje picked a smooth, washed-up stick and threw it into the surf for the collie to retrieve. The dog scattered the sand'lings which were following the ebb and flow of the neap tide. She continued, 'Joe thought he was dead, drowned. Would you tell me more of it?'

Doorjte waited.

'He all but was. I had heard news of the flood, of course, and that there was much loss of life. At first, I did not think of Tom. Then I remembered he had been travelling by cart in the area worst affected. He was going to van Reit. You know of this?'

'Yes.'

'I had hoped for a message from Veere and began to worry when nothing came. The dead and the dying were so many that they were fetched and left on boards in the Nieuwe Kerk. I did not intend to go. I did not want to admit to any of it, but one day my walk took me there. Too few nuns attended; many bodies were fully covered in white sheets. Others were separated to an area where families and their physicians could nurse them. There were untended bodies in the middle, between the rows of the dead and the living, as if in purgatory. They were robed in mortuary linen, but their faces were left uncovered. Many were dead in their eyes. I started with the sure dead, row-by-row, one-by-one, peeling back the cloth and looking into their faces.

Doortje let out a gasping cry and sobbed. 'I'm sorry. I'm sorry. I have never spoken of this. There has been no one...'

Grietje reached for her hand. 'Do not go on.'

'I need to. I need to.' Doortje whispered. She continued after a further moment of quiet.

'The stench was awful, not just the human smell. Worse than a putrid sewer, death has its own scent.'

'Body after body I looked, I looked and prayed. I did not know the words of prayer or to whom I was praying. Many had the scarring of the cold and were blackened. You saw his face?'

157

'Yes.'

'As I moved towards the living and the expectant dead, I sensed him before I saw him clearly. I walked straight past another two or three others and there was his face. No doubt, no colour, black scarred, skin white from cold and lack of blood. A nun saw me and came over; she held a resigned look. Yet he was not dead, there was a thin rasping breath. Life's beat drummed slow and his body still held on to his soul. That was the beginning. I did not leave his side. I took advice from physicians and the pharmacists; most of them gave no hope. But I could not leave him; I rubbed his limbs daily, I rubbed him, I anointed his skin, all of it. I even tried breathing my life into him through his mouth, such was my desperation. Days beyond days passed, and he did not leave us. I wanted him home. If he was not to survive, I would not have him to die in those sacred but repellent confines; the air was wretched and cold, and there had been talk of plague. I had two men carry him to my house on a board. Sorry, I will not extend this pain much longer, Grietje. I placed him by the fire and continued my administrations. Then one day, one day an early morning ray of sun caught his face and his eyes moved. The next day he took a spoonful of warm soup.'

They were sitting beside each other. Grietje changed the hand that held Doortje's and put her arm around her shoulder. They sat for a timeless moment.

'I, we, have not an aim. We live day to day. There is contentment. Tomasine is our delight, our cause, our reason. Without her there would be little else. We find our little pleasure in the life of this village. There are no questions and the people are kind. Tom teaches the children and helps the fishermen with their accounting. He likes to contribute, to do work, but without any ambition at the moment. We should go back, I suppose.'

They had covered a good distance. Doortje called the dog, which had been enjoying its freedom.

Grietje spoke first. 'The money Joe left.'

'Yes, oh, yes. Please thank him.'

'There is more if...'

'You mean the house. We needed to pay off debts, the boarding house, and the move to the village. And my mother has expenses. The money allowed that and to secure the rent for this house. What is left covers our needs. We are fine. The village is mostly barter and exchange. We contribute enough to merit food and fuel. That is all we require.'

'Joe believes Tom is due more. If you have need...' Grietje offered.

'Thank you. Not at present. As Tomasine grows we may ... we will do what we can. Will you come for supper?'

'Gladly, but will Tom not...'

'I don't know. If he wants to talk, he will talk.'

'I will not raise anything. I have one question which you may find odd. Well two, actually.'

'Yes?'

'From what you say, Tom has not travelled far?'

'No, we have stayed in the village.'

'He has not been to Delft? He has not seen the lawyer Janssen?'

'No, why?'

'It is odd. I am not at the bottom of it.'

'Is it important to us?'

'No. it is a minor issue. I have engaged another lawyer in his office. I have met Janssen. You have met him?' asked Grietje.

'Yes, once.'

'How did you find him?'

'He was a vibrant and charming man.'

'Too charming?'

'Perhaps.'

'It is of no matter. He is quite ill now.'

'I am sorry.'

'It is of no consequence. I was just curious.' Grietje knew she toyed with the truth.

'What was the other question?' asked Doortje.

'Why do the street children call Tom, *David*?'

159

'When he at last managed to get on his feet, as you can imagine it was not easy getting him out of the house. The fishermen and others helped selflessly. They lifted him up and down those steps every day and they made me a barrow chair, so I could push him along the street.' Doortje's voice slowed and grew low again. 'For a long time, he could not talk but it was not his mind: he waved his hands and could scratch pictures on paper. It was just that his voice did not work. Eventually, a single word, and the word he said was *David*, and it was his only word for a while. Most days I took him out, the children would follow us; they would chatter and help me push the chair. At that time, all Tom could say was *David*. To them, he was *the David*.'

Grietje had remained composed throughout the walk, but now she wiped the wetness from her eye. 'Tomasine is a beautiful, happy child.'

'Thank you. In the circumstances she is our miracle. Please, tell me about your painting.'

Grietje leapt on the opportunity of safer ground and told of her ambitions and her continued contact with van Reit and her friend Henry's commission.

When they stopped by the house they parted warmly, with Doorjte saying she would prepare a good supper, but apologised for having no wine to serve.

Three hours later Grietje returned wearing her green dress. The evening was pleasant; the conversation stayed clear of difficult topics. Grietje had brought a jug of wine from the inn which softened the awkward moments. Tomasine, who sat with her mother, was fed at the table. Tom asked of van Reit and was pleased to hear of his better health. Grietje told openly of his ambition for a school and her aim to capture him in paint. Grietje was surprised to see that it was Tom who lifted the child and took her to bed. Later, she overheard him tell a fairy story in the next room, his voice stilted. The cat had followed them but was deposited back; Doortje distracted her with the remains of their meal.

After Tom left, Doortje asked, 'Will you tell van Reit?'

Grietje met her eyes. 'No, I will tell no one. I wholly consider myself under Joe's confidence in this matter. In truth, I feel the guilt of an intruder. It is only that Joe has shared so much with me and I know things that he will not tell, even to his wife, I feel a part of it. Yet I play no part. I will tell Joe of course, unless you don't want me to.'

'I felt such a release today being able to talk to you. We have friends here yes, but no questions are asked, and nothing is said. I am so pleased that we have talked. I hope you can come again.'

'I am happy to. My own family and friends have suffered; many were lost in the plague. It is only my painting that stops me from feeling alone in Delft. I too would value the friendship.'

'But you have all these men!' remarked Doortje.

'Hah, men! I fear they invoke the best of us and the worst of us. I have had recent luck with Henry, van Reit is a treasure and of course Joe; at the moment, I cannot find a safe place within myself for Joe.' Grietje changed tack. 'They are building a new church?'

'Yes, the old one is in such disrepair, it is not used. There is no minister which suits us, as we cannot be married. Tomasine is not registered. We do not worry; we will deal with what comes when it comes.'

'There is no Council, no authority?'

'No, there is a landowner, but he does not interfere. We are such a small community; we just help and look after what we have. Everyone is fed, every child is shod. Tom's teaching of the children has been welcome; it is just a few hours. There are some who travel to attend a church, but they do not bring it back with them.'

'A world without God that does not feel far from heaven,' Grietje observed.

'I don't know, he sends many storms and sand to silt the harbour and we are bleak in winter.'

'Doortje, I have one small request?'

Doortje nodded.

'Can I return to sketch Tomasine, for you? I find that even the masters' painting of children is a poor representation of their life. I am keen to try.'

'She will not sit still.'

'That may be the problem. I can bring the cat.'

'Of course you can.' Doortje got up from the table and walked to Grietje and surprised her by kissing her quickly and gently on the lips before reaching over to pick up the dirty plates.

'Well, cat and I must to bed. I will sketch the old church tomorrow morning then set off before noon.'

Doortje clutched her hands. 'Have a safe journey and do come back.'

'I will, I promise.'

Tom Binnie

FIFESHIRE 1733

Chapter 14

The estuary crossing was so smooth that David, who had found a comfortable sack of grain, needed a nudge awake from a seaman when the ferry approached Dysart harbour. It was still dark as he walked to the school, not long after the ninth hour. He spent an hour at his desk reviewing the boys' speeches. This time the pile included three sheets from Smith. Those papers were not the tidiest, but David could see the piece was well structured; he had grasped the key points and there was a persuasive tone in his phrasing.

The boys were pleased and not surprised to see him. Among them, there was a rising undercurrent of excitement: the preparations for the rehearsal and the play's performance began to intrude on each day's teaching. Tuesday afternoon was wholly taken up with the enterprise. Samuel and his wife's efforts were essential as they arranged the room, clothed the players, and dealt with a continuing series of minor questions while David and the thirteen boys of the Senate concentrated on the staging and the oratory.

The efforts that had gone into the costumery produced a tableau which would have graced a professional production. Mrs Smith's word's echoed in David's mind: *you are not without support here.* Smith had the look of Caesar. Where in this small town had someone found a thick royal blue robe embellished by a golden silk scarf? David did not know. Smith himself, who else, had formed and chanced a leafy crown to wear on the back of his head. On stage there was a crimson backdrop, and silver goblets on a white-clothed table; it was beginning to look like the last supper. David hoped it was not a metaphor.

Eventually the boys were settled, and the second class formed the audience. Smith walked on last. He stood, and the others were seated. They were much of the same height.

David held up the signal to start and looked to Samuel; he raised his hand to keep the quiet in the room. One of the boys in the audience, robed as he was primed to pose a question, stood up. David did not know him.

'What is it, Grant?' asked Samuel.

'Sirs, Caesar needs a box. He's not tall enough.'

The others laughed.

'Sit down, Grant.'

David nodded and Samuel left the room.

'Boys, we are going to proceed one question and speech at a time. I will stop you by raising my hand, and when we are done, we will do the whole thing again. Those with a speaking part will go with Mr John for the first part and return to see the full performance.'

'Can we attend on Friday, sir?' a stray voice shouted.

'There is not enough room. Today is your chance to see it.'

There was a mild groan. Samuel struggled back in, carrying a wooden crate. Smith plus his chair were raised a couple of feet. Smith smiled at his enhancement and the audience laughed again.

'Don't fall off, Smith,' instructed David.

Smith rose and announced, 'Caesar does not fall!'

David rearranged the boys; the taller were at the centre, each side of Smith.

'He may not have the height, but he has the nose for it,' whispered Samuel in David's ear.

'He is just the man,' replied David. 'It looks magisterial. I hope the performance matches the setting.

They rehearsed and rehearsed and rehearsed; some were tiring. David had to remind the boys that it was a serious act, and that the performance was important for the school. It was near the sixth hour when David said they were ready to go through the whole piece unaided. The other pupils were brought back in; very few had taken the option of leaving.

There were pauses, mistakes and forgotten lines, but David let it run and the boys got through it. Not many of them had seen a

165

staged play; their only guide was the travelling players who occasionally arrived with the fair. When it was over the boys clapped, and the actors looked pleased and confident. Smith had done a good job.

'It's good enough,' said David.

'I'm impressed,' replied Samuel, 'the boys have gained an air of Roman swagger as they have rehearsed their lines.'

David was not sure how the burgh Council would react.

Friday arrived in a moment. After a short morning prayer, David made the boys go through their speeches once again. The rest of the school was a bedlam of preparation. The second classroom had been set up as a dining room; a group of parents had contributed food and organised the reception of the guests. David knew nothing of this. There were even jugs of ale. He wondered if the minister would attend.

David tinkered with the players' dress, the order of the questions and the setting of the stage. All present became aware of the increasing level of noise coming from the yard and the other room. Several boys excused themselves to use the bucket. David maintained the calm as much as he could.

On the half hour before twelve, parents, merchants, Council members and others filed into the classroom theatre. David stood close to the stage, his back to a window. The cast were ready. The boys who would interrogate the platformed Senate took their seats. The room began to fill, then overfill – had anyone counted? The standing room at the back became a crush, the space to the sides of the seating was filling up. The front two rows of chairs, reserved for the councillors, was the only free seating.

David was glad to see Mrs Oswald, in apparent good health, arrive with Mrs Smith and take seats at the front. They had the minister Erskine sandwiched and tamed between them. David spotted Peat the lawyer, Hogg the merchant, members of the Ramsay, Douglas and Drysdale families, and even his friend John

Anderson sitting further back. At the last, the Council officials entered and took their seats, some still holding tankards of ale.

The Senate entered from the back and squeezed down one side of the room to take their places on the stage: the room began to quieten. A rustle at the back and another family crept in. David looked up at the disturbance and there was a flash of familiarity. A tall, well-dressed gentleman, two girls whom he knew, and one more, wearing a cape with a hood covering most of her face. He became certain of this girl's identity when he saw her hand was held by Mary Grieve.

The classroom door opened again, and the hubbub quelled. The boy did not squeeze through; instead he waited for a corridor to be made for him. The crowd parted, and he slowly made his way to the front. His head high, his look of disdain: it was an imperious Caesar who stepped onto centre stage.

Smith's closing speech digressed wildly from his script, but it stirred all, even David. As he delivered his closing line, '*Me serve hic est omnium*', the boys in the audience stood to lead the clapping. Many others followed. The was a mixed reaction from the front benches. Gradually more stood to applaud, leaving only a few in their seats. Mrs Smith and Oswald stood, thereby dwarfing the seated Erskine. David moved quietly up the side of the room towards the door. He grabbed Joseph's sleeve as the Grieves were first to the exit.

'David, brilliant, I hope you're not cross. I have a boat at the harbour. We will wait on you.'

'I will not be long. I will thank the boys and come straight away. Joseph?'

'Yes?'

'Thank you.'

David managed to find and thank the boys, Samuel John and his wife, Mrs Oswald and Smith, and some of the other parents. He shook hands with many but was at pains to avoid the minister and the committee members. He left as soon as he politely could, fetching his bag from the cottage before untethering his horse.

The Grieves had not arrived by ferry: a sleek schooner, with a painted upper deck and uniformed crew, sat in Kirkcaldy harbour, incongruous against the mêlée of small fishing boats. As soon as David jumped on board, the railed boarding plank was raised, and the mooring ropes were cast off.

The Grieves had gathered on the aft deck. Joe appeared. 'If there is blame, David, it is those three!' he said, pointing to a trio of impudent faces grinning up at him.

'Papa! It was wonderful. But why didn't *you* speak? I wanted to listen to you.'

'It was not for me, Rose. It was for the boys and the school.'

'Are you cross with us for coming?'

'Not at all. I am very pleased to see you.'

In the light afternoon breeze, the mates raised full sail and the boat lurched, as it slipped through the waves like a sharpened skate on ice.

Joe went to speak to David.

'Do you have your own navy, Mr Grieve?' David asked.

'Alas, no. It is the Company's ship. You would be surprised how useful it is.'

'I can see!'

Joe grinned. 'It pays its way in business, costs us nothing as sometimes speed is everything. We have had some adventures on it.'

Rose walked over. 'There is a cabin, Father. Come and see the cabin.' Rose followed Grace and Benthe below deck.

'David Miller, this is Captain John Russell.'

'Sir,' responded the Captain, taking David's offer of a hand.

'You have a fine ship. Does she cross the sea?'

'Yes, sir. We have been as far as the Mediterranean and travelled down the west coast of Africa.' Russell nodded and returned to the helm.

'What an opportunity, Joe. The world suddenly seems very small.'

As the ship headed for Leith, David went forward towards the bow. The light was beginning to fade, and he could see the glimmer of the lights on the far shore. Joe came along the foredeck to join him.

'Your father used to do that.'

'What?' This time, Joe's mention of his father did not affect David detrimentally.

'Stand at the rail. I remember it well on the sea crossing. It was the worst of weather, a storm. He stood at the bow of the merchant ship. All sails were up, the ship rising and falling in the swell, the wind and rain lashed all on deck. His hands gripped the rail and he was transfixed. The captain had two hands fetch him in. He received a firm rebuke.'

'In my distant recollection, that does not sound like him.'

'No, I agree. It seemed out of character. I think that is why I recall it so clearly. He told me later, he liked the way that it made you lose your senses.'

'Ironic that it would lead to the death of him.'

Joseph did not respond. Instead he invited David below to join the others and have a drink.

They all sat awhile drinking a fizzy wine, then Rose whispered that she felt queasy.

'We'll go atop and look for the harbour,' said David.

He took Rose to the bow and they stood to look again for the harbour lights. There were many now. The wind was stronger, and David wrapped his arm round her.

'Do you enjoy this?' he asked.

Rose responded with a wide grin.

David pointed. 'The lights are all the harbours on the coast. Which one would you like to go to?'

Rose looked ahead and then she looked up. 'I want to sail to the moon and visit all the stars. With you.'

Holding his daughter tight, David looked up to see the iridescent sparkle of the winter night's sky.

Rose broke their silence and the mood. 'I'm fine now, can I go back to the others.'

Tom Binnie

DELFT 1711

Chapter 15

On the journey back from Monster to Delft, Grietje had time to
reflect on her visit. So much of it was unexpected. Her mind was
now occupied with thoughts of Doortje more than Tom. Doorjte
still held her youth, and despite the poverty of her dress, she was
beautiful. There was a composure, an understated elegance.
Doortje had a brief encounter with an older married man, and
within a short time found herself with a child and a man who was
barely whole, who would not survive without her. Doortje did not
look behind nor ahead; she did not express doubt or self-pity. Was
it something in the man or something within herself – Grietje
could only surmise. Grietje knew one thing: at twenty-one she
would not have followed the same path. At that age her first choice
had always been to walk away, to escape.

It was cold in the studio when she walked up the stairs. *Katje*
was reluctant to be put down, she kept looking at the cold fire in
disbelief. Grietje set the kindling and left the room to put the cart
round the back of the building before she returned the hired horse
to the stables. Back in her room, she found the fire had caught, and
she hung a blackened pot of stew over the newly glowing coals.
Grietje chided herself out of her sombre mood and made plans for
her studio. She would put in a proper staircase, along with a
second fireplace on the ground floor. She would see Meijer about
her funds in Veere; her coins and notes were running low and she
had no idea how much the bank held.

Grietje met her lawyer late one morning. Meijer was pleased
that she did not want to raise the issue of Janssen and van Reit.
Instead it was a matter of dealing with the transfer of money from
the bank in Veere. Meijer had said it would take a few days, and

she would need to travel to Veere to sign the papers, never the easiest journey. He was delighted to accept her invitation to lunch. 'And I promise, there is no hidden intent,' she assured.

Meijer that brought up van Reit at the end of their meal. 'I talked with my father, in the abstract, without naming names.'

'Oh?'

'He said that they could force a judicial review quickly in such circumstance, where there is a medical foundation. If the counsel is declared incompetent, then, *evident sui*, they cannot raise an objection. Where it is only a matter of lay opinion, even if held by another lawyer, then the courts become involved and the process can be lengthy and uncertain in outcome. As I say, I am sure he would guess I was alluding to Janssen, but he has no knowledge of van Reit or his involvement.'

'Thank you, Rolf, I fear that neither would seem a good option for van Reit.'

'At least Teuling and I addressed the issue as a problem for the practice. This we had not done nor appreciated before, and Teuling has been spending the late hours going through the accounts of Janssen's private clients. He says nothing to me apart from asking the occasional question, but I can tell he is troubled by it. He has only nine more months to serve, and his qualification depends on Janssen's signature.'

'I see.'

'Can I ask one thing of you?'

'Yes?' replied Grietje.

'May I see some of your work?' Meijer smiled.

'Is it necessary for your legal representation?'

'Absolutely.'

'In that case, we had best meet next at the studio.' Grietje laughed.

'Thank you, mevrouw.' Meijer bowed.

Early on the day of the seasonal visit, Van Reit's and Henry's carriages stood outside the studio door. Grietje, Henry and three footmen stood inside in the warmth waiting for the Meijers to arrive. Grietje had a case and several packages secured on the top of van Reit's carriage. Rolf, his two children and his pregnant wife Mila arrived in a third carriage, but they had agreed to travel together in two.

Rolf introduced his wife, Mila, and his children to the others. 'And this is Luuk and Lotte.'

'Grietje, it is so kind of van Reit to include us. Are you sure that...'?

'He was delighted, Mila. You will be made very welcome. When I told him of my kitten, he insisted that she come too, although I do not know what his hounds will make of her. She may amuse the children in the carriage.'

Henry clapped his hands. 'Are we all wrapped up?'

And they set off, Grietje, Henry and Rolf in the first and the others in the second.

'You have the papers?' Grietje asked.

Meijer patted his case.

'And is there any other news?'

The lawyer looked to Henry.

Grietje assured him, 'Henry is in my confidence and he is familiar with the background. Do talk freely.'

'It was from a further conversation with my father. I believe you know him, meneer.

'He may not remember me. He acted in a complex business arrangement where I was marginally involved. I am pleased to report that it all went smoothly,' Henry replied.

'I am glad for that. Well, regarding the building of the school, my father thinks that they, that is Meijer & Meijer, if instructed, could proceed with that action. A new mandate would have legal priority over any other. There would still be the problem of extracting the funding through Janssen, but he did not see that Janssen would have any legal ground for refusal. It would simply be an authorised payment of monies due.'

Grietje responded, 'That is useful. Do you think Teuling would put that to Janssen?'

'I think he might, but we cannot predict how Janssen would react.'

Henry thought on it. 'We need some leverage.'

Grietje scolded 'This is a delicate matter, Henry.' He bowed his head in false shame.

When they were halfway there, Grietje transferred to the other carriage, joining Mila and her children, allowing the two gentlemen to talk. She suspected Henry would produce a flask from his cloak.

As the carriages drew up at the house, van Reit, wearing an extravagantly embroidered waistcoat, a green jacket and blue breeches, was standing in the doorway. He met Grietje with a beaming smile. The others stood in wait while he embraced and greeted them one at a time. The children giggled, excited by their release from what they viewed as a long journey.

'We have a house full,' the host declared. 'Welcome, welcome, but come in from this cold.' Van Reit knew each name, 'Mijnheer Meijer and Mevrouw Meijer.'

'Sir.'

'And you must be meneer Egerton. I have heard so much, I feel we are friends already.'

'I do hope so, sir,' Henry replied and then he whispered: 'Grietje will not let us away with anything less.'

All fires were lit, all lanterns, lamps and candles were bright, the house was ablaze.

Van Reit gained their attention. 'The servants will show you to your rooms, then please join me in the drawing room once you are settled.' He reached for Grietje's hand and held her back. 'Thank you so much, my dear. I have my physician joining us along with his son, daughter-in-law and their children. I have had to employ more staff. This is like it was. This was my life, and I never thought it would be this way again. I will dip in and out, of course, but I will make sure you are all well looked after.'

Grietje could not find a reply and embraced him. Van Reit continued. 'Does the lawyer have the papers ready to sign?'

'Yes.'

'Fine, we will get that out of the way. You and Henry and I may talk late. We will see.'

'Sir, we will serve you in this. Please share your burden, and we will assist if we can.'

'You are the kindest soul.'

'There is something else, of a lighter nature. I have brought Henry's portrait. It is overdue and he is impatient to see it. But I also want you to view it. This action belies my confidence, but I would like to present it to him tomorrow, before the dinner perhaps.'

'How exciting. Of course, of course you must.'

'I cannot express my nervousness. I know that true artists never admit to such.'

Grietje was given her familiar room. The door was opened for her, and she was met by a bashfully grinning Sara and a full fireside bath.

When soft-skinned, sweet-smelling Grietje in a new fine cotton dress made her way down the stairs, the drawing room was bustling. The children, who were close in ages, were beginning to test their freedom in the strange new house. Servants moved swiftly and quietly around; each glass was never left to become less than half full. Trays of treats were served, savoury for the adults and sweet for the children, and Henry it seemed.

Grietje, Mila and the physician's daughter stood and shared family details, while the men gathered to tell old tales of politics, religion and wars. The children chased each other around the room.

'Oh, they will never sleep...' wailed Mila as her glass was refilled. 'But I will.' She laughed.

Van Reit walked the room, spending more time with the children than the adults. Henry lent a hand, as their host struggled to become erect from being crouched too long and too low.

'I am fine. I am fine, but thank you,' van Reit protested. 'We should sign these papers. Would you mind prompting mijnheer Meijer and the others for me?'

Van Reit looked over the papers and found they were as he had requested. Grietje did not have the status to act as a witness. Van Reit asked a few questions and all the pages were then signed. The witnesses were not required to read the document, they were only attesting the signatures. The business was quickly done.

'I will rest easy tonight, gentlemen. Thank you, now let us to dinner.'

The children were removed to eat in the kitchen, and the adults arranged themselves around the table for the dinner. Van Reit chatted amiably with Henry, roaring with laugher in response to one of Henry's fables. Henry could tell a good story.

The physician's family left the table early to attend their children's bedtime, and van Reit left shortly after. The others withdrew to play card games. The doctor played the harpsichord.

The next day brought a late breakfast. The minister arrived and held a short service, which the whole household attended. Midday brought a frosty country walk with the children and the hounds. Grietje showed Meijer and Henry the artists' *huizen*. The afternoon allowed respite, a rest before dinner.

A few small presents were exchanged in the drawing room before dinner, and at the last two servants brought in an easel and a large covered painting.

Grietje stood and called for quiet. First, she presented van Reit with one of the small drawings she had sketched in Monster. She was particularly pleased with its form and had had it framed. He looked at it closely and nodded in appreciation; his face held an enigmatic smile. Grietje then sat in a chair beside a puzzled Henry and held his hand. Van Reit paused for quiet to gain the attention of all, then pulled the edge of the covering cloth. There was noise, then the room applauded with a shout or two of bravo and other words that Grietje could not discern. She heard no sound: her eyes and attention were only on Henry's reaction. Grietje knew he would be kind, but she wanted to discern his instinctive response. He looked, taking it in, initially, then it became clear he was moved by Grietje's portrayal of him. 'It is wonderful, my dear.' He wiped an eye.

'Do you like it?' Henry nodded. 'Are you sure?'

'Yes, yes.' he squeezed her hand. 'It is perfect.'

'She has your likeness, meneer, there is no doubt in that,' remarked van Reit as the chatter in the room took hold.

Henry laughed. 'Even the hounds ... my chart, square and compass, hah! And I remember that bottle.'

The others gathered round to congratulate them both.

'Is that how you see me?' asked Henry.

'Yes.'

'I would that others did.'

'If they don't, it is they that are in error.'

'Thank you, Grietje, this is far too good for my rooms in Delft. With your permission, I shall transport it to England. I shall find a place in the stairwell or one of the grand rooms of Oulton Hall.'

There were sore heads and frogged throats as they gathered to take their leave the following day at ten hours. Grietje gave Sara, who was very sorry to see her leave, a small present. 'I'll be back,' she reassured. Grietje travelled with Henry in his carriage with Meijer, who was clearly avoiding his children. For the most part, she slumped against Meijer, barely waking to say anything at all.

'My feet are sore,' she complained.'

Grietje was still in her finery, having firmly dispatched Sara to bed, despite her desire to stay up. Grietje had gained bed for only a few hours before having to rise again.

'You did not miss one dance,' replied Henry.

'Oh, the dancing. Who played the music, who were the players?'

'Two servants played flute and viola. I think one of them is atop, and the doctor joined in with the harpsichord.'

'Did I see Sara dancing?'

'Your maid, yes. You took her up yourself, and you also seemed to be fond of that footman,' Henry teased.

'Oh dear, and where's my cat?'

'She's here, Grietje. Just rest now. Our heads are sore too.'

Grietje slumped back into peaceful repose.

The carriages rolled up at the studio in the late afternoon. Half asleep still, Grietje forgot to wait for the footman. She stumbled, missing the carriage step, only to be caught by a passer-by, who helped her up and, along with the arriving footman, supported her to the door.

'And what time do you call this, mevrouw?' the tall stranger rebuked in a low, scolding Scottish tone.

At the sound of that voice and the familiar scent of damp tweed and tobacco, she jolted fully awake.

EDINBURGH 1733

Chapter 16

The Grieves, David and Rose squeezed into one carriage for the short ride from Leith to Canon Mills. Arriving at the house, the children quickly disappeared into its depths. David held Rose back to say that he would look at her work the following morning. 'And did you meet your new tutor, Mr Hume? Did he attend?'

'Oh, yes. He was fun. He came two days. Joe, I mean Mr Grieve, liked him too.'

Rose's answer did not include any of the responses he had anticipated.

'Well, I shall look at what you have produced tomorrow.'

Rose shot off upstairs, leaving David to join the others at the dining table.

Joseph, Mary, David, two of the boys and their mothers, enjoyed an informal supper. Mary tried to rein Joseph in, explaining he was over-exercised by the day's adventure. Joe was on good form.

'We were well prepared, David. We guarded Rose like a Stuart Princess. The Town Guard would have no defence against my sailors. They were well armed, I tell you.'

'Well, I am glad then, that she was undiscovered,' David replied. He never knew the full truth of it when Joseph made jokes, but there was always a grain.

'Rose said you met with Mr Hume?' said David, changing the thread. His question only added to Joe's exuberance.

'Indeed. He was a fine fellow, not at all what I expected.'

'Do tell me more?'

'I sought to measure his suitability on your behalf. I hope you don't mind, but I did not gain the chance. You must seek that answer from Rose herself.'

'And?'

Joe was becoming hesitant. 'He was the sort of chap, David, lively and entertaining, not at all like a school...'

'Joseph Grieve!' Mary exclaimed.

'Sorry, not at all like a ... like a Presbyterian minister.'

'I am relieved, I think,' David commented.

'You can easily fall into conversation with him, and – and I do apologise – I suggested that he and I talk over lunch. In order to examine his character, you understand. Well, we got half-way down the second bottle...'

'That is when I discovered them,' interrupted Mary. 'We sent him away after lunch and he returned the next day and spent a full day quietly in the study with Rose.'

'Thank you. I shall examine Rose's efforts tomorrow.'

'But David,' Joe did not want to lose the tale. 'He had such a good opinion of things and explained, with thoughtful reasoning, each side of an argument across many subjects, religion, politics, education. It was just that ... well, he seemed to get lost when I asked for a conclusion.'

'I am not unfamiliar with that feeling.'

'You may laugh ... well, I hope you do. We agreed, in sum, that I would make the better philosopher than he, and he had the greater ambition to be the successful merchant.'

'That's enough Joe,' said Mary firmly. 'David, tell us what you thought of your boys today. I understand that they were speaking about the merits of your school.'

'It was indeed, and to exhibit the boys' talents. There are Council members and some parents who do not appreciate the school's position. Nothing will persuade the obstinate, but it may have influenced others.'

Mary looked at Grace's pained expression. 'Not these two, I'll wager. All right girls, you may leave.'

David continued. 'I was pleased and a little surprised at the interest of the audience today. I have previously been of the impression that the community is ambivalent. Today was encouraging. A school is as much a part of a town as the church.

Sadly, in creed, there can be confrontation over certain issues. Now Joseph, tell me more of your beautiful ship. Where have you sailed?'

'Oh, don't get him started. I think gentlemen, you will find a ready bottle in the library. We ladies will stay to discuss more delicate matters.' Mary called for them to leave the table.

When David came down for breakfast, Rose was already in the library holding a cup of coffee eating an unusually sweet flaky bread that required no butter.

He joined her at Joseph's desk. 'I will look through the work I set you first.' He was still eating. 'Have you tried this bread?'

Rose nodded and handed him her papers. Her work was neat and error-free, as far as he could judge. 'Very good, Rose, now tell me of Mr Hume's lesson.'

Rose was excited to tell her father. 'We went through the translation you left with me on the Tuesday. I had done the most of it. Mr Hume showed my mistakes and helped where I had become lost, so I worked that afternoon and evening.'

'And he returned the next day?'

'Yes, first he had me stand and read the pieces I had done, and I also read from books he had brought. I hadn't seen them before. It was difficult, but I learned new verbs.'

'What were these books?'

'I have them here.'

Rose offered two slim volumes to David from a pile on the desk. 'They are more about the ordinary people living in Rome, not gods, wars, or religion.'

'Interesting, will you read me a passage now?'

Rose did as she was asked and read part of a letter by Circero.

'Can you translate any of it?'

Rose worked her way through the writing, aided by her father's prompts.

183

'I liked the other book better. It was funny.'

'The plays of Plautus. I know of it, but I haven't read it.'

'Mr Hume and I read parts of *Aulularia*. It was a comedy. The servant and mistress switched places. I didn't understand much of it.'

'You were content then, with Mr Hume's teaching?'

'Yes, Father. Will he come back?'

'As he is in such demand in this house, how can he not? You must do my pieces first and then follow Mr Hume's task.'

'I will, Father.'

'You may go. Remember, there are visitors this afternoon and Mary would like us to lunch with them.'

'Yes, Father.'

David was interested to meet the young man who seemed to have charmed Joe, Mary and his daughter.

That afternoon, Joe, Mary and Rose went to the door to receive on hearing the carriage arrive. Mary insisted on Rose standing beside her. The carriage door was opened for Mr Adam and his wife, followed by their sons: John, Robert and James. Rose smiled in recognition.

John was, rudely, the first to speak. 'I have brought a friend.'

Mary nodded and both families looked to the carriage door to see *Caesar* climb down to join them. Rose jumped up and down and applauded and the others joined in, laughing.

With Rose being the only common link, Grace and Benthe were subdued at the lunch table, as were the Adam boys in the unfamiliar house. Not Smith, however, who never seemed to bow to anything much.

Once they were released into the countryside, accompanied as ever by the hounds, the children charged off ahead of the adults, on some impromptu imaginary mission. The barriers of shyness and embarrassment were breached.

Rose lagged behind and Smith waited to join her. He was so full of questions, although they were personal and not some query of nature or industry.

'Why are you not in school? Are you not coming back? What happened with the soldiers?'

Rose was not going to be interrogated. 'Slow down, Adam. Tell me first, how is it that you are in Edinburgh?'

'Oh, my mother is here for a week. She has meetings at the Assembly. I shouldn't say, but it is something to do with our minister. She arranged for me to stay with the Adams and they were invited here.'

'Did you know I would be here?'

'Only today. Mrs Adam and Mrs Grieve had exchanged messages.'

'How funny. Anyway, it is a nice surprise. You were very good in the play.'

'You saw it?'

'Yes, I was hiding at the back.'

'It was more fun when we were rehearsing. Was your father pleased?'

A shout from the group ahead of them. 'Come on, you two! We've found a river.'

Rose just waved back to them.

'Yes, I think so. He is a bit off these days. He has much on his mind.'

'Are you coming back to school?'

'I don't know. My father won't say. I have a new tutor here.'

'Will you tell me what happened?'

Rose looked to the front and then behind to see how close the rest of the party were. 'Not now, later maybe.'

'Come ON, you two!' came a shout from the front.

David walked with Joe, Mary, William Adam and his wife, who was another Janet. One hound stayed close to Joe's side. Mary pulled David aside. 'Rose enjoys the boys' company.'

'Yes, they spent last summer together. Along with the Oswalds, the Adams are as cousins.'

'You are aware she is growing up?'

'I am constantly reminded yet confounded by it. I have no guide. I had no mother nor sisters, and sadly no wife now.'

Mary squeezed his arm. 'She needs to be aware of older boys, especially if she is unchaperoned and in the public eye. I know that Smith is a few years younger, but he will grow.'

'He is a brother to Rose. I am very fond of him myself.'

'Just take care, David. It is the way others may view it. Not here, but elsewhere. She could be adversely affected by an innocent act, such is our society.'

'I am aware, Mary, thank you. She *is* headstrong.'

'She is a wonderful girl. The next few years will not be easy for either of you.'

'I am also aware, particularly here in Edinburgh, she needs linens, dresses, shoes, hats and the trifles that girls indulge. I will leave her an allowance, but if you could advise?'

'It is all in hand. You don't need to be concerned on those matters.'

'It was only yesterday that a white smock and pair of boots were her only need.'

'That is the way of it.'

Mrs Adam joined them, and after greeting her, David paired with William, as Joe and his hounds charged ahead to seek out the younger walkers.

'William, may I impose on you, despite the shortness of our acquaintance?' David asked.

'If I can help, sir, I am happy to.'

'I may build a house in Kirkcaldy. I think I will be there for a few years yet. It will not be of a scale to interest you, but could you recommend a trusted builder to me. I have my lawyer, Mr

Peat, looking, but I fear he does not have the experience of such matters.'

'I can do that easily. I will write a list before we leave. I would look myself, but my current book is overfull and demanding.'

'I congratulate you on that.'

'It will not last long. I am benefitting from the vagaries of fashion. Tell me, where do you live at present?'

'Cramped in the janitor's house. I desperately need some other place.'

'But, David, you must then use Gladney. We are out of it.'

'I couldn't, sir. It is a kind offer but...'

'You must. It is a burden to me. I keep it up, but we are never there. It is a good house with all furniture. Truly you would be favouring me.'

'If you are sure, sir. It does seem a most convenient solution.'

'For both of us!' William offered his hand and David shook it. They caught up with Joe and the children, who were standing with another group. Joe spoke loudly in their direction as they approached.

'Sirs, we are being arrested for trespass!'

The laughter of the group followed.

'William Adam and David Miller, this is James Balfour of Pilrig and his son, also James. We are not always on good terms.'

The senior James Balfour bowed in reply. 'Grieve talks ill of me because I was recently quicker to some land than he. It was a rare victory.'

The ladies joined them as Balfour continued. 'You have walked a fair distance, let me sustain you. Pilrig is just behind those trees.'

'It would be very welcome, sir, but we must not trouble you.' Joe replied.

'Not at all, not at all. You will find my wife will be very glad of the company.'

Joe and Balfour were in close conversation as they led the way to the house. Rose and Smith kept David company.

'Sir, I have letters for you from my mother and Mrs Oswald.'

187

'Thank you, Smith.' David would open them later.

Pilrig House was an elegant and prosperous house, which leapt into life on their arrival. The children descended on the kitchen, waking the cook from her afternoon rest. The ladies convened in the drawing room for tea and the men were served beer, mutton pie and cheese in the library. The men first talked of the house. William Adam had not been to Pilrig before. But the conversation soon moved on to the intrigues of the Scottish merchants and the banking world. David picked up that the Balfours' wealth came chiefly from their nearby gunpowder factory. Joe and James had resumed their discussion of investment in land. Joe brought David into the conversation. 'We would not battle so often if your bloody school did not eat up so much of it.'

'My school?' questioned a surprised David.

'Your old school,' clarified William who knew of David's background. 'Heriot's has much money and powerful allies.'

'Too much,' added Joe.

'I assure you, sirs, this is not my doing,' said David in defence. He then queried, 'Why such competition, is the land for mining?'

'Mr Adam has the closest ear,' said Joe.

William responded, 'It is the least guarded secret in the burgh. The subject of many a coffeehouse conversation and yet not one paper, Council minute, nor ledger account has been recorded. Not a single mention of it.'

'Then pray, what is the chatter, sir?' David asked.

'There is much talk of a new town, to be built to the north of the loch.'

'Ah, I can see why that would demand your attention,' said David.

James highlighted the issue. 'The land will become valuable immediately. if the Council even admits to its consideration.'

'*New Edinburgh*,' suggested David.

'*Josephtown,* if I have my way,' replied Joe.

'It is not the Americas, Grieve,' chided William.

The businessmen talked on, and David removed himself to find a more interesting conversation with the younger James Balfour who had stood to examine his father's library of shelved books.

'You studied at Edinburgh?' David asked.

'Yes, philosophy. I then spent a year in Leiden.'

'It must be beneficial to travel. I never have. Circumstance has not led me in that pursuit.'

'It is surely not too late?' offered James.

'Perhaps not, and what occupies you now?'

'I am an advocate. I also do some teaching at the university.'

'Both worthy employment. Tell me, do you know of a David Hume?'

'Yes,' James laughed, 'Very well, you are acquainted with him?'

'I have not yet met him, but he is tutoring my daughter.'

'He is a good man, sir. I know him well. As students, we had much principled disagreement; it was never accompanied by personal discord. He is a rare breed.'

'Then, I must meet him. Mr Grieve, my host, has tried to turn him to the trades.'

James laughed at the idea. 'I know presently he is short of funds.'

'I am a curious scholar myself, what was the essence of your disagreements with Hume?'

'The intrinsic behaviours of man, sir. In that we oppose.'

'On that subject, I am at quarrel with myself.'

'At present, theology is a divided land. I find the law a safer place.'

'I commend your choice,' David replied.

The younger James looked to the shelves and pulled out a volume. 'Have you read Hobbes, sir?'

'No.'

'It is a worthy read, but a sorry discourse. I fear my friend Hume is too much under its influence. We have spent long hours over it. I am sorry to admit there are some well-formed arguments.'

'Then what is the problem?' asked David.

'To an extent, they contradict our faith. But it is the root of the argument that disconcerts me. The questions that led to its founding. Hume himself admits to this struggle.'

Mary knocked on the door and came into the room.

'Joseph, the children! We must take our leave. It is getting dark.'

Balfour senior replied, 'I have many carriages. Do stay awhile, your company is most welcome.'

Joe and William nodded in approval as Mary sighed and left the room.

The gentlemen continued in their talk. It was near nine bells when the Grieve party, with seven tired children, set off for Canon Mills. The hounds were unleashed to chase the carriages, which they did in great delight, barking excitedly when the carriages stopped to pay four pennies at the toll house. At Canon Mills, the Adams swapped carriages and headed uphill to their own town house. Mary chased the other children upstairs. 'Church tomorrow, early breakfast.'

David had a concern. 'Where is Smith, is he accounted for?'

'Yes, David, he left with the Adams,' scolded his hostess.

DELFT 1712

Chapter 17

'Joseph, what...' Grietje groaned in surprise. Henry was laughing. 'Henry, you knew, you knew! This is the worst time. I am in no state. Off you go. I shall meet with you both later.'

Henry assisted, 'Come Grieve, meet Meijer.' They shook hands as Henry shouted, 'We will sup at eight hours, Mevrouw.'

The footman followed Grietje up the stairs to her rooms with bags and the cat.

It was after the ninth hour when Grietje arrived at the Mechelen Inn and found them at a table in the back room. She wore a bold smile.

'*Goedenavond*, gentlemen.'

'We weren't expecting you until breakfast,' remarked Joe.

Grietje sat down and reached out to clasp Joe's hand. 'It is a surprise if not a shock. I am glad to see you, Joseph.'

Joe smiled and squeezed her hand in return. 'Henry has been filling me in. My days have been mundane compared to your adventures.'

'You have not yet heard the half. But did you sail in winter?'

'Just the French channel, then overland to the Dutch States,' Joe replied.

A maid arrived to take their order.

'I cannot look at a glass of wine,' Grietje confessed, and along with Henry, she shared their stories of the celebration with van Reit, leaving any business until the morrow. Joe had taken a room at the inn and Grietje was relieved that she was not to be faced with Joe standing beside her at the bottom of the stairs to her chamber.

Joe and Grietje met at the *koffiehuis* early the next day and for two hours it was business, Grietje going over the details of her conversations with van Reit, Meijer and Janssen. Grietje asked Joe if he wanted to see the studio.

'Of course,' he replied.

'I have to tell you, Joe, I no longer live alone.'

'Ah, will there be someone else there?'

'Not exactly, wait and see. You will meet.'

As they walked, Grietje renewed the comfort she always felt with Joe. It was as if he had only been removed from her one night. A street away, a baker blew his horn signalling the readiness of a fresh tray and they responded to the call then picked up cheese from a market stall. The monger recognised Joe and they exchanged pleasantries.

Arriving in Grietje's room, the cat jumped up to hide under the nearest chair at the scent of a stranger.

'This is *Katje*, she has adopted me. Let me show you the studio downstairs, then I will plate the bread and cheese.'

Joe was interested and impressed. Grietje pointed out that none of it would have been possible without his money.

'You worked for it. You earned it.'

As they came out of the studio door to head back upstairs, Joe diverted round the back. Grietje was following him when he stopped suddenly and exclaimed, 'What?'

'What is it, Joe?'

'The cart!'

'That's my cart. Oh, sorry, yes.' She realised.

'That is Tom's cart,' Joe said, as an old sore became inflamed.

'Yes, I should have warned you. It was returned to the driver's widow, Esmée. You remember it was Henrik's. She passed it on to me. Let us talk upstairs.'

Joe had not seen the cart since the flood. He walked forward to touch the worn wood and run his hand along the metalled wheel. Joe did not speak again until they were both sitting at the table.

Grietje gave a fuller account. Joe came out of his thoughts. 'I was taken aback. But if that is the cart, then where are the paintings?'

'There was only the cart. I went into Esmée's shed. I didn't ask about the load.'

Joe's memories came back in flashes. 'I am thrown. I wasn't there, of course, but the cart would have been packed with the paintings Tom had bought from the dealers. If they found the cart, the paintings should have been nearby. What happened to the paintings?'

Grietje thought on it. 'The dealer would keep a record. That is a start.'

'Yes.' Joe stood up.

'Now, Joe?' asked Grietje.

'Yes, I can't sit on it. You don't need to come.'

'Of course, I do, and I will, but sit! Let us plan our days first.'

Joe sat down like a scolded child. 'Ja, mevrouw.'

Grietje and Joe visited the two art dealers after noon. A list would be prepared for them, and they would collect it before four. The air was pleasant, and they took a walk along the canal paths towards de Kolk.

'Joe, why have you come?'

'I have almost forgotten. I have brought some business for you. There is much of it, so we can talk over the details later. I have a fold of drawings of English houses. Edward Clerk supplied them along with a list of porcelain pieces to be patterned. I don't know the process. I would like you to deal with it here. Perhaps Meijer can deal with the formal arrangements, contracts and so forth. You will be paid of course.'

'I want to paint but I do need an income. So, yes, yes please.'

'There is a lot of it,' Joe cautioned.

'I can hire others?'

'Yes, we have the budget. You and I can go through it, with Meijer if you trust him. It would help to have a lawyer administer

194

the arrangement. You can act for me, but we will also need accounting. Although you have the measure of it, there is still much you can learn.'

Grietje welcomed the prospect of Meijer's involvement. 'Meijer has been helpful in dealing with Janssen. He will value this business. You can ask Henry about him.'

'I have already. Henry and I are visiting him at four. We will make sure he understands his position. It might be better if you do not attend.'

'Whatever you think best.'

Joe continued, 'I will collect the lists from the dealers and later we can sup together?'

'Yes, and I will make something for you if I can catch the market.'

They both smiled. 'Just like old times,' said Joe.

In the evening, Grietje served a mutton and plum pie with wilting greens. *Katje* sensed that Joe did not like cats and promptly plumped herself on his lap throughout the supper. Their conversation had been of the new business arrangement. Grietje felt unnerved by the size of the trade, but Joe reassured she was only required to oversee and write to him once a month.

'Let Meijer and the accountant do the work,' Joe instructed.

Apart from Joe's finding of the cart, there had been no mention of their previous visits to Delft together. She wondered if Joe had now managed to put Tom out of his mind. She wanted to tell Joe about her visit to Doorjte in Monster but was unsure of how much to say.

Grietje brought the paintings into their conversation. 'Do you have the list Joe, can I see?'

'Yes, in my bag.'

'You left it at the door.' Joe looked down at his lap. 'I'll get it for you.'

'Just take the papers out. Three or four sheets near the front.'

Grietje came back to the table and looked though the list, cursorily at first, then...

'Wait Joe, I know some of these. I have seen them recently.'

'What, where?'

Grietje checked through the list carefully before continuing. She took a breath as she caught the cause of the evasive unease that had niggled her from the start of her move to Delft.

'Joe, these paintings, or many of them, are hanging in Janssen's offices. But wait, let me think.' Grietje stood up and walked the room. Joe was relieved when she picked up the cat from his lap and stroked it as she paced.

'What is it?' Joe asked.

'Shh, just let...'

She stood in front of the fire. 'I need to tell you things.' Grietje could not avoid telling Joe she had met Tom.

'As I said, many of these paintings are with Janssen.'

Joe shrugged his shoulders. 'Well then, that is surely good?'

'No wait, just listen.' Grietje put the cat down at the hearth and fetched four scrolls from a cabinet by her bed. She broke the seals of the unopened ones.

'These are agreements of sale. Yes, look. They are the same paintings.'

She handed a scroll to Joe.

'They are in Dutch.'

'Look, you can see the names are the same.'

'What does this mean?' asked Joe.

'These show that the paintings were transferred to Janssen and authorised by Tom.'

'What, he sold them?'

'There is no price mentioned. But it is worse. You see, they are signed by Tom and there is a date.'

'I see a scrawl.'

'Exactly. I have to tell you, Joe, I went back to Monster and saw Doorjte.'

'Yes?'

'Tom has never been back to Delft. He has not seen Janssen and he never signed these papers. In fact, he does not remember anything of these paintings.'

Joe stayed quiet to take in what Grietje had told him.

'Are you saying, Janssen has stolen the paintings?'

'You and your company own these paintings, the ones on the dealer's books. Tom physically did not sign them away. I checked the date. Tom was never in Delft and, more importantly perhaps, he was severely incapacitated at that time.'

Joe was beginning to understand. 'I have already accounted for their loss. On paper they were worth a considerable sum. Do you have any more wine?'

'No, we have drunk it all.'

'Then we shall go out!'

'Joe?'

'I need a drink, a walk and a drink.'

They put their cloaks on and headed to the inn.

'Let's pick up Henry on the way,' said Joe. 'He can give us some dispassionate advice.'

They caught Henry in his night clothes. He quickly dressed and followed them to the inn.

'This is astonishing. You are saying a reputable lawyer, albeit an ageing and incompetent one, has stolen a goodly sum in paintings?'

'Shush, Henry, shush,' worried Grietje, looking around.

'We are saying nothing yet,' said Joe.

'Could it all just be a mistake, a misunderstanding, a verbal transaction before Tom's accident?' suggested Henry.

'If so, where is the money?' asked Joe.

'These papers,' questioned Henry. 'The written agreements. Where did they come from?'

The men looked at Grietje, who stood up to avoid answering immediately. 'I need to find the wench.'

She returned and, sitting at the table, turned to look shyly downward.

'What!' exclaimed Henry after her admission. 'You stole them... from Janssen's office! Hah!'

Grietje nodded.

'What a girl. And you have employed her, Joe. I'm not sure if that makes you very clever or a fool.'

'Me neither,' replied Joe.

Grietje feigned embarrassment. 'Shush! Both of you. You must not tell anyone, especially Meijer.'

Joe replied, 'But then we have no case.'

It was Henry who answered, 'Yes, yes, I think you do. You have the dealer's word and papers recording the sale to Tom.'

'Yes,' Grietje acknowledged.

'Then you calmly make your claim. Do not give any impression that anything is wrong. Grietje was received into the office.'

'Offices,' corrected Grietje.

'And she saw the paintings. Did Meijer see you look at the paintings?'

'Yes, we discussed them.'

'Excellent,' Henry continued, 'They will look for the papers. Then, hey! no papers. No evidence of the transaction. No counter claim.'

'What about copies?' asked Joe.

'Let us hope not. If you were committing forgery, would you make more than you needed?'

'Perhaps not,' he replied.

'Bonded in secrecy,' Henry raised his glass. Grietje joined but was subdued.

Joe noticed. 'What is it, Grietje?'

'I have become worried on the other matter. If he would do this to Tom, an invalid, what has he done to van Reit? It is all beginning to make too much sense, is it not?'

Henry sympathised. 'I'm afraid you may be right.'

Joe interjected, 'Let us do as you suggest first, Henry, and I thank you for that, sir. You are invaluable. Grietje, just bring up the issue of the paintings with Meijer. He can only look into it and we shall judge his response.'

Henry had a question. 'What if the paintings should disappear in the meantime?'

'That is a concern, but I'm not sure what we can do, other than give Meijer a short time to reply. I thought at first Grietje could go on her own, but if I could possibly oblige you, Henry. If we have a third-party witness of the paintings, then I cannot see how they would have the grounds to oppose our claim.'

'Of course, Joseph, of course.'

'I will pay you.'

'No, no, you mustn't. I am more useful if I retain my independence.'

'Then I can only express my...'

'Stop, stop. I hugely enjoy this company.' Henry opened his arms. 'You both know this, and I feel more alive when I get involved in your adventures than at any other time.'

'Our adventures! Not I, Henry, I am not the...' protested Joe

'Oh, be quiet you two!'

'Whisky tonight, I think.' Henry summoned the serving girl.

It grew into a long night. Only by holding Grietje tightly between them did Joe and Henry manage to escort her home without falling over. Henry could sing well, Joe croaked a Scottish ballad, and all Grietje, who had no tone, could conjure up were a few bawdy songs from her days serving in the tavern. The three pledged to meet early the next day, before Grietje kissed each of her escorts on the cheek and crawled up the stairs to her bed.

FIFE & EDINBURGH 1733

Chapter 18

On the Monday following his weekend in Edinburgh, David reached the pier just before noon. He was carrying more money that he had ever seen in his life. Joe had sent a second footman to escort him to Kirkcaldy, but David agreed to the company only as far as Newhaven.

'If I have an escort, that will draw more attention, not less, Joe.'

'You make a fair point. Carry a pistol at the least, for my peace of mind.'

David acceded reluctantly and heeded Joe's advice to distribute the notes about his person.

'Have a small note ready to give up to a bandit,' he instructed.

'I am travelling to Fifeshire, not the Balkans.'

The journey was unremarkable and trouble free. David hoped that Mr Peat's offices were furnished with a secure room. He found himself in a lighter mood than he had been for a considerable time. There was to be no teaching in the school for a fortnight or more and he had the determination to press on with his new arrangements. He was keen to meet with Mrs Smith and Mrs Oswald in response to their insistent request; after the exhibition, he had been too worn to face any interview. They were his conduit to the workings of the burgh Council and the church. He admired the two women and, although not always in agreement, appreciated their common sense and frank opinion. He saw that they had both stood to applaud the play; he thus hoped for a pleasant visit. First to Mr Peat's offices, to make arrangements for a change in accommodation for himself and Samuel John. Then an evening of writing letters to the Council.

Joe had sat with him on Sunday afternoon. Free from the over stimulation of the family, Joe had soberly expressed interest in David's plans. He was well used to dealing with lawyers, councils and banks, in all manner of contractual agreements. He offered

David sage advice. Yet he also talked about fairness, balance, and pragmatism.

'Be sure of your goal, David. Do not lose sight of it. You have a written contract from the Council. Read it carefully, with your lawyer, it is bound in law. It forms the boundary of what you are able to achieve. But you can usually negotiate within it. If they cannot meet a written obligation, then ask for something else in compensation.'

'I take your advice, thank you,' said David.

'If you are unsure, send me a message.'

'If necessary, I will. Thank you.'

He was at Mr Peat's again on the Tuesday morning, followed, in the afternoon, by tea with the two ladies.

'Dr Miller, I am so very pleased to receive you.'

'And I you, Mrs Smith. I fear I have been neglectful of late.'

'I know you have had your reasons. We will have the company of Mrs Oswald. As you know, I am on my own. A visit from a single man may start rumours.'

She made not so much as a twitch to indicate her jest. David liked this lady. He saw how Smith's smartness had been cultivated.

'Good afternoon, Mrs Oswald. I am glad to see you in good health.'

'I am out of it now, David. I am pleased to see you well also.'

Mrs Smith called the maid to fetch tea. 'We have some news to impart that we think will interest you, then we can talk on any other matters. We know we are nosy old biddies, so do not feel obliged to answer all of our intrusions.'

David smiled as Mrs Smith continued. 'I was in Edinburgh last week, as you know, to visit the Assembly. It was the end of a long process, but finally the deed was done.'

'You have my attention.'

'Mr Erskine has been removed from the Presbytery. He is, thus, no longer our minister.'

'That is news. Of course, I will not express pleasure, but I confess to relief,' said David.

'It was not just the incident with Rose, there has been a catalogue of events. Mrs Oswald and I worked hard to influence the man, but he had not the character for the job. He is gone.'

'You have a replacement?'

'Yes, Alexander Adam has returned. He was not happy in his new position and he had a keen deputy ready to take up the role.'

'Erskine has left the church?'

'He has resigned. He will find another path.'

The maid brought in a tray.

'Now, do you have news you will share?' asked Mrs Oswald.

'I do. I would ask for your confidence.'

'You have it.'

'Be reassured that I will stay schoolmaster as long as the Burgh will have me. This was decided before today, but your news of Mr Erskine does reaffirm that I have made a good decision and, hopefully, it will ease my own and the school's relations with the church.'

'We are very glad to hear that, David,' said Mrs Oswald.

'And to bespeak my intention, I have taken Gladney House for a year in the first. I will not burden the Council for the rent.'

The two ladies nodded in approval.

'I will, however, press the Council for a janitor who will have use of the school cottage and I will find accommodation for Mr John who is currently living in one room with his new wife. I have presently written to the Council to this effect.'

'It does not seem unreasonable, but...'

'Mrs Oswald, please do not burden yourself with this. I will find a way through it. As you know I am grateful for your continued support.'

'And Rose?' added Mrs Smith.

'She will stay in Edinburgh, until the summer at least. I'm sure you both will understand that I have learned that the needs of a growing woman are far greater than I alone can provide. There are talents and graces that go beyond what is found in a schoolroom full of boys and a quiet home with a bachelor father.'

'I thought she was content?'

'She was, is, but I think she must be given other opportunities. Do not be overly concerned. She will return often, particularly when we are installed in Gladney. Indeed, I hope we shall be able to entertain you both quite soon.'

'That would be most welcome,' Mrs Smith replied. 'Dr Miller, you seem very confident of this. Is there something that you are not telling us?'

'In time it will become obvious, so I will tell a little of my personal circumstance. My intent and determination are secured by an inheritance I have recently come into. It allows a freedom which hitherto eluded me.'

'Oh, I hope there has been no death?'

'No. It is an old bequest. Now let us lighten the conversation. What did you think of my boys? I hope you were proud of your son, Mrs Smith.'

The ladies soundlessly clapped their hands. 'Pride is a sin in this house, Dr Miller,' rebuked Mrs Smith.

David laughed.

David's last mission before returning to Edinburgh was to meet up with John Anderson and Sir Peter Rigg. He found that it would not be possible in the few days he had left. He would arrange something else. In the meantime, together with Peat, he discovered a furnished cottage that would suit the Johns, and before he caught the ferry later in the day, he sought out Samuel in his room in the High Street. It was Samuel's wife Flora, however, that answered the door.

'Dr Miller, Samuel is not in. He is out walking the clifftop. Is he required at the school?'

To David, Flora John looked barely twenty years old.

'No, no, I have brought news for you both.'

'Em, would you like to come in and wait. He will not be long.'

'If I may.'

It was a small accommodation for a family. It was kept clean and tidy and there was a warmth to it: a narrow bed, two soft chairs, a blackened pot hanging above the fire, a table overflowing with papers, a sink under the single window. Mrs John offered David one of the two fireside chairs and swapped the pot for a kettle.

She saw David looking around. 'It is small, I know, but we manage.'

David swallowed hard. It was perhaps a cumulative effect, but he could not hold back an emotional response.

'It is not that, Mrs John, it is not that. It is small, yes, but I see you have made it truly a home, it is your home. Our cottage in Cupar ... my Janett and I, was not any bigger. I am just reminded; it had taken me by surprise. It was our home for many years. Rose was born in it, we were content.' David wiped an eye. 'I'm sorry, what must you think of me? Tea would be lovely.'

In that moment, Flora saw why her husband so admired his employer. Not far below the masterly surface, she saw a depth of emotion he could not always control.

'What is your news, Dr Miller? Is it bad for us?'

David, now using his kerchief, laughed. 'No, no, I have found a new house for you both: a cottage, two large rooms, a scullery and a sheltered garden. There is no rent to pay. Samuel will have to walk a bit further to school that's all.'

'In truth!' Flora exclaimed.

'Yes, yes. I would not jest. It has a view of the sea. In Linktown. We can walk to it if you like when Samuel returns.'

Flora got to her knees in front of the fire and held David's hand.

'Thank you. Now you shall be the first to hear our good news,' she put her other hand on her belly.

The door opened quickly.

'This is a not an expected sight!' remarked Samuel.

'Samuel, Dr Miller has brought some news,' replied Flora.

'It is a surprise, but this is a welcome visit, Dr Miller.'

'David, please, both of you. I am not at my desk. Will you tell your husband the news, Flora?'

'No, we are all going for a walk.'

And they did.

The early morning ferry carried David back to Edinburgh, as Flora and John had insisted the previous evening that he join them at their small table for supper. It had been an intimate, convivial and, for him, rewarding occasion as he shared the Johns' delight of the new house and their anticipation of parenthood.

This day he had arranged to meet and lunch with David Hume, who would tutor Rose in the morning. He had invited James Balfour to join them and he looked forward to the rare opportunity of an academic discussion. Hume, he had been told, was a bright and amenable character. David was impressed by the care he took to frame his arguments. No vagaries or exposition, he would clearly and concisely defend his position. The problem was, and he admitted to it, he could make an exacting case, just as competently, from the contrary point of view. James Balfour noted that he and David Miller could just sit back and watch Hume tie himself in knots. Although they laughed at this, David saw there was substance behind this struggle; at times David Hume appeared unnerved.

Table civility was lost when Joseph, who of course knew of the lunch, arrived back, earlier than was usual, from his office. All semblance of structured discussion was confounded as Joe, demanding another bottle be served, claimed exasperation to be working hard all days to sustain three intellectuals who, he added, 'just run round in circles.' Joe commanded the stage and teased them all. He did make some fair points, but none of the scholarly three would admit to it. Come the eighth hour, Mary had to interrupt, again, and thank the guests. In the hall, David Hume thanked David for engaging him and said how much he enjoyed teaching Rose.

'She is a clever and able child. I do not see any distance between her and any boy.'

David answered truthfully. 'I confess, this troubles me. Is her future confined because she is a girl?'

'We know in practice it is, yet I cannot defend it.'

James had overheard. 'It is still, but they allow female students in Leiden.'

Both Davids looked to James to continue; even Joe listened with interest.

'There are not many. They sit at the back of the theatres, hidden from the male eye. They are instructed to dress demurely and must be accompanied by a matron when they meet their tutors. They are not permitted to graduate. But yes, there are a few females that attend classes.'

'Extraordinary,' said David Miller, 'Is there no official objection?'

'There is great opposition, academic, theological and political, and some unpleasantness, but there it is.'

'We are only just getting girls to attend schools, and none, as far as I know, in a grammar school.'

Mary dispatched the girls to pull at their fathers' hands.

'Forgive us, Mrs Grieve. Thank you very much indeed for looking after us so well. I will take you up to town, Hume,' said James as they all shook hands in parting.

David and Joe shared a late supper.

'Would you consider sending Rose to such a place?'

'I have only just heard that it is possible.'

'Now that I think of it, I should have realised,' remarked Joe. 'I have spent a lot of time in the Low Countries, and I believe I have heard of this before. Years ago, I didn't pay it any heed. It is different there, David. Society, particularly for women, is different. But Rose? I know how dear she is to you, as to us all.'

David made a further trip to Kirkcaldy before returning to spend the Christmas period with Rose and the Grieves in Edinburgh. Mr Peat had become somewhat obsequious and was bowing to and serving David in a new manner, despite David's protests. David could not tell whether it was because Peat had an eye for good business, or that David's new-found wealth had brought its own respect. He did not like it.

He called on Samuel and Flora, who had already moved into the cottage and were delighted to entertain him one evening. Mrs Smith and Adam had gone to their relatives in Strathenry for the festive break and so David called on Mrs Oswald in Dunnikier. Mrs Oswald had been instrumental in his move to Kirkcaldy, and out of respect he wanted to ensure that she fully understood his intentions and his continuing commitment to the town.

'Of course I understand, David. When I heard of what happened, and I do not ask the full details, I would not have blamed you for moving away as soon as you were able. We are just sorry we will not see so much of Rose.'

'We hope to spend the summer here, so I hope you will not have lost her altogether. I will move into Gladney in January. I have not told her of it yet. She may not see it until Easter.'

'I am sure she will be delighted. Is she settled in Edinburgh?'

'I fear too much so, Mrs Oswald. I ensure she is studying, but that, I realise, is insufficient for a young lady. I believe she must become more accomplished if she is to be content and marry well.'

'And she is with friends of yours?'

'Yes, old family friends; she is very much at home.'

'Then I appreciate she is better off. Now is there anything I can do for you?'

'You have done far too much already. You could perhaps tell me one thing, has there been any reaction to the play?'

'The boys' performance was well received by most who attended. They were surprised by it and many would like more of its kind. Perhaps something in the summer?'

'I would be glad to arrange such, a lighter entertainment may suit.'

'The Council were somewhat divided, but they do see what you are about.'

'That is all I ask, then they can make an informed decision.'

'Let us hope it favours your intent.'

David spent the rest of the time preparing schoolwork for the spring trimester. He met with Samuel at the school to satisfy himself that they could both spend the following days at rest, without any pressing concerns. He could not be late back to Edinburgh; his daughter was taking him to the town, to order a new suit before attending a church service.

The festive days in Edinburgh passed as a moment, such was the activity, visits and visitors, food, walks and more food. Apart from the odd tired tantrum from one or other of the children, a most pleasant and comforting nine days was enjoyed. David's relationship with Joseph remained eminently cordial.

On the night before his departure back to Kirkcaldy, over a late-night whisky when Joe was talking about his family, David innocently asked, 'Joe, who is Benthe, where has she come from?'

Joe hesitated and, just for a moment, David saw him withdraw. Then he stood up, grinned and slapped David on his shoulder.

'Time for bed, sir ... she is one of the family. One of our family. I confess I have tales to tell you, and we will get round to it, but not tonight.'

Joe thought further as he went to dampen the fire. 'You and I have this in common. I have come to realise. It is a bond that should never separate us.'

Joe turned his head and looked at David who was still sitting. 'What is it?' asked David.

'We believe that all children are born innocent and created equal. The Good Book may tell us this, but you and I, we believe it. It is our own creed.'

David saw that this was true. It riled him slightly that Joe had made a fair point. Then, to his own embarrassment, probably the debating Hume's influence, he realised Joe's position.

Twenty years earlier, a younger Joe took care of an orphan boy and made sure his progress was unhindered by the lack of a home, parentage or wealth. What matter the origins of Benthe, Tomasine or even himself? He had even run to Joe when his own child was threatened. Joe and Mary did not ask questions; they did not discriminate nor judge. As much as they were able, they would always look after the child.

Tom Binnie

DELFT, 1712

Chapter 19

Grietje and Henry met at nine hours. Henry had arranged their meeting with Meijer an hour later, ostensibly to discuss a number of minor issues, disguising their real intent. Grietje would lead with a simple enquiry.

Meijer welcomed them and fortuitously showed them into the office where Grietje had discovered the paintings. Grietje told Meijer that she had recognised some of the paintings from the dealer's list, and simply requested a receipt from Janssen's bookkeeper. Meijer knew nothing of this and looked at the copy of the list Grietje had handed him. 'Can we be sure these are the ones and the same?'

Grietje replied, 'No, but the dealer would leave his mark and number on the back, hopefully with a date, exactly for that reason.'

'Let us look,' said Henry.

Meijer and Henry lifted each of the paintings off the wall as Grietje pointed to them. There was a small label in the corner of each of them. Meijer went to find a glass. One by one, they checked the paintings off the list.

Meijer admitted to being puzzled by it and suggested that he would go through them with Teuling. Henry impressed the urgency of the matter, and Meijer confirmed that Teuling and his clerk, who had spent many hours sorting through Janssen's accounts, would quickly follow up their enquiry. He did not foresee a delay.

Grietje asked to look upstairs before they took their leave. Meijer left to fetch Teuling and they all went up to Janssen's room on the first floor. Janssen was not yet risen, so there was no confrontation. The stairwell and the office held many works of art. Grietje asked a somewhat taken aback Teuling, if he had any recollection of the transaction.

'No, I remember these paintings arriving and being mounted on the walls, over a year ago now. We do much of the dealer's work so a simple receipt would be done by the clerks and would not stand out.'

'You will have a copy?' asked Grietje.

'Yes, without doubt. I will just need to check the files. I need a little time. I'm afraid, meneer Janssen no longer keeps an orderly house.' Teuling gestured to the desk.

Henry and Grietje talked quickly to each other in English. Then Grietje spoke. 'You appreciate our concern? Grieve and Lockhart have no record. We shall return at five hours after this noon. Meneer Grieve is leaving for Veere in the morning.'

They parted amicably. As the door was closed behind them, Henry whispered, 'Joe is only going to Veere for a day.'

'I did not lie!' said Grietje, 'and I don't think they will move the paintings.'

'Well just in case, I have the maid at the *koffietafel*'... Henry pointed to the street corner ... 'well paid to send a boy to my rooms if they do.'

'We two enjoy this sport, too much, sir.'

'Alas mevrouw, it may yet be our downfall.'

'As long as it is ours and no one else's.'

'Well said. Seriously Grietje, what made you remove the scrolls? Joe and I were curious.'

'There were two visits. I saw them on the first and spotted Tom Miller's name. When I thought about it and from what I already knew it seemed odd. I remember Joe's tale of being chased away by Janssen, with a sword when he enquired after Tom. I was curious and thought they may reveal something. So I took them.'

'Would you sit with me awhile in my rooms?'

'Not now, but I shall return, if I may, after three hours?'

'I look forward to that.'

Grietje and Henry returned just after five hours, and a solemn-looking Meijer opened the door on their knock. He braved a cheerful disposition. 'It is not satisfactory news I bear. Please come in and sit.'

Teuling joined them in the office. The walls still held the artwork apart from a few they had taken down and left leaning against a cabinet.

Meijer took the lead. 'Teuling, myself and two clerks have raked the records thoroughly. We have found no record, nothing. We weren't disheartened, as the accounts which Teuling kept over the period would show any transactions, in and out. There should be two records in the ledgers and an entry in the daybook. We have the values from your list. We have no record, not even a date. Teuling is upset that he did not question the arrival of the paintings. He apologises to you both.'

Henry waved his hand in dismissal.

'Where does that leave us?' asked Grietje.

'Well, uncomfortable as you can imagine. It is worse for the office.'

Meijer looked to Teuling to get his agreement in what he was about to say. 'We are in your debt. If you could treat this in confidence, we would be obliged.'

'I'm still not clear, Meijer,' pressed Grietje.

'Teuling, representing Janssen, and I agree that with no papers to show ownership of the paintings you have a legitimate claim. Possession is important, but in this case, possession alone would not stand up. I have taken advice on this.'

'I see, then who do they belong to?'

'Not Janssen, nor this office. I know this is unlikely, but we must cover all possibilities. Could they have been gifted?'

Grietje looked to Henry and then thought for herself. 'We have the record of sale to Tom Miller. Do you have a date for their arrival here?'

'We think January or February, the year past.'

'Not before then?'

'No, later perhaps but not before.'

'Tom Miller was lost in the previous December. He could not have been present,' said Grietje. 'We can find out and I can trace the cart that held the paintings. Is it not likely the paintings were returned here because Janssen was involved in the sale? It might be possible to find this out.'

Meijer agreed. 'Even if they went to the dealer first, they would have forwarded the paintings to Janssen.'

Henry played the diplomat. 'What if Janssen had a few crates of artwork arrive on his doorstep and simply acted as custodian?'

That made even Meijer laugh. 'That, sir, is the most generous view.'

Grietje responded, 'We would take that view if that is Janssen's offer. We have no wish for embarrassment or the courts. You are my counsel, what would you advise?'

'I cannot advise on this. Teuling will approach Janssen, of course, and will press for his agreement.'

'Now?' asked Grietje. 'It is important.'

Meijer nodded to Teuling to leave. 'As your counsel, I can say that regardless of his agreement, Janssen has no case. There was no evidence of any attempt to contact Edinburgh, the dealers or even the concierge in Veere. I would hope to avoid a rift.'

Grietje saw that Meijer was forlorn, and looked to Henry, who intervened.

'I will leave you now, Grietje, we will convene with Mr Grieve later at our evening table.'

'Thank you, Henry,' said Grietje, then turned to Meijer. 'Rolf, I can see you are upset with this. You were not involved, we understand this. Your service to us, and the company, is still valued and required.'

'Will meneer Grieve agree with you?'

'I know that he will.'

'That is reassuring but if I may confide...'

'Of course, please go on.'

'We have looked at the accounts and find that they are in a poor state. Janssen has borrowed against the value of these paintings. Teuling has not been informed of many transactions – all these scribbled pieces of paper on Janssen's desk. The puzzle of it is where the money has gone. Even this building is mortgaged. Janssen stopped earning some time ago, yet the outgoings continue. He lives a deluded life.'

'Tell me how it will affect you and Teuling.'

'It is not a happy state. I cannot say, perhaps...'

'Look, let us leave this place. I do have some questions for you on this. Speak to Teuling, then you and I can meet elsewhere, in one hour? My studio, we will not be disturbed there.'

Grietje stopped off to speak to Henry and then at the market to buy fresh coffee grounds. As she walked along her street, she saw a diminutive figure curled up against the cold, crouched by the door of her studio. There was a bag at her feet. Begging was not tolerated. Although there was something oddly familiar about this girl. Grietje went to her door.

'Mevrouw?' the girl called.

'Yes... Sara! for god's sake, Sara. What are you doing here?'

'I have a letter, mevrouw.'

'You are freezing, come in, come in. I have not yet lit the fire.'

Sara turned back to fetch her bag. She held her head down when she reached the top of the stairs.

Grietje was restarting the fire. 'Have you been abandoned?'

'No, the footman will return at six hours. The letter, mevrouw.'

'In a minute, just tell me.'

'The master has sent me to serve you. He thought I would be of use and could learn more here.'

'De heer van Reit?'

'Yes, mevrouw. I am to return if you will not have me.'

Grietje paused, smiled, and said firmly, 'Sara, you are god sent.'

216

Sara was looking around and took off her cloak.

'As you see I am not well settled. I have so little time and you will be of great help.'

'I will set the fire, mevrouw,' Sara said, taking the kindling from Grietje, who put her arm around the maid's shoulders and gave them a squeeze.

'But Sara, we'll have to be very careful.'

'Oh, why, mevrouw?'

'It might be fun!'

Sara glowed pink and attended the fire while Grietje filled the kettle from the large pewter urn.

The loud knock startled them. Grietje had all but forgotten Meijer. He was early.

'Sara, I have a visitor due. But you can stay.'

'I will answer, mevrouw.'

Sara took a little time and came back up the stairs alone.

'It was only the footman, I told him to return without me.'

'I should tell you, Sara. I am no lady, there is no luxury here. Is this what you want?'

'Yes, mevrouw.'

Within the half hour, the room had warmed and Grietje showed Sara how badly things were arranged. They both tidied as best they could.

'I have not had the time to get proper furniture, or a bed and dresser for the other room. We will sort it out in time.'

'I can sleep by the fire, miss.'

'No, Sara, you will share my bed until we have two. Now, I want you to find the market. I will write a list.'

Sara curtsied as they heard another knock from the street door. Sara answered and returned to announce Meijer. 'Mijnheer Meijer, mevrouw.'

'Thank you, Sara.'

'What a sizeable room,' remarked Meijer.

'Apologies for its state. I have not had the time.'

'And you have a familiar maid.'

'That is a surprise to me also. Now, please have a seat and let us talk freely of our worries.'

Meijer confessed he was concerned for himself and Teuling. Any taint on Janssen and the practice would affect them. His intention was to grow the business with Teuling and tolerate Janssen's eccentricity. The history, the building and its location served him well. Even the paintings in the offices gave an impression of status and security to clients and attracted new business. If he were not placed there, he would be a lesser known notary in a market of many.

'But what about your family's business?' Grietje enquired.

'I do not wish to use or depend on them. I acknowledge, I am lucky to have them.'

'As I said, we have no desire to make the matter of the paintings public.'

'I appreciate that. Our problem, the business I mean, and I confess it, is that Janssen has not worked. At present the income from myself and Teuling does not cover the mortgage. We pay a good amount to the business, but it does not match the interest; the debt increases by the month. It is not largely my debt: Janssen is by far the majority partner. I'm sorry, but Teuling and I have only just learned of this.'

'How is the debt secured?'

'On the house and, I'm sorry, the paintings.'

'That are not yours?'

'Exactly.'

'But how...?'

'I don't know. This is not your burden, but you need to know this for the sake of my representation. There is no reason at present, that I cannot continue work for you and my other clients. In the future, there may be difficulties with the office.'

'Did Teuling speak to Janssen?'

'Yes. Janssen would neither acknowledge nor deny the acquisition of the paintings. He shouted *receipts* a few times, that is all. It is of no matter. But I do have something of import.'

Meijer took a breath. 'After the heated exchange about the paintings, Teuling raised the matter of the debt. Then much to his surprise, Janssen acquiesced to the questioning and signed the papers without further protest. Teuling said Janssen was lost in the issues. The anger within him had dissipated and it was more a request, not a demand, from Janssen that Teuling, *sort it out.*'

'Will you and Teuling be able to *sort it out*? What will you do?'

'I will help Teuling. He is prepared to be open about it now. He has realised that his reputation as well as the practice is at stake here. If it is not carefully handled, it would be detrimental to both our futures. Even my father has expressed concern for my name. The first is to account for the assets. I believe Janssen has more paintings than those on your list, and we will balance those and any other assets against the debt. Only then can we form a plan.'

'Rolf, from what you say, you could just leave. Why take this on?'

'My wife has pressed the same question. I can only say that a man must follow his own path. I have no other answer.'

'I have one other concern, Did Teuling find anything of van Reit's legacy? You can imagine that the discovery this day has added to my worry.'

'There is nothing on paper. We have copies of van Reit's legacies and codicils, as far as we can determine, their current agreement, which awards Janssen the Power of Attorney, stands. Before you ask, this can be changed, with authority from van Reit, to my father's practice or to whomsoever he chooses.'

'You found no meddling with the account.'

'There is no record of any recent transactions. There is no accounting book: that is not so unusual as the bank will keep the definitive record. I can suggest to Teuling that he contact the bank. There is nothing of value under our own security. There is a large fold of letters regarding the building of the school. We may need a further instruction to go through them.'

Grietje heard the street door open and Sara climb the stairs. Grietje invited Meijer to join with Joseph and Henry at the inn, but he desired to spend a quiet evening with his family. Meijer stood to leave and thanked Grietje for her time and patience.

With Sara's assistance, Grietje readied herself for the evening.

'Mevrouw, the master sent a trunk with me. It is downstairs, shall I unpack it?'

'Your master is far too generous with me. If it is materials for painting, leave them downstairs. Anything else can be brought up here. I will be late, so do not stay up. Go to bed when you are tired. I will be beside you when you wake.'

Sara curtsied. 'Mevrouw.'

As Grietje walked the short distance to the town square, she realised she had found little time to talk with Joe. She was sure it was not a considered act by either of them, yet neither did they take a step to contrive a circumstance where they could be alone together. Perhaps this was the safest course. She did, however, want to find the opportunity to talk to him further about her visit to Doortje and Tom. She also knew Joseph wanted to go over the details of their new business. Meijer would be involved in this.

The evening supper was, they acknowledged, more subdued than their usual sessions when Henry joined them. Grietje and Henry reported their findings and thoughts to Joe, and the three all had plans to travel. Joe to Veere, Henry on his own business to Amsterdam and Grietje to Voorne to see van Reit and then on to Veere. She would meet with Joe and Meijer there, to set up the new business arrangements and transfer the banking for Lockhart & Grieve to Delft. The timing meant they would not travel together.

Grietje climbed the stairs after the midnight hour, exhausted. She felt a release more than sadness at her parting with Joe and Henry; she was back on her own calendar. Grietje would take some days to herself before travelling to see van Reit. She found Sara waiting up, sitting by the fire.

'Sara, I told you to go to bed.'

Sara shook her head. She insisted on undressing Grietje and washed her gently with a warm bowl and cloth.

'What are these smells?'

'They were in the trunk, mevrouw.'

The embers were a dimming glow. Once Grietje was under the blanket Sara undressed and tentatively slipped in beside her, taking only an edge of the bed. Grietje made sure she was covered.

'Sara.'

'Mevrouw?'

'How many years are you?'

'I'm seventeen years, they say, mevrouw.'

PART TWO

EDINBURGH 1737

Chapter 20

'Father, I do *not* want to spend my days chit-chatting with the ladies, playing pianoforte and auctioning myself at parties to become some red-faced Earl's brood mare!'

Rose slammed the door as she stomped out. David was at a loss. It was worse the few times she had visited Gladney. It was easier when she was in Edinburgh. Mary calmed her. '*It's just a case of finding the right man, Rose,*' she would say. But David knew his daughter well enough to know that these kinder words would not placate her.

The door swung open again. 'I am sorry to shout and stomp, but Smithy is this moment preparing for Glasgow, and he is only fourteen. Robert and William are working in their father's business, as are the Oswalds. David Wemyss is attending Oxford.' Rose paused to restrain her rising tone and continued more moderately. 'May I not go to study at a university?'

'Rose, there is no possibility of you sitting in a university lecture room in this country. You can continue to be tutored at home. Why not travel? I have said you can go to London for the summer?'

'Why not Paris?'

'Oh Rose, I don't know.' David felt perplexed. 'I just don't know.' And he didn't. Rose had seen the paths of others ahead of her. Grace, Benthe and other girls she knew, were excited at the prospect of a young man and looking forward to the liberties of running their own house. Rose had been shocked to see how quickly babies and children arrived; some she had heard of produced three before the age of twenty. Or was it what she had seen on the streets of Edinburgh, very young girls with suckling babies on a doorstep with a brood at their feet. David had difficulty with this picture and had turned away from his daughter's questioning looks when they passed such a sight.

223

He hoped that their visits to London or Bristol would have been enough to satisfy her curiosity. She was fortunate that Joseph, not David, gained her invitations to visit important houses. That had now become her life, and what would have thrilled her three years ago was now dismissed from hand. Would an earlier constraint in Kirkcaldy have altered that path? Perhaps. The deeper admission was that he knew she was right. He knew that he had been driven by his own ambition for her and strove for equivalence in her learning. He felt the impostor of pride when she impressed the tutors and bettered the boys. Was that because he had no son? He did not know that either. It was a problem made worse by money. She knew only too well they were no longer poor.

It may not be coincidence that their rift began during the outbreak of contagion, when Flora John moved into Gladney with her baby, some fifteen months previously. No one had seen the affliction coming and the infection affected the Scottish East coast suddenly and severely. '*From the East,*' they said. Samuel quickly became infected by the disease. The school closed; several of the boys went quickly, too quickly. There was barely a footstep on the streets for four months. Goods were delivered to the harbour and left at the pier. The swift action worked; no cases were reported in Dysart or Kinghorn. And it was unusual that Samuel, a fit and healthy adult, who had looked well on his way to recovery, was struck down, horribly at the last.

During Samuel's incarceration, David offered his home to Flora to keep the baby and herself away from the infection. Samuel stayed in the cottage and was nursed by others. Flora sent notes of love and care every day until one day there was no reply. The next day, she heard that Samuel had gone.

David had thought of escaping to Edinburgh at the first word of the disease, but he knew he might carry it, so he stayed. He also felt his duty was to be near the pupils and their parents. He got early word of every heart-felt loss and sat quiet in the evenings by the fire praying for no more. Each one smarted with the memory of Edward and his brother at his school. With a child, it is the loss of a future that pains. Flora quietly consoled him and tended to her infant and her own loss. He prayed for Edinburgh to be kept free of it. Joe kept his family, Rose and the servants sealed up for a month, all business transacted by letter.

The odd thing was, and it was odd now he reflected on it, after Samuel had passed, Flora did not move back to the cottage. She and David were near six months together in Gladney. It had become their habit, and in a circumstance when their souls were bared. She did not offer, and he did not suggest. It was an unspoken undertaking of unvoiced intention.

By the time the threat of disease had lifted, he had not seen Rose for half a year. Flora had taken over much of the running of the house; the housekeeper was glad of her administrations and their lives developed into their own benign routine. Until, that was, one Saturday night when the child had settled, the house was quiet. Mrs Lyall had taken time away to visit her sister, and David had, unusually, poured them each a second glass of wine at the supper table. The fire was dampened, and candles extinguished, the outer door was bolted. A few minutes after bidding each other goodnight at the top of the stairs, Flora crossed the upper hall and crept uninvited into his bed.

David had only known Janet. This was a different experience. They both wanted comfort, but Flora, he found, knew how to give pleasure and take it for herself. There was no modesty or inhibition; if he had read of the act in a newssheet, he would have called out *shameless*. The shock of it took all other thoughts away, the embarrassment, the guilt, the morality. All pushed aside in the care, the caressing and the kisses, until the morn. After their climax they reprieved to weeping soundlessly into each other's tightly enwrapped arms. No words were said. He remembered only a momentary sleepy soft kiss, and when he awakened late his bed held only one; yet now it felt empty.

225

Nothing was spoken of the next day. The house carried on in its routine. David felt he had travelled to a different world in the night and had been returned, except for the occasional extended look he caught from Flora when they were alone. He dismissed it as a momentary aberration. *The devil's work*, he would call out. *It shall not repeat*, but he couldn't get the memory of it out of his head. It plagued him in the night.

A chance conversation led to a repeat.

'How is your sister keeping, Mrs Lyall?'

'Well enough sir, but she is on her own now?'

'You should visit more often. I will allow the time. We are not a busy house these days.'

The housekeeper, her head down, nodded.

'Mrs Lyall?'

'It not be the time, sir, it be the coach fare. She lives in Falkland.'

'Oh, Mrs Lyall, I should have considered. I will stand the fare. Visit as you wish. You tend a good house for us.' His kind offer was burdened by guilt.

And the suppers were regularly repeated. Not every week at first, but then after a month a single exchanged glance; their half-eaten supper remained on their plates. Still it was never discussed. David's moral compass was not just in a spin, it was ablaze. There were Sundays with no attendance at church. Flora did not lapse; she would not risk God's misfortune on Samuel's child.

As the quarantine relaxed, the burgh school resumed, and it was a reluctant David who travelled to Edinburgh at the weekend. The joy, and there was great joy, at seeing his daughter, suffered rude interruptions of thoughts of Flora John, waiting in Gladney for him to return.

In the weeks that followed his weekends in Edinburgh, there began touching and caresses around the house. They were careful to be discreet, but Mrs Lyall was a wise woman.

'Dr Miller.' She caught him on a Friday before she departed early for Falkland. It was probably his insistence that, some weeks, she spend two nights with her sister that raised her suspicion. He designed to have these Fridays with Flora and leave for Edinburgh early the next day.

'I know it is not my place and I hope you will forgive me, for I am very happy here.'

David suspected what was coming. 'But?'

'There is fisher-wives' talk. It is a small town and you are a man of good standing in it.'

'Mrs Lyall?' David pretended to ignorance.

She continued undeterred. 'She is a precious creature and you must do right by God, else set her on another path.'

'You are right, Mrs Lyall, it is not your place.' And David walked away from her admonishment.

Later, as the coach arrived to collect her, it was David who waited in the hall to apologise.

'Mrs Lyall, I am sorry. That cannot have been an easy subject for you to broach. I hope I am man enough to have heard you, and I thank you for it.'

On the Fridays, when they were together for three days, Flora exhibited a girlish liveliness. She became subdued however, when over supper, David said he wanted to talk to her properly.

'Flora, we have not talked nor spoken of our intent, and I feel, reluctantly, that we must. I am at pains to disturb the joy we steal these few days. I have never known their like.'

'I am content, David.'

'It is others we must consider.'

'Oh.'

'Flora, you will never want for anything...'

'No!' she shouted at him. 'No,' she shouted again.

'But we are not wed.'

'Well?'

'You, you would not wed ... an old man. You would not wed me?' he puzzled, and her demeanour changed.'

Oh, you big ass!' Her voice was still raised. 'Of course I would.'

They struggled to make it up the stairs. Their consummation was immediate, and through their recovering breathlessness, she asked, 'If you would have me?'

David rolled off the bed, raked a drawer to find an old ring from his childhood that he had long outgrown, and knelt on the floor at the bedside.

'Flora, will you be my betrothed?'

'Yes, kind sir, I will, wholeheartedly ... you silly oaf.'

David had frequently mentioned Flora in his letters to Rose. He had taken care to use a progression of terms, *safety, health, care for, company, friendship and companionship*, and so on. Rose, who was wrapped up in her own world, had not referred to their situation in any of her replies. He suggested to Flora that they keep their news to themselves until he could tell Rose in person. He worried for it, concerned that he may cause more distance between himself and his daughter. He was not certain how Rose would react.

Mrs Lyall was the first to know. Flora told her immediately on the Monday morning in the kitchen when she returned from the visit to her sister.

'I'm delighted for you, dear. I could see it in the both of you. I am glad he came to his senses. And if you don't mind me saying' – it was her favourite phrase and she never waited for an answer – 'not a moment too soon, lass.'

Flora smiled and turned to leave, but she was puzzled.

'Mrs Lyall, I'm sorry, what do you mean?'

'Oh, I'm speaking out of turn. Your condition. You look well on it?'

'I still don't understand?' prompted Flora.

'Oh, lass, I've lived too long. Another babby. Do you not yet feel it?'

Flora's face went white, then red, then she saw sense.

'Mrs Lyall, you are mistaken. There is no...'

Mrs Lyall just smiled. 'I hope I haven't shocked you.'

Flora left her and went upstairs to her room, but she found herself sitting on David's bed instead, without thinking of her intention. She had felt her breasts swell and an occasional flutter in her groin. She had put it down to their frequent coupling. She couldn't be, she thought. With Samuel, it had taken her so long to become pregnant, and the birthing wife had said she would not have another. At the time, that news had broken her heart. She couldn't be pregnant. The thought of it though. The thought of it spawned a swirling storm of confusion. The reality of it, if it were true, would bring her delight.

David was due to visit Edinburgh at the next opportunity. Flora pressed him to take his leave early on the Friday. He was sensitive to her suggestion, but she insisted that he should spend time with Rose before bringing up word of their engagement. David saw the sense of it and caught the early ferry on the Friday morning.

The Grieve household was as vibrant as ever. David felt at home and had become naturalised to being a member of the wider family. One consequence of this was that, apart from Mary, his warmest welcome was from the hounds. Rose immediately expressed delight on seeing him arrive, only to quickly disappear upstairs, as the girls were preparing for a visit. Mary assured him that Rose had passed the week soberly and studiously. It was the dawn of Friday that initiated the first turn of their social whirl.

Since his self-confinement at Gladney, Rose had not found much time for him on his few short visits.

'Rose, I must speak with you.'

'Yes, Father?' she replied, exhibiting a degree of impatience.

'I mean at length...'

'Not now, please, we are to attend a ball.'

'Tomorrow then. You and I shall take the hounds for a long walk.'

'Oh, Father, I...'

'Rose, that is what we shall do.'

Rose, on hearing his firm tone, gave way.

'Where is this dance?'

'We are to attend Hopetoun. It is an hour away. That is the cause of the hurry.'

Grace put her head round the door. 'Rose!'

'I'm coming!'

Despite the situation, David found amusement in seeing the girls' excitement.

Joseph caught David in the library, writing in his journal.

'David, good to see you. I would like to catch you today.'

'And I you, Joe.'

'Is all well at the school?'

'Yes, the new tutors have settled in. The contagion had a sobering effect on the school, the church and the burgh. We are not quite recovered in mind.'

'But no more cases?'

'None for a couple of months now.'

'I am glad of it. Shall we wait until the girls have left, then we can settle in here before the evening?'

'Yes. What is this ball, in Hopetoun, Rose said?'

'You remember Edward Clerk, a family friend of his? He is hosting a celebration for one of the nephews. Eighteen years, I think. It is the launch of a new ballroom, one of William Adam's, and they were desperately short of suitable girls. He was on the point of offering a bribe for our brood.'

David laughed. 'They were reluctant to go?'

'Hah, for two weeks, there has been talk of nothing else. I can't say how many dresses have been paraded. I tell you, my next investment in the High Street will be a dress shop. There has been pianoforte practice, dancing and songs. No end of it. Rose was excited because she believes her friend Adeline is attending.'

'I'm sorry that I have missed these preparations.'

'Don't be, it was becoming tiresome. We have created monsters. I would have taken Clerk's money if he would have kept them. Edward and his wife will look after them there and return them safe in the morning. I'll leave you now and talk later.'

David realised how the long parting had left him adrift from all that was happening and important in Rose's life. Her letters had become shorter and of no consequence; there had been no mention of this event. It was much to his regret but could not have been helped. He was envious of Joe and Mary's closeness to her, but he appreciated their intimate adoption of Rose into their house. He knew, at Rose's age, these would have been very difficult days for him as a parent on his own. She belonged to this world now, not the quiet life of a schoolmaster's only child.

A maid brought a pot of steaming coffee and something Joe called Dutch biscuits. The departure of the girls in three carriages brought a divine silence to the house. Joe came into the room followed by Mary.

'This is serious?' asked David.

Mary answered, 'Perhaps it's a little sensitive. You have news for us also?'

'Yes ... of the same nature, I suspect.'

Mary took the lead, 'When you first came to visit us with Rose, do you remember there was another woman in the house? Joe and I think she was at the supper table that day?'

'Yes. Now you mention it, I do.'

'She is coming to stay with us again. Arriving tomorrow, we hope.'

David interrupted. 'And this is a concern?'

'Well, we hope not. It is just that she is from Holland. Joe met her years ago when he was searching for your father.'

David kept his silence and Joe took up the story.

'She works for me. She is employed to manage the selection, design and purchase of Dutch earthenware for export. Primarily, she is an artist and spends most of her time painting. You will have appreciated her work on our walls.'

'So how does this...'

Joe raised his hand in request for David's patience. 'She is well acquainted with Tomasine, who is accompanying her to Edinburgh. Tomasine will not stay with us, but we thought you should know of this visit. You must, of course, make your own decisions. That is the sum of it.'

Mary spoke again, 'David, Joe and I hope that we three are robust enough to withstand any discomfort. We would discuss any matter that troubles you.'

'Thank you, Mary, Joe. Can I ask her name?'

'Of course. It's Grietje, Grietje van der Meer.'

'Is she Benthe's mother?'

Mary smiled. 'Oh no. She brings with her a companion, Sara. It is Sara that is Benthe's mother.'

'She has red hair?'

'Joe can tell you that tale over whisky, I think. She *is* one of ours, David.'

David's mind drifted to take this news in.

'David, David!' prompted Mary. 'Shall I stay for your news?'

David jolted back to the present. 'Yes, Mary, please do.' He had difficulty bringing up thoughts of Kirkcaldy. Should he stall? 'My news is family news also. I hope you find it good news.'

Mary looked to Joe as they waited. 'I wrote to you that my regent, Samuel was tragically taken in the contagion. His poor wife and child came to my house for safety during the confinement. I can tell a longer tale, but I'd best be blunt. She had no one to return to and, she and I have become fond of each other. We are now betrothed.'

Mary let out a squeal, 'David, David!' She ran to his embrace.

Joe barked in shocked amusement. 'This is no jest?'

'No, this Saturday last. I am as shocked as you are!'

'You didn't bring her. You must bring her,' cried Mary.

'Rose knows nothing yet. I tell you first and ask for your counsel.'

'You have mentioned her to Rose?' queried Mary.

'In letters, yes, but she has yet to respond to any of my signals.'

Mary, who was still standing beside him, pulled a chair over and sat holding his hand. 'Oh, Rose will react, of course, but she will be fine. You are doing the right thing. I have no doubt.' She looked again to Joe, 'We are truly delighted for you. What is her name?'

'Thank you both. She is Flora. I will talk with Rose tomorrow.'

Mary advised, 'You must ensure that Rose is firm in your love, even if she reacts unkindly.'

As they stood to leave, Mary walked on ahead.

'You are a quiet one, Dr Miller,' remarked Joe.

'I had very little to do with it.'

'I understand that feeling. Regarding the other matter, I have never talked to Tomasine about your father. When Lockhart died and you inherited the business, I felt my job was done, in some sense. You may choose to pick up on it. That is clearly your decision. Grietje kept in touch with Tomasine's mother, but I have not discussed any of this with her for many years.'

'Thank you, Joe. I think I have grown beyond it. There are questions. I don't know if I would pursue them given the opportunity. As to my sister or half-sister, if we meet, I believe I am settled with this. I am naturally curious. I hope I would welcome my father's blood.'

Now tell me of this girl, young, you said?'

'Later, Joe, later.'

'I'm holding you to that.'

Chapter 21

Later that day, after supper, Joe and David found themselves once again with a whisky bottle in the library of Canon Mills house. The younger diners had taken their leave.

'So, Dr Miller, how did this betrothal happen?'

'I would tell you of it, it may help to arrange my mind. If we are sharing confidences, however, tell me first of Benthe? There is a good reason I ask.'

'Let me top up your glass.' Joe stooped to poke the fire. 'Young Joseph has always involved himself in the business, as you know. Well, I dispatched him on a trade to Delft once, unsupervised, and I don't need to really say anymore. If you meet Sara, you will understand the young man's weakness. He has served his time on it. As you also know, Mary and I would never abandon a child. It caused Sara the most heartache. Joe was engaged and Sara was very young. When the child became aged, oh, must have been four years, I think, there was sense in Benthe coming to live here with us, and now we are all settled to it.'

'But Katherine...?'

'I confess it did not rest well with her. We had to tell her, and as you can imagine it was not easy. When Benthe came to us, Katherine had birthed Grace, and another was on the way. No mother will blame a child and, over time, Benthe and Grace ... well you've seen them. I have learned that children, in these matters, do not look to history or any other things. Unlike the men and women, they will become, they will readily accept another child on its own terms, not on those of others. We lose much when we lose the child in us.'

'We are all children under God,' said David.

'It was my idea. Mary was against it. Grietje and I were in discord, but I asked Grietje to fashion a sketch in crayon and when Mary saw the bairn with the ginger mop, she just said, *Bring her*

home, Joe. Grietje and Sara have always been made welcome here.
She uses the barn in the grounds, at the end of our garden as a
studio. Have you seen it? For now, they choose another life.'

'And Benthe?'

'She knows Sara as her mother. They write often. She has not
asked as to her father. I lead a simple life, David.'

David responded with a wry smile.

'Now tell me of this young wench?'

'I should wait until you meet. We were thrown together by the
outbreak. We both wept and mourned the loss of Samuel. I was
greatly fond of him. Her boy, Ben, brought us away from too long
mourning the dead. Over time, a habit between us formed. It was
my housekeeper, Mrs Lyall, who recently pointed out the
irregularity in our living arrangement, and although I am quite
shocked and unnerved by the consequence, I am very happy.'

'So, you proposed to make an honest woman of her.'

'I will not tell you anything, other than it was she who
propositioned me.'

Joseph laughed. 'But did Janett not propose to you also?' David
nodded. 'You are a quiet, studious, moral, contemplative and
respected gentleman and you have young women falling over you.
Where did I go wrong?'

'You have the perfect wife, Joe, and you know it.'

'Let us then toast our beloved women and daughters. Past,
present ... future!' Joe raised his glass.

'Oh, do not tempt fate.'

'So, you asked about Benthe because Flora, your Flora, has a
child and Rose...'

'Yes, whether or not I can expect upset, I will tell it plain. I
know it's late, Joe. Tell me more of Gre..., Griet, how is it?'

'Grietje, it took me a year to get it right.'

'She is a woman employee of yours and an artist?'

'Yes. We met, as I say, when I returned to Holland to look for
your father. She was familiar with the porcelain industry and the
art markets. She was an instrument in the success of the venture.

235

She still is. Grietje is strong and capable in business. She has an accountant, a lawyer and a manager working under her. We have good trade still. A market in fine goods, quality rather than volume.'

'A woman in charge?'

'Yes. It is not so usual even in the Dutch states, but it is tolerated there. Women can legally own property and business. I do not say it is easy or without trouble, but there is no law against it. She has been a close friend for many years now. Presently, she will stay with Sara above her studio and join us for occasional meals. The children love her and will be pleased at her return. When she is here, she teaches them drawing and excites them with exaggerated tales of her travels.'

'Then I look forward very much to meeting her. And I will likely chance a meeting with my stepsister. I have the school break in a few weeks: may I come and stay again?'

'Of course, David, the room is yours, and do bring Flora.'

'It may be a bit early to throw her to the...'

'Wolves?'

'Hah, no Joe. I haven't yet found the word. Perhaps, first, you and Mary might visit us at Gladney.'

'We would be delighted, whatever you think best.'

Joe entertained David with a story from his escapades in the early days in Delft. He took care not to mention Tom.

Rose and the girls were late back from Hopetoun and exhausted. David suggested that the two of them sit together in the drawing room rather than walk out. Rose took the first hour telling him of the house, the ball, the music, food, and the dancing. 'Father, we had a delightful time. The dancing was arranged. I wasn't adept, but it was of no matter. I met all manner of people. I can't remember many of them. Some men asked if they could call on me. I shook my head. Father, I didn't know what to do. I am too young. I do not want to be courted. Some men were quite old, already with families.'

David felt the irony.

'Rose, when I was held to the house, I thought much on the future. I wrote to you on this and I told you of Samuel John.'

'Yes, it was terrible news.'

'And I wrote of his widow, Flora.'

'I remember. How is she and the child?'

'They are much saddened but resigned to it. I have come to enjoy and value their company in the house...'

'Oh.'

'...and I desire that to continue. You understand that other than the school I am quite alone at Gladney.'

'Do you want me to return?' Rose did not disguise her fright at this.

'Not unless you wish it. That is not my point.' David now held his daughter's full attention. 'You are always welcome to return, Rose, at a moment's notice. Gladney is your new home, although I understand it may not feel like it. I don't think there is any longer a threat to you in Kirkcaldy. I see you happy and engaged here; I assume this is where you want to be. You have grown in ways I could not have taught you.'

'If you want me to return, Father?'

There was resignation in her question.

'Your place at my side will always be there, Rose, don't ever doubt it. We, you, must think on it, but I would not have you serving my needs for the rest of your life. You must live by your own choices.'

'I think I understand. If I stay here, will you continue to visit?'

'Of course. It may not be every week, and you will be able to visit Gladney often. You may choose to stay longer when the weather is pleasant.'

'Then why?'

'Well, Flora and the child, Ben, he is named, live in the house, and I welcome them there.'

'Yes, you said.'

'Recently there has been talk in the town. Remember it is not Edinburgh; the minds are smaller, the church.' Rose was quiet.

'Rose, I would wed Flora.' There, he had said it.

'Father ... I don't understand.'

Tears came and Rose silently left the room to go upstairs. David remained sitting, and when the hour bell rang, Mary came to see him.

'Let her be, David, she will come around.'

He left it another hour and then went up to find Rose in her room. She was not there. He found Grace. 'Have you seen Rose?'

'She has gone to the barn with Benthe.'

David was stuck now. Strangely, the one person he wanted to talk to was Janett. It occurred to him that Rose probably had exactly the same thought.

After another half hour, he put on his jacket and boots and headed to find the studio and meet Joe's visitor. It was further from the house than he had expected, and on a path he hadn't taken before. This early in the year, much of the ground was still sodden and a slip in the brook earned him muddy trews. After thirty minutes of walking, he found the building, a much-altered barn. There was no road to it, only a couple of grassy paths. There were two high barn doors and a smaller door within one of them; he banged on it. The woman who opened the door had enough of the look of Benthe for David to realise who she was.

'Sara, is it ... is Rose here?'

Sara opened the door for him. There was a wooden partition and a second door. David walked into the warmth of two roaring fires and the enticing smells of baking and coffee.

Rose, Benthe and another, who, dressed in breeches, a waistcoat, and long boots, looked like a man, were sitting by one of the fires eating from plates on their knees.

'David, hoi, I am Grietje.' The tall, handsome, older woman held out her hand in greeting.

'Hello'

'Please join us. There have been a few tears. Would you like some coffee ... or a whisky?'

'Coffee would be fine, thank you.'

Grietje placed a spare chair beside Rose and continued. 'I am sorry for the heat. I am trying to dry the place out.' Grietje looked at Rose. 'It all came out in tears. I think she just needed someone to talk to. I offer my congratulations.'

'Thank you.'

Rose allowed her father to hold her hand. 'I am better now, Father.'

'We can talk later. Tell us more of the ball.'

Sara brought David's coffee and delicate pastries.

'This coffee is not bitter, and these sweets!' David exclaimed.

'Both from Holland. We are not allowed to import them, but I bring a small supply for myself and Edward Clerk.'

'You know Edward?'

'Yes, quite well. We work as a pair. I procure goods mainly from Holland and he sells to the English, French and, more recently, the American markets.'

'I see, and what then, pray, does Joe do?'

'He sits at his desk, counts his money, and goes out for lunch.'

David could see she talked in jest. 'But you paint, here?'

'I do, and that is my passion. I hope to spend more time in Scotland, but I have apprentices in Delft, and they demand my attention.' She laughed. 'I want to paint a hill! I can see some from here.'

'Do you have any female apprentices?'

'How perceptive, sir. Indeed, I do. Two, and Tomasine of course.'

'I don't know any of this, Tomasine paints too?'

'She is a talented draughtswoman, but it is not her vocation nor her destiny, I think. You know she is in Edinburgh, did Joseph say?'

'Who is Tomasine?' Rose interjected.

David made sure to answer first. 'A friend of Joseph and Grietje.'

'Girls, go and put on the dresses you brought for me to see. Sara will help,' instructed Grietje.

'I thought one shock for Rose today was enough. She does not know of Tomasine. I will bide my time before introducing a new aunt,' explained David.

'I understand, two in one day. Do you intend to meet with Tomasine?'

'I think now I will. When she was younger, I did not want to explain and introduce her to Rose, if she was to be a rare relation who would not play a part in her life. She is growing faster than I can measure. I didn't realise until today that you were well acquainted with Tomasine.'

'Yes. I watched her grow up. Joseph and Mary do not ask of her. They only wish to know if she is well. It was the death of her mother and her own curiosity that brought her to the funeral. I can't remember the name.'

'Lockhart.'

'Yes, that was it. She was invited to the ball.'

'Did she meet...?' asked David.

'No, I don't think so. They travelled separately. I suppose, they may have stood ignorant of each other in the same company.'

'Through Edward Clerk?'

'Yes. Tomasine, it seems, is a prize highly sought after. She says she will only accept a Duke or a Prince... I see the jest is not to your taste.'

'It is not your jest. I am becoming aware of the duty of the parent of an eligible girl. Rose, when we spoke earlier, told me of offers to call and of other invitations to parties. She is seventeen.'

David stood up in his exasperation. 'She has gone from twelve, sitting reading the bible on my lap, to, to ... this!'

The girls walked down the stair in full finery. The stark background of the old barn and the firelight seemed to enhance their theatrical entrance. The girls paraded, fanned themselves and danced an unaccompanied gavotte. The three adults clapped.

'You look beautiful, Rose, Benthe,' commented Grietje.

The girls curtsied and disappeared back upstairs.

David was still standing at the fire while Grietje sat and Sara cleared up. 'And the families, not just the men, talk of them like prizes. As if they are for trade in a beast market. I'm sorry. I confess, I have tired today.'

David sat down again, surprised at his own outburst but also how comfortable it had been to talk to this strange woman whom he had never met. Maybe that eased this release of his disquiet.

'It was ever thus,' said Grietje.

'Did you go through...?'

'No, not in this way. I almost said I have never married. It was short and so long ago. I do not come from a family of wealth. Many of my family were taken by the plague when I was Benthe's age. The bartering of my future was not refined; it was less pleasant.' David was shocked yet impressed by her forthrightness. 'I know we haven't met, but Benthe has written to Sara and myself and there have been many lines taken up with tales of Rose and some of yourself. I do not feel unfamiliar with you. Many years ago, Joe would talk of you as a boy.'

'Does Tomasine want anything from me?'

'I don't know. These times, she very much keeps her own counsel. I am no person to advise. She may have become aware of her lack of family.'

'May I ask, do you or Joe support her?'

'Hah, no, there is no need. I think she is wealthier than all of us. Has Joseph mentioned de heer van Reit?'

'Not that I recall.'

'He was a wealthy Dutch merchant. He passed some time ago and unbeknownst to any of us who knew him. He left funds in trust for Tomasine until she became of age. A substantial sum.'

'The reason?'

'I was close to him and I am still not clear on it. He had no family surviving him and he gave much to charity. Van Reit never met Tomasine but knew only of her circumstance: that she was a talented child born out of wedlock. Perhaps something in his past. He was a wonderful man and a dear friend to me.'

The girls and Sara came back down. Grietje stood. 'David, I would happily talk more with you. We will meet again soon, I hope. Will you walk Rose back? Benthe will stay here tonight, I think.'

David and Rose both thanked Grietje. Sara gave Rose a bag of pastries. 'For Joseph, but only if you don't tell Mary,' she whispered Rose embraced them all before walking out into the twilight with her father.

Rose walked quietly with her father. He was fortunate that Rose knew the way better than him. She put her arm through his.

'What an extraordinary woman, have you met her before?'

'No, I like her,' Rose replied. 'She was comforting but also firm with me.'

'What! What did you do?'

'I was upset because of what you had told me, and she asked about it. She asked a lot of questions and made me think. In fact, she was like a bit like Mr Hume.'

'Really, in what way?'

'Well, she asked questions to make me see my folly.'

'What sort of questions?'

'I can't remember them all: does your father love you – yes; do you love your father – yes; do you love Mary and Grace and Joe and Benthe – yes; then the tricky one: is your father allowed to love other people? And: do you want happiness for the people you love; does your father deserve happiness...' Rose became upset again.

'It's fine, Rose. It is fine.'

'She is right, Papa. I do not feel it, but I know it to be right. Just allow me a little time. Can I please ask one thing?'

'Yes.'

'Can we visit Mother's grave in Cupar?'

'Of course, I would like that too. Rose, there is nothing that can or will replace your mother or change my enduring love for her.'

They walked through a small wood.

'I don't remember this path.'

'Trust me, Papa. What did you talk about with Grietje?'

We talked about girls growing up. It's something I do not know.'

'I used to think you knew everything.'

'So did I.' Rose looked up at him. 'If I could snap my fingers and take us both back to Cupar and live in the schoolhouse with your mother, then I would do so. I was happy there; we all were. When things change in life, you have to do the best you can. And life will never stay the same: people grow, people change, things that you try to avoid, things you don't anticipate, happen all the time. All we can do is the best we can. No one can take your mother from us, and the love which we enjoyed will be with and within us as long as we live.'

Rose squeezed her father's arm.

'If we had stayed in Cupar, Rose, just us two I mean, we may have been quiet and content. Would it have been better or worse? I cannot answer, and I don't ask that of you.'

Rose knew her father meant well but sometimes he was too much the schoolmaster.

'The baby?'

'What baby?'

'Mrs John's child, did you say his name is Ben?'

'Yes.'

'If you marry, will he be my brother?'

David looked to see a familiar impish smile.

243

'Yes, step-brother but, yes, you would have a very little brother and he would have a big sister.'

Rose did not appear unhappy at this unforeseen consequence.

DELFT 1713

Chapter 22

Early February 1713, found Joseph, Henry, Meijer and Grietje around a late table at the Toren Inn in Veere. Henry arrived last and insisted on playing host. The others had mostly completed their business and were exaggerating their stories for Henry's amusement.

Meijer had presented the best report. Janssen had eventually agreed to give up control of the legal practice. Under the threat of selling his country house, Janssen had relinquished the town office and accommodation, which would now be occupied by Meijer and his family. Janssen has removed himself from Delft to the country, while retaining only a minority share in the business. Meijer has borrowed substantially to buy up some of the debt, and the rest was secured on Janssen's country house which was remarkably mortgage free. The process of selling Janssen's paintings and silverware was underway. Meijer's empathy did not stetch to worrying how Janssen would service his fraction of the remaining loan.

Joe left the paintings in the custody of Meijer, as there was nowhere else to store them safely. He did not want to add to an already oversupplied home market, and in time would seek Edward's help to obtain a valuation from the English market.

Grietje had obtained signed papers from van Reit, in the hope of imparting momentum to the building of the new orphan school in Delft. She confessed she wanted the uncertainty to settle so she could find the time and the peace of mind to paint. 'I am not a business-woman,' she exclaimed. The men looked at each other.

'What, what?' asked Grietje.

It was Henry who chose to reply. 'Well mevrouw, if *you* are not a business-woman, I do not know of anyone who is!'

'Oh, stop it. I will manage Joe's earthenware and I will paint van Reit's portrait. And I will stroke my cat. That will be my idyll.'

The men laughed, shaking their heads.

'What!'

'Well, we will just...'

'... wait and see.' Joe completed Henry's sentence.

Henry apologised and rose to retire to his room at the Toren. The others stood to bid him goodnight and readied themselves to leave. Meijer was rooming at the Scottish Conciergerie and left.

Joe and Grietje were alone.

'Where are you, Grietje?'

'I am in my own room. Do you not remember?'

'I had forgotten. It seems so long ago.'

'A lifetime.'

'So much has changed in such a short time. Shall I walk with you there?'

'Yes, thank you, as long as you don't pick another fight.'

They pulled on their cloaks and stepped into the cold. That temporal wave that comes only with the night-wind blew time away, and they were back. The wind and the sea crashed against the breakwater. Joe put his arm around Grietje, and she rested her head against his shoulder as they walked in unhurried steps.

When they neared the buildings that overlooked the harbour, Grietje asked, 'Are we still the same people, Joe?'

'I don't know these things.'

'I think I am the small boat caught up in the wash of a flood driven inland. I am being held afloat in an unnatural place for but a moment of time. I wait, almost impatiently, for the flood to recede and be found far from the shore.'

'Do you have what you desire?'

247

She turned her head to look up at him. 'Most things yes... I have what I can have.'

'And is that enough for you?'

'Yes, Joe, it is. Not long ago my answer to your question would have been no, but now I have more than enough. And it is you that brought me this fortune.'

'Greta.'

She laughed it was the old name he used before his broad Scottish accent could get his tongue to pronounce hers.

'Yes, sir?'

'Let me tell you what Meijer said. I asked him why he chose the challenging path of dealing with Janssen and keeping the business afloat.'

Grietje interrupted with a laugh. 'I have asked him too.'

'Well, I'd wager he did not give you the same reply.'

'Go on.'

'He had been suspicious of Janssen, yes, but he left Teuling to deal with it. He led a comfortable life and sat in the security of a good family. Then this female whirlwind spun into his office, full of energy, determination, and life. And when he saw you dressed as a man, he realised he had been living half asleep. Teuling too, saw that nothing would change for the better unless you made it happen. And that if you are young, you should take the risk.'

'They do me too much credit.'

'No, Grietje, they don't.'

'I have no dependant, no risk. It is easier for me.'

'I understand that, but I know this path. You are driven to fight on the behalf of others, if not yourself.'

They were passing the Scottish Inn at the harbour. Grietje nudged Joe towards the door. 'Do you think we left some whisky in that bottle?'

They found a quiet table. A maid brought a full bottle and two glasses.

'At last,' Grietje said, putting her hand over Joe's. 'I have you alone. I have things I need to tell you and the whisky will help us both. You know I went back to Monster?'

'Yes. I am not sure why.'

'No, neither am I, but when am I ever? Anyway, I went to paint. I stayed at the inn, and yes, I saw Doortje and then Tom.'

Joe was attentive and showed concern. 'Do I need to know this?'

'Yes, Joe, I think you do.'

Grietje took her time and told Joe the story as Doortje had related it to her. 'Joe, she discovered Tom near dead in the church...' Grietje gave Joe the details of Tom's long period of convalescence with Doortje and the difficulties of their situation. 'Remember that Doortje was barely twenty years when she met Tom. She was attractive, bright and fun. She laboured in the lodgings and dutifully looked after her mother and grandmother. She may have thought to have some excitement with Tom. I don't know. But after the flood, when she sought him out, found him, and nursed him for many months – she nurses him still – she stood by him and the child. I saw not a flicker of regret or selfishness in her countenance. Whether she does it out of love or duty, I do not know. He appears as an old man, prematurely grey haired, barely out of invalidity. They both adore the child, who is a delightful creature. And they lead a simple life.' She saw Joe was moved by her tale.

'Did you speak to Tom?'

'Not in a meaningful way. We were polite. He has hidden the past from himself – it was not mentioned. I liked her. She does not have anyone close.' Grietje let Joe digest her words. 'I have told van Reit of Doortje and the child because he asked. I did not mention Tom to him, only you can do that.'

'Have they made use of the money I left?'

'Yes, there was some debt and they have no proper means, but the village works by exchange, they live on the benefits of their contributions.'

'Tom also?'

'Yes, he keeps books and does some teaching.'

Joe shared his thoughts. 'These paintings, the ones in Meijer's office. I do not want to look at them. They were on the cart. It still seems extraordinary that they should turn up on Janssen's walls. Remember how he confronted me?'

'Yes.'

'My instinct is that these belong to Tom. I bought the company cheaply because these paintings were lost. For the company to claim them does not feel honest.'

'You are still troubled by David and the fate of Margaret?'

'Yes.'

'Do you want my reflection?'

Joe looked over to her, 'Yes, you have seen them. Do not appease me. How do you see it?'

'You know I do not judge. I have lived through too much for that and I have no church. I do not think that Tom has yet found himself well enough to confront it. Yes, he may be hiding from it, but what would a good man have him do? Leave the woman who has nursed him back to life, and the child who he has fathered to a poor existence? To return to what? He is mostly in a chair, Joe. How would he benefit David's life?'

'Better a dead hero than the living cripple?'

Grietje chanced a smile. 'Joseph Grieve, you are a wiser man than you pretend.'

'It does not rest on my shoulders.'

'No, but we both know, it resides in your conscience.' Joe refilled the glasses; the bottle was now below the half. 'Joe, I think in time he, they, will have to confront this and, remember this was your first thought, they will do it in their own time. That is their right and not yours.'

'I understand that view, but it is not clear.'

'Does the boy, sorry, does David, not fare well?'

'He does.'

'Does he trouble or burden you?'

'The opposite.'

'Come we will take the bottle to my room. We are the only ones keeping the wench awake. We can talk of lighter days now.'

As they walked the dark street, Joe expressed his gratitude. 'Thank you for telling me. You were right, I needed to know. I will make sure they have a good income from the paintings. Unloading a cart full of oils and canvas would not serve them well.'

Grietje paused for a minute. 'I do, though, fear I have erred and may have caused them trouble. It is on my conscience.'

Joe saw Grietje's admission held a small smile. 'Tell me.'

'I told van Reit about the village – he always asks about Doorjte and the child – and the unfinished church. There was no intent. He was quite taken with it and expressed concern. He said he would deal with it. I brought an instruction from him to Meijer.'

'Why is it a bad thing?'

'They are unmarried. Tom and Doortje are living as man and wife, with a child. Yet, he still has a wife, doesn't he? Doortje knows this and expressed a real concern to me, should a minister be appointed to the village.'

Joe managed a laugh. 'Well, God can judge, that is his job. I will happily hand the burden over!'

Grietje took a slug from the bottle as they walked and handed it to Joe.

'Whisky solves all life's ills!'

'Until the morn,' she replied.

Joe slept in Grietje's bed that night. They found the comfort of old in each other's arms. Grietje understood, they both did, that it was a fond glance back at the past, not a pointer to an unintended future.

EDINBURGH & KIRKCALDY
1738

Chapter 23

The spring breeze which disturbed the blossoming fruit trees turned into a strong wind of change for Rose by early summer. She had chosen to ignore the fact that Grace and Benthe were a year older than her, and their maturity had brought new considerations into their lives. Rose had never lost the habit of listening in halls; she had influenced Benthe into the same behaviour. Downstairs in the hall, they overheard raised voices from upstairs. They crept as far up the steps as they dared, where they could hear much of young Joseph and Katherine's family disagreement. It was the repeated shouting of Grace's name that gained their attention. Rose could only catch phrases: 'I want my own place; you've promised this many times; she is eighteen now; she wants to entertain and sit with other young ladies.'

Joseph's reply was of one form, 'She can do that here.'

Katherine again, 'No! she cannot. How could she explain?'

'Explain what?'

'Who all the children are? Who the women are, that share a bed at the end of the garden, and David and his new woman and child? Oh, why are we still living here?'

Young Joseph replied, 'We cannot afford this living, these rooms, servants and carriages.'

'I don't care. I need my own house, or the children and I will go elsewhere.'

At the sound of the door latch, Rose and Benthe shot along the corridor and into a bed chamber, collapsing on the bed in giggles. Rose sensed Benthe's response was more muted than her own.

'Do you think Grace will leave?' asked Rose.

'They have argued like this before. I don't know. Rose, I have something to tell you that you may not like.'

'O Benthe, what is it?'

'I may leave for a while.'

Rose stopped her play-acting and gave Benthe a pleading look.

'Benthe you can't... especially with Grace...' Rose found herself shocked and in tears.

Benthe pulled her into her arms and held her close. 'I will come back. It will only be for a short while.'

'But where are you going?'

'I want to go with my mother and Grietje, to Holland for a while.'

'Oh no, for how long?'

'Six months, perhaps, I don't know. I promise I will come back.'

Rose sat sobbing.

'Rose, we are grown now. I am eighteen. I cannot remember Holland. We three cannot just idle our days here for the rest of our lives.'

'I am not idle.'

'I know, but you too have to think to your next years What will you do? Your prospects are not bleak. You have a new family and you have not had much time to enjoy your new house.'

'That is what my father says.'

'You are very lucky to have them. I have no prospect of a brother or sister.'

'You might!'

'No, Rose.' Benthe wondered at Rose's naivety. 'I will come back, unless...'

'What, what?'

'Well, not straight away, but maybe you could come and visit us.'

'To Holland?'

Benthe embraced her. 'Rose, we can look forward to adventures if your father will allow. We will write and meet all around the world.'

'We can't. He would never allow it.' But the thought cheered Rose.

David found it easier to go to his school directly from the morning ferry. It was a long day, and near the sixth hour after noon when he returned to Gladney. Flora was trying not to look anxious. She didn't move to embrace him.

'Mrs Lyall has left a pot. I said we would attend to ourselves.'

'I am hungry and exhausted. A bowl of stew will revive me.'

Flora turned away to fetch the supper.

'Wait,' called David. She stopped. 'It was fine. As fine as it could be.'

'Really? I thought…'

'What? That I would have doubts. No, not one.'

'…that Rose might upset you.'

'We will talk over supper. Have *you* had doubts?'

'No, David. I want you as my husband.'

'Flora, you shall have me.'

Over supper, David took time to tell of his past days in Edinburgh with her. It was a summary, to fully describe the theatrics of the Grieve household was near impossible.

'Rose was shocked when I told her, as were the others.'

'You told the Grieves?'

'Yes, they wish you well and are looking forward to meeting you. Rose and I talked but there was another woman there, whom I had not previously met – an old friend of Joe and Mary's. She listened to Rose carefully and talked through her anguish in a way that I could never have done.'

'Who was she?'

'She is a visitor from the Dutch States, a quite remarkable woman. Then ... poor Rose ... her friends, sisters really, told her of their plans to leave Canon Mills in the summer.'

'Oh, the poor girl.'

'Well, our news was no longer her greatest fright.'

Flora reached for David's hand. 'If you need to go to her.'

'She will be fine. It has made her, and me for that matter, consider her own future.'

'What *are* your thoughts on the matter?'

255

'An empty page, at the moment. She has time yet. I will return in a fortnight at the start of the school break.'

Flora came back into the room after clearing the pots.

'May we abed now, sir?'

'What about Mrs Lyall?' Flora's forthrightness still shocked him.

'She has told me, now we are betrothed, that she has no eye on our behaviour.'

David was exhausted but would not decline her need. She sensed this and demanded from him nothing other than the most natural of responses. Afterwards, as they lay entwined, she asked him, 'Do you have a mind for a day?'

'I have thought on this. There are demands. I have people who request meetings and some whom I would like to invite to the house. It would be more seemly if there were a married couple to receive them. I do not press you, but I see no reason to delay past the month that I would allow for Rose to settle. Do you wish more time?'

'No, sir. For us, the confinement was a convenience. Out of it we cannot continue as we have been. I fear any longer a wait, and I would have to move away for appearance's sake.' Flora returned David's embrace.

'I do not have a thought as to place: here with all attending, Edinburgh where you are not known, or shall we escape to Gretna?'

'I don't care,' Flora replied. 'Am I really to be the mistress of all this?'

'And more. Are you to marry me for my wealth?'

'Well, it's not for your looks or temper.'

'Oi!' David exclaimed before punishing her with a tickle and she soon became lost in his kisses once again.

The following day, David sat at his school desk after the class had given their translations and were quietly reading through another text. He was preparing a test for them and looking for some challenging phrases. '*Sit homo sto super opinionibus suis*,' and it stayed with him all day.

He returned to Gladney at four; Flora was feeding Ben at the kitchen table while Mrs Lyall prepared supper. Ben giggled when he saw David. Mrs Lyall left to attend to some other work.

'Flora, you would be happy here?'

Flora laughed. 'I think I have made that plain.'

'I mean staying in the town with the schoolmaster and this house. It is comfortable but you are young, there are other...'

'David what are you saying? I know you enjoy your visits to Edinburgh. Do *you* want something else?'

'I asked myself that question today... No, I don't. I confess I am not a very exciting scholar. I love my school, the pupils, my books and, despite past events, I like this town. I can make a difference here.'

'And?'

'And I love you of course, I was thinking in terms of my occupation.'

'I mean, you have not asked for anything.'

'I would like friends to visit, a good horse or two, perhaps, occasional travel but largely a quiet life. Would that be enough for you?'

'Would it be enough for you, you mean? You bring back so many stories from the Grieves, is that not the life you desire?'

'No, it is a more contemplative life that is my own. I don't report to you the hours I spend hiding in my room there.'

'David, this is all I wish. You, Ben, and to live here is all I need and desire.'

'Then here we stay?'

'Yes.'

'Well, let us wed here. Let us invite the town. Let us not shy nor shelter, the schoolmaster shall be wed! Will you allow such boldness!'

'On one, no, two conditions.'

'Which are?'

'A new dress such as the ones you buy for Rose. I will need her help.'

'And?'

'We need her approval. My wish would be that she attends. I know I have not yet met her, but I saw her often around the harbour, usually with the Smith boy.'

Mrs Lyall returned to the pot on the fire.

'This is a cheery table, what are you two up to?'

'We are planning a wedding, Mrs Lyall, and you shall attend!' said Flora.

'Oh, my dears.'

David's days in Kirkcaldy were spent on school business. He was inundated with requests for places in the school. His exhibition, it appeared, had worked well. The Saturdays filled with domestic business, and on Sundays, David, Flora and Ben attended the kirk together. David's first appearance left him parrying questions for an hour after the sermon. None involved his domestic situation. Flora took Ben back on her own. Mrs Smith was the most anxious.

'Dr Miller, I pray for a few moments...'

'Mrs Smith, of course. Can I just finish here, then I can walk back with you?' There were more concerned parents to see.

David thanked Smith's mother for her patience as they made their way down the hill to the High Street. 'I am sorry it has been so long.'

'The town's affliction affected us all. I am concerned for Adam. He misses Rose in the classroom and has started wandering again in self-absorbed chatter, when his nose is not in a book. Your daughter is a good influence on him, and, yes, I know I did not welcome her attentions, initially.'

'I have seen the change.'

'Is she not to return?'

'I intend that she will spend more time here, yes. Certainly, over the summer, but she will not return to the school. She is seventeen now and I confess I am at a loss for her next years' occupation. But as for Adam, I do have intentions of which I hope you will approve.'

'Well, you both must come to Strathenry in the summer. Will you join me today for a small lunch?'

'Yes, thank you.'

They sat at the grand table in, what was, a sadly dark room on a fine spring day. The maid quickly served soup with bread accompanied by a platter of meats and cheese.

'I have not discussed anything with Adam without speaking to you, but it is clear he is now beyond my schooling. Well beyond, I may say, and I take some responsibility for that. As you say, he is getting lost in unguided consideration.'

'What do you suggest?'

'He has an interest in so many things: farming, Oswald's nail factory, shipping, the mines... I could go on, but he is young, and his mind reaches for the abstract, the generalities. Once he has understanding of specific issues, he finds them trivial and bores of them.'

'That is my son, Dr Miller, in those words, you have him.'

'So, it is the university for him if you will allow, Mrs Smith. Whether his destiny is law, the church, study or government, he needs to learn reason, logic, ethics and structured thought.'

'To St Andrews then?'

'This is your decision, but I have exchanged letters with some of my university acquaintances and in their, and indeed my own, minds the recommendation is Glasgow.'

'Oh, that is quite far. Not Edinburgh?'

'I have spoken recently with an old friend and a young student of Edinburgh. Presently, they find it a poorly led, staid and tired college. They are attracting very few young students.'

David paused for Mrs Smith to take in his suggestion, then continued. 'On Friday next, two Professors from Glasgow are to appear at the Assembly, and they have consented to interview Adam if you agree. That would not be a commitment, but they would be in a position to offer a funded place.'

'Dr Miller, this is all a bit too quick.'

'I understand. It is just an opportunity, to save you both a journey.'

'Can I let you know?'

'Yes, I am to meet with them in any case. I will travel to Edinburgh on Friday. Adam can come with me, and I will return him, hopefully along with Rose, on the Tuesday.' They sat in silence awhile; the maid cleared the plates.

'Dr Miller, what I am about to do may shock you. I hope I may trust your confidence and not incur your judgement.'

David was disconcerted but curious. Mrs Smith went to the dresser and opened a cupboard door. She came back to the table with a brown clay bottle marked whisky and two glasses.

'It is for my nerves, you understand; he is all I have.'

David showed that he did and nodded in acceptance of her gestured offer of the second glass. He glanced up at the portrait of John Knox, before joining Mrs Smith in tasting the peaty drink.

'It is all of a sudden. These professors, what are their names?' she asked.

'Loudoun and Fergusson. Loudoun supervises the matriculation.'

'Do you think he would gain entry?'

'Mrs Smith ... I have no doubt.'

'Oh.' And she took another sip.

Flora was in the front garden throwing a ball for Ben to chase. There was an early white blossom on the fruit tree; blue and white bluebells sprinkled the grass.

'Dr Miller, did you get lost?' Flora frowned then embraced him openly.

'We are not public yet!' he warned.

'So much school-work. This is a day of rest. Wait!' She sniffed. 'Whisky. You have been drinking! Where, how?'

'Shhhh...'

Flora pretended at shock. 'Am I to marry an inebriate?'

'It is worse when I tell you where and with whom.'

'Tell me!'

'I am sworn,' he teased. 'I will save it for my supper tale.'

'You think you will get supper now?'

David chased them both around the garden, much to Ben's delight.

Chapter 24

Friday mid-day found David, once again boarding a ferry to Edinburgh. This time he was accompanied by Smith. Flora had come down with Ben to wave them off. David confessed he found his companion good company. Smith was well-read and would willingly converse on almost any subject; he retained a sense of wonder about God's world.

During the short journey, Smith kept getting up from their bench, in front of the wheel, to examine something he did not understand. He bothered the master with questions on navigation, moon tides and the effect of wind direction. He exhibited not a hint of discomfort in travelling with his schoolmaster.

'Where shall I stay, sir?'

'In the Grieves' house. You visited there before.'

'Will Miss Rose be there?'

'Yes, and the Adams' boys will join us on the Saturday.'

David's answer seemed to please him. 'What will the Professors test me on, sir?'

'Latin mostly, you know your *Historiae Romanae*. Did you bring the *Encheiridion* I gave you?'

'Yes, sir.'

'And probably some Greek.'

'I have been working on my Greek, sir.'

'Do not appear inattentive, Smith. Your poor habit can disguise your intent. Be more of a Caesar!'

'Sir.'

They hired a cart in Newhaven to take them directly to the College. Smith and David awaited the visiting Professors in Robert Hunter's office. David then spent the interviewing hour with Robert at a local inn. It was near two hours before a college porter arrived to summon them back. Their visitors were to attend a dinner with the presbytery and could not delay their departure.

John Loudoun shook David's hand, thanking him, David thought, with an acknowledgement of satisfaction. Smith, for once, was quiet.

'Thank you for the use of your office, Robert. All I can do is pay for the ale and promise to stand you a dinner, another day.'

'You are welcome, Dr Miller, and good luck with that new bride!'

'Sir?' said Smith as they walked down the High Street.

'You did not hear that, Smith!'

'Sir.'

It was still light, and they walked the good hour it took them to travel over Calton and down through Bonnington to Canon Mills. David thought Smith deserved a respite after the long interview and did not press him for a record. Smith was open eyed at the bustle of the large burgh: the heavy cart traffic, smartly dressed burghers, street pedlars, and uniformed soldiers. He gazed up in awe at the height of the buildings in the High Street when they walked through the low Cowgate. As they neared Canon Mills, David asked him how he had fared.

'Do you think it went well?'

'I answered their questions. Em, will there be supper, sir?'

'Yes, there will be supper.'

David took the objecting Rose to the library after their greeting. Her mind was more on talking to Smith than her father. He took advantage of this distraction to tell her of his plans and give her time to adjust to the prospect of returning with him to Gladney. Before he mentioned this, he saw that she was not her usual exuberant self.

'Are you well, Rose?'

'Yes, it is...'

'Tell me, Rose.'

'Well, Katherine has arranged a formal weekend for us. Tomorrow, the ladies, and that seems to include me, will dress up and are to read, sew and take tea. We will sing in the evening.'

'That is fine, it is not uncommon.'

'But only the men, and the boys, will get drunk at dinner, tell their funny stories and play silly games.'

'That is the way of it. You are grown now, suddenly it seems.'

She came over and sat on his knee, leaning into him. It had been some time since he had been able to hold her that way.

'It may not seem the right time to tell you, but I want you to return to Gladney with me and Smith on Monday. For a few weeks at least. We will come back to Mary, Joe, Benthe and Grace within the month.'

Rose did not immediately protest. 'Will Mrs John and Ben be there?'

'Yes, you will meet them. I am keen for you to meet them. They will soon be your family.'

Rose looked up and David responded with a squeeze. He could tell she was being brave.

David offered her consolation. 'Mrs Smith has asked us to visit Strathenry this summer.'

'Oh, will there be horses?'

'I think it's about time, now that you're nearly eighteen years, that you have your own horse. Don't you?'

'Yes, please, Father.' Rose's smile was genuine. 'Can I see Adam now?'

'Yes, but you cannot be with him or any of the boys alone.'

'Father!'

'I know, but it is unseemly.'

'But he is only fourteen. He is...'

David finished her sentence, '... probably going to the university after the summer.'

Rose was downcast.

The Friday supper was an informal affair. David saw that Rose had contrived to sit beside Smith and they spent most of the meal in close conversation. He saw them both in good cheer; she could make him laugh.

Saturday brought an industry of preparation for the arrival of the Adams and the other guests. The large drawing room was decorated and flowered for the ladies. Additional maids had been brought in for the event. The girls were engaged in trying on gowns and chattering about the boys.

David escaped. He borrowed the hounds, who now knew him well enough, and set off through the open countryside in the direction of Leith. He found a long rise with a view to the North. There was a dark sky in the distance. When the afternoon sun dipped its beams under the clouds, it brightened the waves near the shore, and occasionally farther out, the white crests streamed along the darkest water's peak like a silvery sea serpent fleetingly revealing its bright presence, only to disappear again down to Neptune's depths.

David sat on a grassy tuft, pulled his neglected journal from his sack and used it to help him collect his thoughts. The dogs were beside him, the older one lying and the other sitting. The youth caught something in the wind, and without any visible means of communication the elder stood. The was a momentary pause, then they set off. Caught by surprise, David shouted them back. They paid no heed. Groaning to stand up, he repacked his bag and followed them. He was not unduly worried, as these dogs would find their way back to Joe from anywhere, but it would be an embarrassment if they returned without him. They were graceful in full run. They did not head back to the house but towards the sea. He saw them disappear over the crest of the headland.

When he reached the brow, David saw that the hounds had arrived beside a person sitting on a stool, occupied at a table. A tall woman stood beside the sitter. The dogs were excited, jumping up and barking. The two figures did not seem unduly disturbed and turned to look up in his direction. Their wave coincided with his own recognition.

'Hello David,' said Grietje as he approached. 'You remember Tomasine.'

Hello, yes, it has been three years I think.'

'Hello.'

Grietje took up the silence. 'I am not finished here. Why don't the two of you go to the studio with the dogs, and I shall follow shortly.'

'We will not leave you out here alone,' said Tomasine.

'Leave the dogs then ... go on, off you go.' And she shooed them away.

As they trudged back up to the top of the slope, Tomasine spoke first. 'We do not need to talk if you do not wish it.'

'No, I'm fine, I think. Sorry, this is a bit of a surprise ... meeting you today. I wrote to you a few years ago, but my life has been upside-down. I have talked with Joseph, of course, and I have recently met Grietje. Things ... I ... things have changed, in my mind.'

Tomasine was very good at speaking with silence.

David continued, 'I look at you now, and I see the familiarity, I see the resemblance ... your mother must have been very beautiful.'

'You are my step-brother. This you accept?'

'I do. I see you in Rose. It is stupid to think otherwise. Not just the look but in the movement, in the manner. Have you met Rose?'

'No, I have not visited the house. Joe would not allow us to meet without your approval. I often talk with Mary, but Joseph stays away from me. I have heard so much about Rose. Would you object? I would love to meet her.'

David stopped. Tomasine also. She turned to face him.

'You are my sister?'

'Yes, if you want me to be?'

He took both her hands in his and stood to look at her directly. She did not shy from his gaze.

'This does not feel real.'

'I heard talk of you as I grew up and started to ask questions. I understand that I am a mystery to you.'

'I did not know any of this,' replied David.

'Joe would tell Grietje stories of you as a boy, then she would tell my mother.'

'How strange.' David released her hands and they turned to walk slowly on. The dogs darted around at any sniff of a rabbit. 'It will take time to get used to this. Will you visit often?'

'Grietje and Sara have been absent from Edinburgh this past year because they were supporting me in Holland. My mother had become very ill and has since died.'

'I am sorry, Tomasine.'

'Grietje has taught me to be strong and independent, and I will be. Other than you and Rose, however, I have no family. So, my answer is, fair or foul, and if you will allow, I will visit often.'

David stopped and again turned towards her. Tomasine took a step to close the gap and they embraced momentarily.

'That was ill-eased.'

'Well, we can yet improve,' laughed Tomasine. 'Will you talk to Rose?'

'We can do that now, together. We will walk up from the barn once Grietje returns.'

'But the ladies' party?'

'Perfect!'

'You surprise me. Is there a devil too?'

'Only a small one, I fear these recent months have disturbed his rest.'

David and Tomasine remained quiet as they neared Grietje's studio. Tomasine had put her arm through David's as they walked.

'You have more questions?' she asked.

'Many, but they will wait.'

267

David sent a maid to bring Rose to join them in the library. As she entered, David smiled at her bright, flower-patterned dress.

'You look fragrant, Rose.'

'Do not humour me, Father. I did not choose it.' Rose curtsied as she noticed Tomasine.

'Rose, this is Tomasine. She is a friend of Grietje and Sara.'

'Oh. I know. Benthe has told me all about your travels. She shows me the letters you send.' Rose blushed as she thought she should not have confessed their deceit. 'Hello!'

'Hello, Rose, I am very pleased to meet you.'

Rose thought Tomasine stared too intently.

'Rose, we have recently discovered information that has come as a surprise to me, and I think it will surprise you too,' said David.

'Oh. I seem to keep saying oh!'

'It is a nice surprise,' continued David. 'Tomasine and I find we are related. She is my half-sister.'

'Oh! That means ... what does that mean?'

'Well, it means she is family and you have an aunt, I suppose.' Rose's puzzlement led to a brighter smile.

'Oh, I think I am happy with that.' Rose ran to Tomasine and embraced her in an enthusiastic clasp. 'I don't know what to say now. I'm going to sing for the ladies. Would you like to come?'

'I would love to, but I am not dressed for it. Perhaps another day. We can meet again soon.' Tomasine looked to David to receive his acknowledgment. David dispatched a reluctant Rose back to the ladies.

'You should have been a diplomat, sir. She is a lovely girl.'

'There is much of her mother in her. Will you sit awhile longer? I shall summon some tea.'

After they sat down, David asked, 'I know nothing about you and am now curious about many things. May I ask about your schooling, what is offered to girls in Delft?'

'There was a schoolroom, in the village. Van Reit added it when they rebuilt the church. Father taught there for a short time.'

David wondered if he had misheard and was lost in thought for a moment. There was much he did not know. He was determined to let the past go. Perhaps her mother had another marriage. That would not be unlikely. In any case, now was not the time to raise this question.

'David ... David?'

'Sorry, I drifted, you were saying, van Reit. He was your benefactor?'

'Yes, on my schooling, I then attended a small school for girls in Delft where I boarded. We studied English, Latin and accounting.'

'All maidens?'

'Yes, there were not many of us. Twelve at the most, all ages in a large house. Then I went to the University of Leiden for two years.'

'This was allowed!' It was more an exclamation than a question from David.

'Very few of us, but yes – one other from my school. We wore a long black habit, a white cloche and held our heads down and hoods up when we were not seated. There was a row set at the rear of the lecture rooms for us, curtained off. We could see the lecture and we followed the lessons. Some lecturers included us; others ignored. There was a sole woman tutor who looked after our studies.'

'You are well in advance of us, I mean this country, in this.'

'And Grietje has taught me to appreciate painting. So, we toured Europe after university: Italy and France, churches, ruins and great houses.'

'Your mother?'

'Yes, and with Grietje and Sara. I had come into my inheritance. The travelling may have brought on my mother's illness. She tired and was not well when we returned. It's a longer story, of course. Now, as you see, I am here.'

'Hopefully we will have time together, so you might tell me more.'

'I hope so too. I think we will. I'm sorry I haven't asked about your betrothal, but I must leave now. I am to attend a dinner in Penicuik tonight.'

'With Edward Clerk?'

'No, Edward is coming here, and I will catch the returning carriage. I am partnered tonight with a nephew of his. I have met him once. I am not very keen.'

Tomasine stood and she held him warmly, kissing him on each cheek before taking her leave.

David's invitation caught her at the door. 'Tomasine!'

'Yes, you will attend the wedding?'

'I'd be delighted, thank you.'

David sat awhile and reflected. He had never felt less alone and rarely felt as buoyed. It was as if he had discovered an island, a rich sanctuary, which he never knew existed.

Rose and Mary had taken the carriage up to the town on the Monday morning. They were meeting Tomasine and going *ladies shopping*, as Rose had termed it. David finished his letters, installed Smith in the library, where he was at his most content, and decided to walk to Grietje's barn. He hoped to find her alone. He found her mixing paints.

'Well, this is a surprise. Come in.' She beckoned and kissed him on the cheek.

'I don't wish to disturb you, but do you have any time to talk before I leave?'

'Yes, by all means. Shall we go upstairs or out to walk?'

'A walk may be best.'

'Then let me get my boots and a cloak.'

They set off in the direction of the sea.

'Do I need to prompt?' asked Grietje.

'No, sorry, I was composing my thoughts. I wanted to thank you for talking to Rose. She gave me a sense of what you had said to her, and I believe it greatly eased her mind. It was not easy for me to talk to her about it.'

'I just happened to be there when it all came out.'

'You did more than just being there. I am grateful.'

'But that is not why?'

'No, I have a question for you, Grietje. I will be direct: Did you know my father?' Grietje did not reply. 'Did you meet him? Tomasine said something, inadvertently perhaps, it did not make sense to me. Joe does not know or does not want to talk to me about it. He is clearly discomforted, and I would not set this on Tomasine. I do not want to cause upset. Only you have a view that is ... I don't know ... detached, not emotional. Will you tell me?'

They had reached the ridge with the view of the sea. An island covered by the white of a thousand gulls broke the vast grey swell; full sun highlighted the ports of the Fifeshire coast and beyond.

'I will, David, if you are patient and promise not to judge. There is no crime. There is no cause for blame.'

'That is not my intention.'

'Let us sit on this rock.'

They found a sun-warmed, sea-smoothed curve in a large rock; their boots sank into the sand.

'Your father, Tom, did not die in the accident,' Grietje began. 'Doorjte, Tomasine's mother, found him in an infirmary on the point of death, weeks after. He was badly affected: physically scarred, half-crippled and his mind was altered, his speech lost. That girl, a maid of nineteen years, took him in and nursed him for many months. Joe and I went looking and, yes, we saw him. I was deceitful. I approached Doortje without declaring who I was. Joe was much troubled by it – I think he has been all his life. He decided to leave them alone.'

Grietje gave David a moment to think, to take in what she had said, before she continued. 'I went back on my own, after Joe had returned to Scotland. I had sympathy for Doortje. The attention was all on Tom's tragedy and his business. I saw Doortje's anguish. We became friends, as you know, yet we did not often

271

speak of the past. Tom died when Tomasine was aged ten years. He slowly lost his breath and then it stopped altogether. He did not suffer in the manner of it.'

They sat together; David absorbed in his thoughts.

'His life was not so miserable a time. His mind became sharper. His speech improved. He learned to write with his left hand. He taught the children and helped the fishermen with accounting and taxes. He learned enough Dutch to get by. And their joy was Tomasine.'

Grietje stopped suddenly.

David waited and then had to ask, 'What is it?

'After all these years, something has just occurred to me. The spidery handwriting – it is nothing, forget it.'

'He did not remember or talk of Edinburgh?' David asked.

'To Doortje he did. She told me of it. At first, he had nightmares and he would call out your name, and Mary's. He would battle the storm, claw at the bedding, night after night. Doortje always asked about you when I told her I had seen Joe. I believe that was to reassure him in the night. He would shout *the boy, the boy*... does that mean anything?' David shivered. 'In time, he settled into this new life. There were small pleasures in it. Doortje said he acted as if he could not look back beyond the accident. If he tried, he found only the nightmares. I could say more, but I think you have the sense of it. Joe made sure they had money, and latterly van Reit built the village church and the school.'

'I keep hearing the name van Reit, yet I do not know how or where he belongs,' said David.

'Another day for that one, David. Your father found him. He was a wonderful gentleman, a master, who left much of his legacy to Tomasine. Sara was his maid.' Grietje hesitated. 'Joe felt betrayed, David. He wanted Tom to need him. I told him it was a selfish motive.'

Grietje stood and stretched her back before continuing. 'I have thought long on this over many years and I have a reflection that I would like to share with you. Let us walk back to the studio and I will feed you.'

David got up from the rock. 'Tom was then as much a father to Tomasine as myself.'

'All that you now know and hold close: Rose, Joe, Mary and their family. Tomasine, Sara, van Reit's churches and schools, my membership of the Guild, Edward Clerk's fortunes, your own school and teaching; your tutoring of the delightful Smithy and his like. All the good over the years that the Grieves have done. All of it, David. *All of it.*' Grietje paused to take a breath, 'None of this would have become as it is now, without your father. Without him living and without him dying.'

'You are saying it is God's hand?'

'That is not my chosen path, but it moves my soul. Does it yours?'

'It does.'

'And if you were to pick a point to change something, when would that be. What would you change?'

Grietje's question did not demand an answer, but David did respond. 'That is not possible.'

They walked back in silence and sat down in the sun on a bench outside the barn to take some bread and cheese. David looked questioningly at the flagon of wine and cups Sara had brought for them.

'I am a European,' Grietje reminded him, picking up the jug to pour.

David felt the need of it.

273

KIRKCALDY, SCOTLAND 1738

Chapter 25

Crossing the Firth challenged David's constitution on the Tuesday afternoon. The water was choppy, and the ferry had to weave its way through a Dutch merchant fleet before it gained clear sight of the Fifeshire coastline. That day, Rose and Smith were the more robust, and never short of conversation. Smith's convenient company these past days seemed to lessen the reservation his daughter may have had about leaving the Grieve household and meeting his wife-to-be.

Mary and Rose had bought three rolls of silk, cotton and linen, whites and creams, along with ribbon and threads for Flora's dress. David had no idea whether they would be gladly received.

Flora, with a wriggling Ben in her arms, was at the house door when the cart stopped. Smith jumped off and David helped Rose down. Smith greeted Flora briefly before running off to his own rooms in the High Street. Ben was already charging towards them when they opened the gate. He stopped abruptly at the sight of the unrecognised girl.

Rose crouched down to him. 'Hello, I am Rose. What is your name?'

Ben ran back and hid behind his mother's skirts. As they all laughed Rose walked forward and offered her hand to Flora.

'Hello Rose, I am Flora, please call me Flora.'

'Hello.' She looked down at the peeping Ben, then back to his mother, 'I hope I don't fright you as much.'

'I have scones and tea ready. Would Smith not stay?'

'I could fetch him?'

'His mother will be keen to see him,' interrupted David. 'He can come again later in the week.'

Rose carried her bag to her under-inhabited room in the south western corner of the first floor. She looked back from the stairs to see Flora give her father the briefest of pecks.

'We are not married yet,' Flora whispered in his ear.

Rose returned promptly to find them sitting in the downstairs room with two tall windows and views to the west. The late afternoon sun was catching the Forth and shading the hills beyond in pink. Ben played with a wooden soldier at his mother's feet.

'My father has a sore head. Did you bring in the silks, Father?'

'Oh no. What happened to them?'

Rose went to find that the cart driver had left them at the door.

'Flora, Mrs Grieve sent these for you.' They were cumbersome. Rose clumsily took them over.

'But these are beautiful.'

'I told her that all material in the whole of Fife was either black or grey.'

David spluttered in drinking his tea, and Flora laughed loudly.

'Will Ben come with me into the garden?' asked Rose.

The familiarity from a few minutes of play by the hearth and the temptation of a ball had Ben following her out to the front of the house.

'David she is absolutely delightful. Is she truly fine with it, with us?'

'It will take some days but, as you see, at least she accepts the change. Knowing her, she will try to make good of it.'

'And you. Did you miss me, and this?' She left a longing kiss on his lips. 'We will have to be good now.'

'You mean I have to wait a month?'

'Sir, how dare you suggest otherwise!' Flora's laugh was cruelly teasing. 'Come, let us join them in the garden.'

Mrs Lyall had prepared a fine supper, and the day maid served it before she went home. Ben was too excited to be put to bed, but he played contentedly on the floor beside Rose's chair.

'Father has found a sister!' Rose remarked.

'Really?' replied a surprised Flora.

'Yes, a half-sister, from Holland. Your surprise does not measure the fraction of mine,' said David.

'And you met her?'

'Yes, she was visiting Grietje.'

'Grietje?'

'And Sara,' added Rose.

'I am glad you are here, Rose. You father has led me to believe he went to Edinburgh for contemplation and to study books. I am beginning to learn another side.' Rose looked very pleased with herself. 'And I had a Mrs Smith call for him here.'

David looked up. 'Rose, would you clear the dishes and then you can tell us of the ladies' afternoon, and please us with one of your songs.'

'She is testing you,' said David, after she left.

'Yes, I know. Don't worry. But this sister, she is really your relation?'

'Yes, I'll tell all later. What did Mrs Smith want? She knows I was away.'

'Oh, she was full of concerns, but did not really express them. You, me, her son. She dared not ask me directly, but I reassured her. I told her Mrs Lyall ran a Godly house.' David laughed. 'And I told her we are soon to be married. Do you mind?'

'No, I am glad of it. How did she react?'

'Relieved, I think, pleased. She is also worried for her son. She would like to see you.'

'Well, we can invite them both for tea.'

'Who is coming to tea?' asked the returning Rose.

'Mrs Smith and Adam.'

'Goody.'

'Now a story and a song, Rose.'

'There is a pianoforte in the other room. I can accompany you,' offered Flora.

'There is?' asked David. He realised, to their mocking, it was a room he had hardly been in. It was large and he had not bothered to heat it. David set a fire while Rose found some music. Flora picked up a curled and sleeping Ben to move him to his cot upstairs in her room. Rose whispered, 'Can I come and see?'

Flora nodded.

By the time they came back downstairs, David had lit the candles and was sitting with a glass of whisky, reading a newssheet he had brought from Edinburgh. After a hesitant start, the out-of-tune piano and high-pitched voice found the same timing. Rose sang an English ballad followed by a Scottish musical rhyme. David then chased her upstairs to claim a little time on his own with Flora.

'I thought you had chosen a quiet life, sir?'

'I do, oh, so much, I do.' Flora laughed as he checked the closed door before sneaking across to kiss her.

Flora moved her hand to his crotch. 'Do we need to set a date?'

'Yes,' David replied in a tone that was higher pitched than he had intended. 'I have no picture of what you would like.'

'As long as you are at the altar, nothing else so much matters.'

'Nothing grand then: *A Penny Wedding*, on a Friday in three- or four-weeks' time. Let those who want to come, come. A morning service: we shall provide for food and drink and shall call some fiddlers to play, then chase everyone home.'

David heard Rose coming back down the stairs; the door handle turned. She ran over to him and hugged him, adding a kiss. She then turned to embrace Flora. 'Thank you for my room,' she said, and left to run quickly back upstairs.

'What did she say?' asked David.

'I put some things in her room: a small writing desk, paper, books and fresh flowers.'

'That's very thoughtful, thank you. I said that she and I would visit Janett's grave. We will travel Friday next. It would just be one night. She was quite taken with Ben.'

'And he with her.'

'When you were both playing in the garden, I realised how little difference there is in your years.'

'Does it bother you?'

'A little, now I've thought of it. Does it not worry you? For the future, I mean.'

'I no longer think that way. Samuel and I, you and Janett, we all at one time had a long future together. I do not know what the future means anymore. So, no, it does not bother me at all, and I shall show you that the night we are wed.' she smiled.

Chapter 26

The following month was the busiest David could recall. Mrs Smith brought Mrs Oswald on her visit to Gladney, and they took up the mantle of arranging everything for the wedding feast and entertainments. School had re-started, and David's sole domestic job was writing letters and reporting on who was to attend the ceremony – all of Kirkcaldy and half of Edinburgh, it seemed to him. Rose was on board, if not with the significance of the event, certainly with the arrangements and the excitement.

A letter from Glasgow University arrived at the school for David. He brought it home before unsealing it. Rose had spotted it and read the Latin on the seal.

'Is it about Smith?'

'Rose, you are now grown enough to stop having an interest in things that are not your own.' David was firm. 'I shall report the contents to Mrs Smith, and if Adam decides to tell you, that is when you will find out.'

It was early evening, and David went to call on Mrs Smith before supper while Ben was being bathed and bedded. When the maid showed him in, Mrs Smith pre-emptively sent the annoyed Adam on an errand.

'It is very good news, Mrs Smith. Adam has been invited to join the semi-bachelor year and offered a fee scholarship.'

'What does that mean, exactly?'

'It is to his credit that he has not been asked to study the two *bejaune* years. He will have three years to his degree. This is very unusual in one so young. He will study under Loudoun, the professor who conducted the interview.'

'Oh my, this year?'

'Yes, from October. I will leave you to discuss it with him when he returns. Please trust that I will tell no-one of this. I think you know who I mean.'

'Thank you for coming, Dr Miller.'

David, Flora and Rose had finished their supper when the maid answered a loud and repetitive knock at the house door.
'It's Mr Smith for Rose?'
'Ask him to join us in here, Ann, thank you.'

On Friday in Cupar the sun blinked over the churchyard and a quick warm wind blew high clouds quickly across the sky. David put his own flowers at Janett's headstone, then left Rose to place hers. Rose kneeled, sitting back on her heels, for nearly the hour to talk quietly to her mother. David sat patient in reflection on the low churchyard wall. He saw some tears, but he could tell Rose was talking as if she was sitting at the supper table and her mother at the stove. When she stood up and came over to him, she was not troubled. She expressed her gratitude to her father for bringing her.

They had both travelled on horseback for speed and brought no change of clothing. Peter Rigg insisted on hosting them both for the night. It had been over two years since Rose had visited his daughter, her friend Adeline, although they had resumed their regular correspondence and talked briefly at the ball.
'Times change, David, times change.'
'Sir Peter, this is kind of you I am sorry for our...'
'None of it,' he waved his hand. 'Come sit with me. We can leave the girls to their own devices before supper. We four will eat at a small table. I do not heat the whole house when there is just two of us. My boys are in London.'
A servant brought a decanter of wine and filled two glasses.
'I thank you for your letters. I see you have become a man of independent wealth. A surprise to you, I gather. But you still choose to teach?'
'A shock may be the nearer emotion. I do intend to teach, and I will. It is my anchor. I have no plans to do anything other, except contribute to some charitable or public works perhaps.'

'There was a legacy, from your father?'

'That is the easiest description, but I am only now becoming acquainted with the whole story and the fact of it. It seems ... rather, it has brought me a sister also.'

'And this was all news to you.'

'Completely.'

'Well, I drink to your health and to your continuing good fortune.'

'Thank you, and to yours, Peter.'

'How is Rose?'

'The young adapt better than the aged. I am at a loss as to what to do with her now. Adeline still travels?'

'Yes, she has a number of suitors and is yet to decide her mind.'

'That seems to be the way of it. My new sister – how odd that sounds to me – Tomasine, has attended a university in Holland. Are you familiar with such *metier*?'

'In my scant experience there are more young women brought up in academic pursuits in Europe than in our kingdom. You are interested?'

'Yes, it was a thought.'

'I think it is due to the greater number of smaller princely and ducal dominions in the continent. There are many daughters of such grand houses. Some are educated, often by private tutors, and they grow up in a more stimulating house – fine libraries, men of letters, attendance at public debates and so on. Many studious young men, who are in need of sponsorship while they study for a faculty position, are keen to take up the role of tutor, whether it be for a son or a daughter of a grand house. There is no shortage of willing tutors.'

'In the arts?'

'Philosophy, science, art, physic, religion, it may be any.'

'I employed a Mr Hume for Rose as such, while she lodged in Edinburgh. He had tutored a number of aristocratic young men in Europe. There was no mention of women.'

'And where is he now?'

'Hah. He has become lost in his own logic, and Joseph sent him to Bristol to become a merchant. He was in need of a reliable income. But what then becomes of the female tutees when they reach full maturity?'

'There is only one of which I am familiar in this country. I know the family well. She maintained a dialogue with a very eminent man. She reads and contributes to his papers and lectures before he publishes.'

'He publishes in his own name?'

'Yes, and I know from old where you are going with this. There would not be an acceptance if her name was mooted, even as an acknowledgement.'

'I would say that is fair in these circumstances, but I am not sure that it is. Can you tell me this scholarly woman's name?'

'Yes, Miss Trotter, Catherine Trotter. She is a Scot. In her youth she corresponded with Locke, no less. Oh, she married, I do not remember her husband's name.' David made a note in his pocketbook. 'She published poetry, for which she is the better known, and a play, I think. Wait, in fact, no, come with me. Bring a candle, would you mind?'

David followed Peter along the corridor through the darkened hall to the library. Well-stocked, floor-to-ceiling shelves held David's attention while Sir Peter climbed a ladder. After a few failed attempts, Sir Peter brought down a thin volume and read the title: '*Agnes de Caftro – A TRAGEDY – Theatre Royal – By His Majesties Servants.*'

He handed it to David, who looked at it and finished reading the frontispiece: '*Written by a young Lady.* Your Miss Trotter?'

'Indeed, that is she. Food for thought, David. Let us summon our girls and find food for our stomachs.'

At the table, Rose told of her life in the Grieve household, and Adeline entertained them with tall tales of her travels. It was the society scandals she animated, rather than her impression of Santa Croce. At the end of the meal, to the girls' groans, they agreed a hill walk after breakfast before their departure the next day.

Peter's perspective was still in David's mind as they donned cloaks and boots before heading out on to the moor.

'Peter, would you be able to introduce me by letter to Miss Trotter? I want to consider options for Rose, alternatives to endlessly taking tea and waiting for a beau. I would value any advice.'

'Of course, I knew Catherine well, although I have not visited the family for some time. Brilliant of mind, sagacious. She will be of your age.'

'Thank you.'

The fresh walk up Tarvit brought memories of their past visits. David took up a theatrical stance on the high rock only to be shouted down by a covering of ears and girlish moans.

'What has happened to our angels?'

'Indeed,' laughed Peter. 'Regarding Miss Trotter, when I awoke this morning, more came back to me. It is odd how the mind still works when the body sleeps. She married a curate, I remember, Cockburn, an Edinburgh man I think.'

'Not Patrick Cockburn?'

'Yes, that's it.'

'Good God, how odd. I knew him – if it's the same man. We studied at the same time. He is a few years older than me. He was a Jacobin if I remember, a bit dour. I hope I do not cause offence.'

'Not at all. I never met him. It's coming back to me now. There was a scandal.'

'With her?'

'No, the curate. He would not sign an abjuration and lost his position. He became a schoolmaster.'

'Ah, the midden for all failed scholars.' David laughed alone at his own jest. 'The character I remember does not quite fit as the husband of a celebrated playwright.'

'An attraction of opposites, perhaps.'

'Do they have children?'

'Yes, many, if I recall.'

David turned to see where the girls were. 'Come on Rose!'

'She refreshes Adeline. It is good to see. Adeline misses her brothers and frets if left too much alone.'

'She is welcome to visit, you both are. We now have a house to accommodate and entertain you. A walk by the sea, a good substitute for this hill. I have sent you both an invitation to the church service, but I don't expect you to...'

'Of course we are coming.'

The longer days allowed them good time to reach Kirkcaldy before twilight. They cantered along the good road from Cupar before slowing to a trot and stopping at an inn. Rose screwed up her nose when she supped a beer with their shared pie. They were soon on their way.

'Father, is Adeline and her brothers like Ben and me?'

'In a sense, except I am not Ben's natural father.'

'Flora's husband died from the contagion?'

'Yes, you know that.'

'Like Mother ... that is sad for them both.'

'For all of us, yes.'

'They are related, Adeline and young Peter I mean, like you and Tomasine then?'

'Yes, exactly. Dearest, I will always be your father, nothing can and will ever change that.'

'Our souls are entwined!'

David returned her smile. For the moment, his daughter had found a place where she was comfortable; something he had struggled to achieve for more than forty years. He had come close, but it had always slipped away. He was reaching for it again.

Rose trotted her horse on, then slowed again. 'What were the books Sir Peter gave you?'

'I will show you at the house. I would like you to look at them. They were written by a family friend of Sir Peter's, a lady. She published letters and plays when she was of your age.'

'Really.'

'Yes, and they have been performed on the London stage.'

'Like Shakespeare and Marlowe?'

'Yes, though lighter in nature, I think.'

'Perhaps I should write a play,' Rose considered, as she heeled her mare.

Ben ran to the gate when he heard the horses draw up. David left Rose and dropped the bags to lead the two sweating horses back to the stables. When he returned to the house, there was a glass of wine by his fireside chair. Flora had rearranged the room so that there were three chairs at the fireplace. Rose was sitting on the middle one with Ben on her knee, looking at a thin picture book that her mother had made. There was the sweet smell of roast duck wafting through the house.

Chapter 27

It was fervent, impassioned, and violently quick, such was their desperation. David at last had Flora to himself, and he held her close to his chest, only halfway undressed, breathing softly from within a sound sleep. David had nothing else in his mind but to go over the day in which he had barely the briefest moment to pause for a single breath of awareness.

The day of the wedding started calmly. The minister had insisted on a service at ten hours morn, with the ceremony following. David rose early; he was looking for the maid to serve breakfast when a loud banging on the door brought Mary and the two girls, who took over the dressing of Flora and Rose. They were followed on the quarter by Mrs Smith, who under Mrs Oswald's direction, brought the organisation of the day. When David tried to question even the smallest matter, the recipient was deflected from answering by some urgency that demanded their more immediate attention. He meekly obeyed the order to be dressed and on the street the half of nine hours. He walked out of the house to find Joe, Tomasine, Grietje and Sara. Mrs Smith, who did not know what to make of Grietje, uniquely attired in tricorn, purple trews and a rich wine doublet, chased the bridal party from the house to the light applause of the gathered onlookers.

Flora wore a simple cream silk dress; Rose was in a white cotton with floral ribbons and Ben wore a corresponding white suit. Grace and Benthe were in floral print dresses. All the girls wore wildflower garlands. Mrs Smith, as ever in a black jacket and long dark skirt, took a guiding position separating the bride and groom and led the party along the High Street towards the church. The cool morning mist had started to lift, and the lack of wind promised a fine day.

High Street business owners and dwellers stood or sat outside their shops and houses to watch the short procession. Small children ran ahead, in between and behind. Rose held David's hand, but she chatted to Smith who was shuffling along behind her, between the giggling Grace and Benthe. The girls waved at the onlookers as they walked along the long High Street.

The guests, who had gathered at the bottom of the Wynd, were joined by others from the town who had walked up from the harbour. A couple of Irish fiddlers stood on a mound and played a simple tune.

David noticed many he knew from the burgh, plus old friends from Cupar. Peter Rigg, John Anderson, the Oswalds, William Adam, John Drysdale, even Edward Clerk: all waited to join the wedding procession as they took the steep climb up the Wynd to the kirk. David also saw that Samuel's elder brother and his wife had come from Dunfermline, Ben's uncle of course. They had brought their two young girls.

Mrs Oswald waited with the minister at the church gate to usher the party into the designated seats. David had yet to gain more than a glance of his bride.

The service started with two bright hymns, and a reading followed. Another hymn, then the minister's sermon began on a low ebb. He recalled the poverty, the potato blight, the food riot, and the contagion that the burgh had endured. 'It is not ours to question why...' He paused for a few minutes. 'Let us pray for those loved and so recently lost. Amen.' He raised the pitch of his voice. 'Our God gives us joy; this is a joyful day, and we will rejoice. And those whom we have dearly loved will look on this happy day and rejoice with us.'

After another hymn and an uplifting reading on the sanctity of the human bond, Mr Adam called first David and then Flora to join him in front of the congregation. They honoured their vows and then the kiss: he remembers the kiss.

The duly wed couple came out before mid-day, and the sun crept out from behind cotton clouds. Younger children threw cherry blossom in the air. David held a good two handfuls of bawbees which he bowled down the Wynd. The smaller children, and some not so small, lost all restraint and thundered, scraped and tumbled after their fortune.

A piper tuned up and led the congregational walk; all that were gathered joined in. A meadow, a furlong from the church, had been shorn and prepared on the high ground beyond the school. A military tent had been erected, and benched tables were filled with food.

David recognised the two innkeepers, who were there to serve the ale, and the women who attended the tables. He squeezed his wife's waist, thieving a second kiss, but they were given no time. He noticed she was as surprised as he by the extent of the celebration and the numbers that came.

Suddenly, Joe was shaking his hand and slapping him on the back, and Mary was kissing ... well everybody. Flora was pulled away by a cousin and some of her own friends.

'She's lovely, David, what a beauty,' confided Joe. 'I'm surprised you didn't scare her off!'

'She knew well who we were.'

All at once he was being greeted, congratulated, and embraced, but he saw it was Flora who was the greater attraction. She looked radiant. He felt the guilt of his own good fortune.

'Father, Father, come and meet...' Rose dragged him to speak to others. Ben stayed with his mother until he had become acclimatised to the crowd, then he found Rose's hand and enjoyed being trailed around and fussed over. David spotted the two of them talking to Ben's cousins and their parents, a most gracious family. Ben, the only miniature in a bright white suit, was easy to locate. David kept an eye and noticed Flora doing the same; they exchanged a smile.

David saw that Sir Peter and John Anderson had found Joe and Edward; the four, along with William Adam, were ensconced in conversation between mouthfuls of hock pie and swigs of a dark ale. Joe was popular. Grietje continued to cause curiosity. And when the fiddlers joined by a kilted man with a whistle, struck up, it was Sara who led the charge to the dance floor with a surprisingly enthusiastic Mr Peat.

Tomasine rescued David from quizzing parents with a plate of food.

'Well brother, how do I find you? A little dazed, I think?'

'Hello, I am not at all sure how or why this has happened.'

'Pray good sir, do not question. I have just met Sir Peter Rigg and Adeline. He said you have been a recent visitor.'

David was gorging on the food, finding himself famished after his first bite. Tomasine put her hand up to stop his reply. 'It was an interesting discussion.'

'Yes,' he mumbled. 'I would like to talk to you about Rose when we are more settled.'

'Flora is lovely, you are very lucky.'

'I know it. Did Edward bring his nephew?'

'You catch me out. Yes, he is here. I confess he is growing on me.'

As the afternoon cooled, Flora used the excuse of a tired Ben to find David and take their leave. It was a short walk to Gladney. Rose and the girls joined them to collect Rose's bags; she was to spend the fortnight in Edinburgh with the Grieves, allowing David to close out the school term and spend time with his new bride in their family home.

Chapter 28

The penultimate week of the school term had was busy for David. He shared a precious and lovely weekend with his new wife, then spent long days in the classroom and his evenings in his study. There was an increasing pile of correspondence to be dealt with, social, educational and now, disruptively, legal and financial. David managed only to respond to the urgent. Flora organised what had become their social calendar. She penned many thank you letters, signing for both of them where she could. The couple discovered a table full of wedding presents, large and small, sitting in what they now called *the piano room*, when they arose the afternoon after their wedding day. The largest was a stunning seascape from Grietje, which they were yet to fully consider, and the smallest was an envelope with a seal, from Joe and Mary, which they had not opened.

David promised Flora he would stop everything at noon of the Friday, sending Mrs Lyall and their maid Ann off to their relatives, so they could enjoy the Saturday and the Sunday with each other and Ben, undisturbed.

The Friday was bright. After lunch, the three of them took a walk along the cliff top toward Wemyss. David decided Ben needed a dog, two in fact, and he wanted to find a horse for Rose. These desires gave some purpose to their outing. They were stalled in conversation by almost everyone they met. David laughed, and Flora reminded him how fortunate it was that they were received in such a manner. They were so overly advised on the matter of hounds and horses, they stopped introducing the topic. Descending into East Wemyss to stop at the inn, Ben became tetchy and tired, so David paid a cartman sixpence to take them all back to Gladney.

As the sun passed its peak, David sat in the garden under a cherry tree and read through correspondence, and Flora coaxed Ben to lie down for a nap.

'Are you happy to sit and read?'

'Yes, I will look through these letters, then find a book. What will you do?'

'I will wash and press your clothes.'

'We have a maid for that.'

'I know, but I want to.'

'Will you first sit with me awhile? It is lovely here with you.'

'Yes, husband. I will bring some sewing, so you can read in peace.'

They had found a quiet place.

'I don't know what to do with gardens, I've never had one,' commented David.

'This one is beautiful, albeit a tad overgrown. I will tend to it so Ben can safely play. We will need to mend that wall.'

They rose late the next morning, despite Ben's early demand for attention. Their idyll was disturbed before breakfast by the sound of a cart outside their gate. Half-dressed, with David and Ben still in the bed, Flora looked out from the window as they heard a knocking at the door.

'I think it's Rose!'

'What!' remarked a surprised David.

'And Tomasine.'

'What!'

David grabbed the clothes that were nearest to hand, and Flora carried Ben downstairs to greet the visitors. David arrived in the front room to find Ben in Rose's arms and Tomasine looking at his bookshelves.

'Hello!'

'Papa.' Rose passed a struggling Ben to Tomasine and ran to embrace her father. 'I was missing you.'

'Rose! It is lovely to see you. It is a surprise but a very welcome one... to see you both.' He let Rose go, to attempt another awkward embrace with Tomasine. 'It is very kind of you to bring her.'

'Well, I wanted to visit too. I shall not stay but I have a few hours before I return.'

Flora came back in, having overheard. 'No, Tomasine, you must stay a night or two if you can. You have come all this way. We have plenty of room and there was little chance for us to talk properly at the wedding'

Tomasine looked to David, who added, 'I would like that too. You have no other assignation?'

'Not of any import. If you are both sure, I am happy to.'

Rose jumped and performed a small clap. Flora went back to fetch the coffee.

'Is there news, Rose?'

Rose looked to Tomasine before answering. 'A bit, I suppose. Shall we sit?'

David interjected, 'We need to organise. We have been very lax. To the market for food, I think ... No, I'll fetch the maid back. Yes, let us first sit awhile, then I'll go.'

Ben, wearing only a top, was hungry and running around the room in excitement. Tomasine and Rose silently agreed that she should explain as they sat down. Rose played with Ben on the floor.

'Simply put, Katherine and young Joseph have all but moved out of Canon Mills. There had been some discussion before, but the arrival of Sara disturbed Katherine greatly, more than Joe or even Mary realised. They have not quite gone but there is ... I don't know the word, tension? Benthe stays most nights at the barn, and Grace is packing to leave with her family. There have been many tears,' Tomasine looked to Rose, who looked down but smiled. 'And we thought Rose, we, should ... come here. I hope that was the right thing to do. There was shouting in the house last night, so we just...'

'I did want to see you, Father,' appended Rose.

'I hope Joe and Mary are not too troubled,' said Flora.

'Joe is suddenly very busy in the office and Mary is applying what balm she can,' replied Tomasine.

David suppressed a laugh as he recognised the behaviour. 'I shall dispatch a letter to Mary straight away. I will now leave you to fetch the maid and arrange the delivery of provisions. Did you travel on your own?'

'No, I have two footmen waiting at the inn. I didn't know how safe we would be, and unlike Grietje, I do not take the risk. But I will attend to the footmen. Shall I walk with you, is it the same way?'

'Yes, let us do that. Rose?'

'I'll stay with Flora and Ben.'

As they walked the path toward the High Street, they received a few quizzical looks, which David ignored.

'I think you are becoming a figure of curiosity,' Tomasine remarked.

'Or fun perhaps. I think it is you they are looking at. Thank you very much for bringing her. Under the circumstance, it seems the right thing to do.'

'I acted before I could think about it. I hope you do not find it presumptuous.'

'Not at all. Rose appears very comfortable with you.'

'And I, her. With this disruption, we have spent much of the last week together. She understands our familial relation and appears to have quickly placed her trust in it. Believe me, I endeavour not to let her down, David.'

'Thank you. I do seek your counsel regarding Rose's future. Flora and I are not well travelled, and I am struggling to advise Rose as to what she should now do. She is not ready to settle in a home and a marriage. This disruption may have brought the matter to the fore. We are happy to have her here, of course, but I think that is not making the best of the opportunities she may enjoy. You have had a different experience, and I wondered if you have thoughts?'

'I have talked with her on this. She has been very curious about my own upbringing. I don't know if that is a good guide. She told me of her correspondence with her acquaintants and is envious of the boys' occupation. She sees Adeline, is it? in a similar position to herself. I would not advise her. I take care not to influence.'

'I am sure speaking with you can only be of benefit. For both of us, in fact.'

They arrived at the market.

'I have to go to the maid's house and bribe her to return. Is it Joe's footmen who accompany you?'

'No, they are mine. I'll tell you on the walk back. Shall I buy some bread or something?'

'Yes, why not, and some cheeses. Not too much, I will get the maid to fetch a goose for supper. Meet me back here on the hour?' They both checked the harbour clock.

Tomasine was standing with a filled basket as David arrived a little late.

'Sorry, I have found a maid and sister. We will be well served.'

'What did you do about the footmen?'

'They will just stay at the inn.'

David and Tomasine started the walk back.

'I have so many questions,' he said.

'I have the advantage. I know more of you than you of me, especially now I have spent time with Rose.'

'Oh no, what has she said?'

'She has sworn me to secrecy, but there are things I will not forget.'

David looked across to catch her smile. He liked this sister. There was an overpowering feeling of familiarity although ostensibly she was a stranger. He believed that Rose had sensed this too.

'Tell me about your footmen.'

'They are from Holland, a father and son. They always travel with me. They served in van Reit's house. You know I inherited this estate of which I had no knowledge. It came with a village and people. There were, are, legal conditions on the house and the people. Grietje and her lawyer guide me through it. As to the footmen, I tell you a confidence, brother. Grietje has always been a little too fond of the father.'

David laughed, 'This is a life I can barely imagine.'

'To me though, I see your life and your wedding. I have no town to attend my wedding.'

'Will you not soon have the whole of Penicuik?' he teased.

'It is much too early for that. I have to be careful about my choice.'

'Seriously though, would you settle here?'

'For the present, yes. The future, who knows the future?'

'That is precisely what Flora said when we discussed our engagement.'

They had walked so slowly that the maids had arrived at the house before them and were earnestly scurrying about, preparing the rooms. Flora and Rose had formed a swing on the tree for Ben in the garden and were tying it up round a branch when they arrived back.

'Can we picnic outside, do you think?' asked Flora.

Later in the day, after supper, Flora took Ben upstairs and David chased Rose up to bed. 'I'm eighteen now, papa!'

'I can still count, Rose. You are not quite there yet.'

He sat with Tomasine. 'When she is here, I realise how much I miss her, and yet, I think I have to let her go again. Or at least give her the opportunity to leave.'

Tomasine did not respond.

'She cannot attend a university in this country, I have made enquiries. She can travel for a short while, but like you, she would need a chaperone and an escort. I haven't got a sense of what would serve her well.'

Tomasine responded, 'She studies, you know this? Every morning, without a tutor. And she writes long missives to Smith. Not letters, more a discourse.'

'You have seen this?'

'Yes, she has showed me.'

'But what is the content?'

'It is a dialogue. The unusual thing, to my mind, is that their points of views, their arguments, are evidenced, justification is given. Smith will come up with a proposition and Rose picks at it.'

'In what sense?'

'She did not show me much of it. She assumed I would not be interested, and I did not want to press her. From the little I read, I got the impression that Rose added a, how to say, human side to Smith's logical analysis. She liked to confound Smith, and it was her squealed expression of that, that gave rise to our conversation on the matter.'

'Good God. I always wondered what they talked about, but never troubled to ask. She keeps confounding me.'

'Her *wee lassie,* is that what you call it, manner, belies an agile mind.'

'You attended a university. Do you think she would settle there?'

'I do not know her well enough. She is not unlike the others I knew when I attended.'

'As I say, there is no prospect of that in Scotland nor England.

'Europe?'

'I have selfishly avoided that thought. It troubles me. Excuse me, I must see what has happened to Flora.'

David left to go upstairs. He returned a minute later.

'She is fast asleep on the bed with Ben, still fully clothed.'

'Well brother, do you have any whisky?'

'You like using that term for me?'

'I'm trying to get used to it.'

'As am I. I will fetch a flagon.'

The Sunday brought a packed church and David hurried them back to the house to avoid Tomasine gaining too much male attention.

'Is it always like this?'

'Unfortunately, when I travel. Mostly, I wear a cloak with my hood up. I'm tall here. I don't stand out so much in Holland.'

As a family, they spent the afternoon looking at the gifts and writing letters.

There was a knock at the door. One of the maids had answered and brought a message for David.

'It is the Wemyss seal,' he observed. He opened it to read. 'Hah, an invitation to sup at Wemyss Castle, *please attend with your wife, daughter and sister.* Hah,' he said again. 'It is not *me* that is sought. You ladies are much in demand.'

'Who is it?' asked Flora.'

'The Earl of Wemyss ... the castle beyond Dysart.'

'I don't know it.'

Rose was interested, 'I do, but David Wemyss is still in England. Will we go, Father?'

'I fear our appearance at church was too well noticed. Difficult not to. It is a month yet. You might be well advised to return to Edinburgh before then, Tomasine.'

'Why?'

'They are staunch Jacobins; Clerk is a Whig!'

As they sat, Tomasine noticed an unopened envelope on the table.

'You have not opened Joe's gift?'

'No, I have kept it. We can do that now?'

David looked to Flora who asked Tomasine, 'Do you know what it is?'

'Yes, but I'm not saying.'

David handed the letter to Flora who handed it back to him. He then gave it to Rose to read out. She stood.

Dear David and Flora,

Many congratulations!

We do not have the words to express our delight and good wishes for your future together. This letter bears our unusual gift.

You may have the sole use of the yacht and crew for one month from the end of your school term. I hope you will take up the offer and use the time to travel and give yourselves a well-deserved break.

You need do nothing to accept or arrange this. The ship will be waiting for you at the harbour in Kirkcaldy on the morning of the first Monday in April. You need only walk up the plank and decide where you want to go. (Just bring it back, please!)

Love,

Joe and Mary.

Rose threw the page in the air and jumped up and down, clapping her hands in excitement. Tomasine and Flora looked at her, smiling, then looked to David.

'Oh,' said Rose, sitting down quickly. '...I'm not coming ... am I?' Rose tried in vain to hide her disappointment.

'It's too much, too generous, far too much...' said David. 'We cannot accept...'

The others did not speak, apart from Ben, who wandered around the room picking up and discarding the paper that had been strewn across the floor,

'What,' said Ben. He had, that week, started to talk.

'What,' he said again, and again, as he continued in his preoccupation. 'What.'

The three watched him in silence.

'What,' again.

David looked to Flora.

'It is his name for you.'

'What?' asked David absently. No one laughed.

'It is the name he calls you. You are *what* and I am *mum*, well he says *dum*, actually.'

'Ben, that is incorrect,' she said in a mocking tone.

'Yes, Ben,' interrupted Rose. 'Father's real name is *why*!'

A moment's silence, then Flora and Tomasine burst into laughter.

David couldn't supress his smile. 'We can't go. It is too much. Where would we go? We'd need a guide.'

They sat silent again and David looked at the face of his forlorn daughter, Flora hiding her disappointment, and a scolding expression from Tomasine.

Eventually, he broke the quiet. 'I suppose it would be seen as rude to refuse, but how can we...'

He never got to the end of his sentence before Flora and Rose ran to embrace him, followed by Ben.

'You want to, my darling?' he asked Flora.

'Yes, I do. We need not take the month if you do not wish it. And you are right, it would be very rude to decline Joe and Mary's generosity.'

'And do we take Rose?' David asked Flora, looking at Rose.

'Yes, of course we do!' she exclaimed.

It was Flora who received Rose's embrace this time.

'Right, let us all sit and think, where shall we go?' commanded David.

Tomasine, who was enjoying their antics, offered, 'If I may, I have an idea.'

'Go on,' said David.

'If I were to accompany you, as a guide, we could travel to The Low Countries and I would show you Veere, Delft, and Bruges, perhaps, and the villages. You would stay comfortably in my house. Also, with your permission of course, I could take Rose to Leiden and show her where I went to university. This would leave the two of you with time to yourselves. It was a thought ... but maybe some other arrangement would suit better.'

Rose's eyes widened.

'Thank you, Tomasine, that is a thoughtful and generous offer. You have the time to do this?' said David.

'Yes, I have the time.'

'Flora and I will discuss it.'

'What!' said Ben, and they laughed.

'A boat,' replied David. 'You will go on a big boat,' then to himself, 'Oh, what have I done.'

Flora asked, 'Tomasine, the painting, the gift from Grietje, is that Holland?'

'Yes,' she replied as she went to retrieve it. 'Rose, will you help please?'

Grietje had painted a long seascape with a single, distant sailing ship, silhouetted by the sun rising or setting on the horizon.

'It is beautiful. Where is it?' asked Flora.

David looked to fully admire the rich, pastel-coloured, atmospheric canvas for the first time.

Tomasine continued, 'It is a composition, not a real depiction. I have not talked with her about it. That is unmistakably Delft in the background on the right,' she said pointing, '...but Delft is not on the coast, so she has just placed it there. On the lower right are the cottages, *de huizen*, at van Reit's house, on Voorne. Beside them she has also painted the cottages in Monster where I was brought up. On the bottom left' –David was transfixed now – 'there are two figures on the pier; they could be on any breakwater, but I would guess, Veere.'

The two figures were indistinct; they were standing, facing the sea: a cloaked adult holding the hand of a child looking out toward the ship. The ship could be turning away or toward the harbour. It wasn't clear, David couldn't tell.

'And this child,' Tomasine said, 'Could it be me... or you, David? I don't know. I'm not sure if Grietje does.'

They sat quiet, moved, by Grietje's depiction of an imagining they could feel, yet not quite grasp. Flora reached for David's hand,

'We need to travel there, David,' she said, 'All of us, as Tomasine has suggested. It is your past, and our future.'

END

Printed in Great Britain
by Amazon

60694958R00180